WHAT HAPPENS TO BAD GIRLS

This time she simply chuckled and brought her knee up higher still, lifting my bottom into a wonderfully ridiculous position, much the highest part of my body and completely spread, to leave everything showing behind and completely vulnerable.

'I've got a little present for you, darling,' she said.

I tried to peer back between my dangling boobs as she reached down into her bag, but all I could see was her legs and the edge of the steps.

'What is it?' I asked, wondering fearfully why she needed me in spanking position before I was given it.

'Shut up and stick it in,' she told me.

I obeyed meekly, lifting my bottom into full prominence by rising up on my toes. The sight made her chuckle, and I felt her fingers touch, pressing down between my cheeks to stretch my already flaunted bumhole wide. Something was going up my bottom, maybe a dildo, maybe anal beads, something to enhance the shame of my spanking, and it was impossible not to purr at the thought of my own degradation.

WHAT HAPPENS TO BAD GIRLS

Penny Birch

This book is a work of fiction.
In real life, make sure you practise safe, sane and consensual sex.

5

First published in 2006 by
Nexus
Thames Wharf Studios
Rainville Road
London W6 9HA

www.nexus-books.co.uk

Typeset by TW Typesetting, Plymouth, Devon

ISBN 0 352 34031 2
ISBN 9 780352 340313

Penguin Random House is committed to a sustainable future for our business, our readers and our planet. This book is made from Forest Stewardship Council® certified paper.

MIX
Paper | Supporting
responsible forestry
FSC® C018179

Printed and bound in Great Britain by Clays Ltd, St Ives plc

Why not visit Penny's website at
www.pennybirch.com

You'll notice that we have introduced a set of symbols onto our book jackets, so that you can tell at a glance what fetishes each of our brand new novels contains. Here's the key – enjoy!

cp (traditional)

cp (modern)

spanking

restraint/bondage

rope bondage/hojojutsu

latex/rubber/leather/enclosure

fem dom

willing captivity

medical

period setting

uniforms

sex rituals

One

My knickers were coming down, which is what happens to bad girls.

I walked to the window, paused just long enough to make sure the little bastards were paying attention, turned my back, stuck my bottom out, lifted my dress and eased down my panties, making sure they had plenty of time to see what I was up to. Percy rose on cue, stepping towards me as I got slowly to my knees, making very sure they could see his back but never his face. As he threw a leg across my waist to stand over me, I knew that all they'd have to photograph would be a broad expanse of tweed and the back of his head, but their lenses would still be fixed to the window. He lifted the hairbrush, also in full view.

'Give me a couple for real,' I asked, raising my bottom.

'Certainly, my dear,' he responded and brought the hairbrush down hard across one cheek, drawing a squeal from me the photographers could probably have heard.

'Ouch, Percy!'

'Well, you did say . . .'

Again the hairbrush smacked down, and I was left with both cheeks tingling and hot as I quickly crawled out from beneath him. It was a pity, because

1

it would be my last chance of a spanking for some time, and I could have done with my bottom properly warmed, perhaps before being made to kneel for his cock with my smacked cheeks stuck out behind as I brought myself to orgasm. Now there was no time.

Percy continued to apply the hairbrush, only now to the padded surface of my dressing-table stool, which I'd quickly pushed in where my bottom had been a moment before. Still on all fours, still bare behind, I scrambled for the door, Percy's voice following me as I reached the bathroom.

'That, my dear Natasha, is a view I shall miss very badly indeed.'

'Not for long,' I promised him, and blew a kiss as I stood up.

Two quick motions and I'd pulled my knickers up and adjusted my dress to make myself decent. Percy continued to spank the stool, producing meaty smacks not wholly unlike the sound of wood on girlish bottom flesh or, at least, so I hoped. Still, it wasn't the only precaution I was taking. With just my shoulder bag, I looked as if I was only going shopping anyway, although they might have wondered why I needed to climb down the fire-escape instead of using the front door, had they seen.

I could be fairly sure they wouldn't, a small risk I judged worth taking. Out through the mews and into Fitzroy Road, praying their lenses were still firmly fixed on my window, over the foot bridge and no car could follow me, down into Chalk Farm Station and I was away, surely? I still made a point of getting off my train at Euston and jumping back on at the last minute, but other than an odd look from a business-man nobody paid me any attention.

By the time I got to Waterloo, I was smiling to myself, convinced I'd made it, away from London *incognito*, leaving the wretched paparazzi to harass some other poor girl who'd made the mistake of letting her knickers down a bit too publicly. So far as Natasha Linnet was concerned, they could whistle.

I had everything worked out. New phone, new email, new cards, cash payments only, until I was safely ensconced in my new home. For the moment it wasn't even in my name, but in Penny's, the one person I knew I could trust absolutely not to betray me, nor to pinch any of the money I'd put in her hands. She hadn't even wanted to accept a commission, but I'd insisted, leaving her with enough to pay off most of the oversized mortgage she'd recently taken on.

From Waterloo to Eastleigh, changing my look in the train, hair up and floaty dress changed for skirt, blouse and stay-ups, glasses added and the sassy, casual girl who'd got on the train got off as a smart young businesswoman. A couple of hours spent fidgeting in the airport and I was in the air, not in a jet, but a tiny yellow thing with three engines and a double row of seats down the middle.

Forty-five minutes later and I had my first view of the island, windblown trees and grass, scattered houses, high cliffs and lonely offshore stacks with the surf breaking against them. There were also fortifications, lots of fortifications, German and Victorian, including one which was now mine or, rather, Penny's, but it would be mine soon enough. I wasn't sure which it was, only that it stood on an islet at the eastern end, cut off at high tide. I could see three like that, any one of which would have been perfect, providing the absolute seclusion I wanted.

It was going to be perfect, the life I had always dreamed of: no job, no worries, just relaxation. Then, once I'd settled in and friends could visit, lots and lots

3

of really dirty sex, without the least risk of being disturbed. I'd be able to do anything I liked, go naked all day, play with myself when and where I liked, give guests the right to whip my panties down for spanking as they chose, and more, much more.

True, the planes came in at just a few hundred feet above the sea, which I hadn't bargained for, but that wouldn't give anything away beyond my going naked, if that. Besides, I'd hear them coming, which would add a pleasant touch of fear without taking any real risk. Even if they did catch a glimpse of me naked, they wouldn't know the half of it.

Landing had me clinging to my seat as we banked over a huge cliff, so low I was sure we'd run into the ground, but the pilot knew what he was doing and put us down with no more than a bump. I got out into wind and sun, more like the Caribbean or the Med than the English Channel, and hot enough to make me want to strip off then and there. I promised myself I would, just as soon as I'd sorted myself out. First that meant a trip into town to pick up my keys from the estate agent.

Penny had warned me the place was pretty rustic, and she hadn't been exaggerating. My taxi was ancient, my driver no less so, a man so fat the suspension was down on his side, while as he drove he kept turning his great red sweaty head to talk to me and let his lecherous, piggy eyes flicker over the front of my blouse. I responded to his questions amiably, following the story I'd worked out to make sure nobody decided to make a quick few pounds by passing on my whereabouts to the papers.

I'd inherited my money, the least exciting way to become rich I could think of, and decided to move to the island for the sake of peace and quiet. Don the driver accepted all this at face value, responding with a dull grunt, as if he had been hoping for something better. The truth, even the upper layers of the truth never mind the fact that I was to all intents and purposes a very successful sneak thief, would have had those piggy eyes popping out of his head, but he wasn't going to hear it.

That was for me alone, not Percy, not Penny, not any of my friends, all of whom believed layer one of the fabrication, that Philippe Fauçon had given me the paintings before he died and that my distaste for the attentions of the press was simply a sensible reaction. Not that I had any scruples about it. It was my big secret, and it made me feel wonderfully naughty, knowing I was such a bad girl, and that I'd got away with it.

Got away with it so far, anyway, because as always my train of thought ended with a stab of worry, not guilt, simply worry. It was still possible for the whole thing to come unravelled, just unlikely. Highly unlikely, in fact, because, although the island presumably ran to such civilised things as newspapers, and therefore Fat Don the cabbie would almost certainly have seen my face, he hadn't recognised me. Given his conversation, and what it implied for his taste in newspapers, he'd probably seen my bare bottom too, a thought that gave me a mild flush of embarrassment and once more turned my thoughts to having my bottom spanked. He would be just the sort of man to do it, physically at least, big and lecherous but old and ugly enough to be properly grateful and so give me the attention I needed, while the whole process of being laid bare bottom across his knee and smacked would be exquisitely humiliating.

Mentally, I knew it would be a different matter. Penny had warned me not to expect too much of the inhabitants. Apparently, a titty fuck was thought

5

exotic and kinky, while the chances of finding anyone who would understand the subtleties of erotic punishment and humiliation were zero. In many ways that was good, but the knowledge that I wouldn't be getting spanked was making me want it more than ever. Fat Don no doubt thought me aloof and untouchable, making me smile for what had been going through my head as I climbed out of the cab in the main street of the town.

He'd called it a town anyway, but by mainland standards it would hardly have passed for a village. Two major streets formed a T-shape, with an ancient square, a cluster of alleys at one end of the bar and a few newer side roads. That was it save for the harbour and the scattered houses I'd seen from the air. Don had dropped me at the 'top of town', where the two major roads met, and the estate agent proved to be at the bottom of the shallow hill. I didn't mind, keen to see where I'd be doing my shopping.

I hadn't expected much, and I got even less. There seemed to be just one of everything, including a general store no bigger than many London corner shops. Pubs were the exception, so numerous I quickly began to wonder if Penny's description of the island as 'two thousand alcoholics clinging to a rock' was a joke after all. Each seemed different too – one clearly for the retired wealthy and full of men who looked like retired colonels and their blue-rinsed wives, another very much a tourist bar, a third clearly where the local hoi polloi congregated.

The last, Andy's, brought a smile to my face. In the window there was a poster, hand written with child's felt-tip pen, advertising a pole-dancing competition that evening with a first prize of one hundred pounds. I could just imagine the blowsy local wenches and drunken tourist girls' desperate and pathetic attempts to pick up the miserable little prize, and their embarrassment as they peeled off, probably just down to knickers and bras.

It was funny, and I was smiling as I continued down the street to where the estate agent stood at the corner. There was a girl behind the counter, about my age, trying to look smart in a white blouse taut over fat peasant breasts. She looked up, smiling. 'Hi, may I help you?'

'Yes. I've come to pick up some keys.'

'Certainly. Which property would that be?'

'*Les Hommeaux Florains.* I'm the new owner.'

Her smile immediately faded, to be replaced by a puzzled frown. She spoke even as I realised my mistake. 'Sorry, I don't quite understand.'

I hesitated, not sure how much I should reveal, when it struck me that there was a way around a lot of tedious and possibly risky explanation.

'I'm Penny Birch, the new owner. The sale went through two weeks ago.'

Her look grew more puzzled still, and hard. 'I know the sale went through,' she answered me, 'but you're not Penny Birch. I've known Penny Birch since we were children.'

'Oh . . . look, I'm sorry. I don't know why I said that. I'm Natasha, Penny's friend, and I'm supposed to pick up the keys. You can call her to check.'

'I will,' she answered, her tone softening marginally.

I waited as she rang. No answer.

'What number are you ringing?' I asked. 'She won't be home yet. Try the university, or better still her mobile. I've got the number, hang on . . .' I looked into my bag to find my mobile, only to realise that my purse was missing. 'Shit! I think I've left my purse in the cab. Look, here's the number.'

I left her to call Penny as I burrowed down into my bag with ever-increasing frustration. My purse definitely wasn't there, and the only place I could have left it was the cab. I could feel my panic rising as I searched, but the girl obviously thought I was a loony anyway and I forced what I hoped was a calm smile as she put the phone down again.

'Penny's in a lecture,' she told me. 'They told me she'll be out in half-an-hour.'

'Great. May I have the keys then?'

'Er . . . no, not really.'

'Why not? You know I'm telling the truth, or I'd hardly have asked you to call Penny.'

She hesitated. 'I don't know that.'

'Yes, you do, and I've got her mobile number.'

'That doesn't mean you're who you say you are,' she answered, now doubtful again, 'and, anyway, she didn't say anything about somebody else picking up the keys.'

'No, but . . .' I stopped, realising we'd been a little too secretive about our arrangements.

She went on. 'We close in an hour. You can wait if you like, but I'm sure you realise I can't give you the keys until I've spoken to Miss Birch.'

'OK, fine . . . no, I'll get my purse first. I'm sure it's in the cab. Do you know the cabbie, Don, big fat guy with a red face, always staring at your tits.' I smiled, trying to make a joke of it and get her on my side, and to judge by the size of her breasts she was sure to get stared at.

'My uncle Don? Yes. I'll call him.'

I felt the blood rush to my face in response to her cold tone, and my own foolishness. After all, in a place where the locals would have had nobody to shag but each other for generations I should have guessed they'd be related. This time at least the phone call was a success.

'He's got your purse,' she told me, her tone implying that I was not only a complete clown but an idiot into the bargain, 'but he's gone out to the lighthouse to collect a fare for the airport. If you go up to the top of town you'll catch him as he goes past.'

I went, and waited, and waited, glancing nervously at my watch every so often. Finally, his battered white Cortina appeared at the top of the road, bumping down over the cobbles and coming to a stop as I flagged him down. His grinning face appeared at the window.

'Hi, love. I've got your purse. It's at my place.'

'What? Can you get it for me then?'

'Sure. Right after I'm finished.'

'When will that be? Hang on!'

He'd driven on, leaving me seething in the street. Presumably he would be back after he'd dropped his fare off at the airport, but that meant going to wherever he lived and I'd miss the estate agent. Cursing bitterly, I hurried back down the road. Penny still wasn't available and I hurried back, just in time to see Don's cab disappear at the top of the street. He was going east, and unless he lived in one of the few houses out of town he would have to stop soon, so I chased after him. There was a crossroads at the top of the hill, just a few houses near by, but no sign of his cab. I stopped, panting for breath.

Maybe he'd be back, with my purse, maybe not. One fork of the crossroads looked as if it went to the bottom of town and I took it, walking between a pair of fields and back in among houses, but not where the estate agent was. I walked on, puzzled, asked a man the way and ended up outside another estate agent, but near the pub advertising the striptease. Finally, I found the right estate agent, locked.

There was no sign of the girl, no sign of anybody, the street empty except for an obvious tourist family. I drew in my breath, trying to calm my temper and wondering what to do. I could go to my fort, but I wouldn't be able to get in, so that was no good. Besides, it was at the east end of the island. I'd have to stay in a hotel, but for that I needed money, which meant finding Don.

I walked back to the pub, sure that such an obvious sleazeball would be known there. It was everything I'd expected from the outside, a dusty, grimy space with a threadbare carpet and decaying glitz passing for décor. To one side, a pole had been put up at the centre of a clear area, obviously where the girls were expected to dance. A few people had already arrived, that or they'd been drinking all day, tough-looking men who were obviously locals and very much at the bottom end of the social scale. Only the barman looked even remotely approachable, and I forced a smile.

'Hi, do you know Don, the cabbie?'

'Sure.'

A laugh came from behind me, and a coarse male voice, attempting to sing a dirty version of a jingle. 'Stripping tonight, she'll be stripping tonight, stripping tonight, she'll be –'

His voice broke off as the others burst into laughter. I ignored them, trying not to think of how it would feel to have to peel my clothes off in front of their leering, drunken faces.

The barman wasn't going to venture any more information without prompting, so I spoke again. 'Do you know where he lives?'

'Whitegates.'

'Where's that?'

'Out towards the lighthouse.'

10

'Not in town then?'

'No. Look, he'll probably be along in a bit.'

'OK, thanks.'

I stepped back from the bar, pondering on whether I should wait or attempt to track Don down. It looked like being a busy night, and he was sure to bring some fares to Andy's, while it was hard to imagine him missing the striptease. I would wait, perhaps outside, where I wouldn't have to put up with a dozen yokels sniggering at me.

As I made for the door, one of them called out to the barman. ''Ere, Liam, she up for it?'

Liam went up in my estimation as he answered, his voice dripping sarcasm. 'What do you think?'

Their voices followed me as I left the pub, the first man defensive. 'Could be. Some posh birds like it rough.'

'Just as well, 'cause they don't come much rougher than you, Frank!'

'I say she'd be up for it,' Frank replied.

'Nah,' another jeered. 'A piece of posh totty like that's not going to get dirty with us, is she?

Others joined in.

'I bet she only goes with rich kids, that one.'

'Nah, rich old gits, more like, with a million in the bank and a bad heart.'

'Bitch!'

I didn't even bother to look round, but sat down at a table outside, wishing I had just a few pence on me to buy a drink, even a glass of lemonade, although a double gin and tonic would have been better. It was hot, even with the afternoon fading to evening, and I was prickly with sweat from running around the town, and badly in need of a shot of alcohol.

A movement caught the edge of my vision and I looked around, slightly worried because of their

11

aggressive attitude. One of them was coming towards me, by far the best looking, tall with a mop of tawny hair and a square jaw, like something out of a Tarzan cartoon. He spoke as he reached me. 'Don't mind those wankers, love. Drink?'

I hesitated only a moment, my thirst and relief at his friendly tone easily overcoming the defensive mood his friends had triggered in me. 'Gin and tonic, please. Thanks.'

There was an immediate echo from inside the pub, three or four voices raised in a chorus, their accent a parody of my own. 'Gin and tonic! Oh I say!'

'I say, Frank, old boy, she wants a G and T.'

My rescuer turned on them as he went back into the pub. 'Fuck off, lads, give her a break.'

The response was a fresh chorus, this time of derisive remarks, but now there was jealousy mixed in with the mocking tone. I pointedly kept my back to them, waiting until Frank had returned with my drink and a pint of lager for himself. Mine was a double or more, and I took a large swallow, allowing the cool, sharp liquid to trickle slowly down my throat, an immediate restorative.

I still wasn't up to flirting, never mind more, and hoped he would postpone making a move on me for another day, although that was obviously his intention.

He had taken a draught of lager and was going to speak when one of the others called out instead, no longer mocking, but a warning. 'Frank, Womble's coming.'

Frank swore and disappeared up the street and around a corner, leaving his pint on the table and me wondering what was going on. The atmosphere had grown suddenly tense, and as I turned I saw why. A man was coming up the street, evidently Womble from his bizarre, pear-shaped body, but I couldn't imagine anyone calling him that to his face. He was huge, well over six foot, and bulky, his clothing bulging with muscle and fat in unsightly combination.

My initial instinct was that here was a possible protector, a man I could flirt with to make very sure indeed that the rest of them showed me proper respect, but the idea faded as he came closer. He was simply too grotesque, too alarming. For one thing, his face was oddly soft, carrying a strange combination of the babyish and the aggressive, which scared me. Like his body, the bulk of his head seemed to have slipped downwards, his fat cheeks and a massive jaw hanging beneath a pointy cranium surmounted by unkempt blond hair. I don't mind big men, but I do like them to look at least vaguely rational.

He was obviously making for the pub, but had seen Frank leave and changed his mind, breaking into a shambling run as he made for the corner. I watched, at once amused and disgusted by the way his monstrous buttocks wobbled to the motion of his legs, also somewhat alarmed. I'd pictured the locals as largely harmless rustics, to be ignored or used for my amusement as I pleased, but there was something frighteningly primitive about Womble. In fact, he barely seemed human.

I went back to my drink, glad Womble was gone and that the incident seemed to have silenced the remaining men. The sun had dipped behind the houses and the heat was beginning to fade from the day, making me glad of my jacket. Neither Frank nor Womble came back, but Andy's had soon begun to fill up, mainly with locals, but also tourists. The two groups were easy to tell apart, the former in work clothes or casual in an oddly self-conscious way, the latter smarter and clearly not on their own ground.

Seven o'clock passed, and eight, still with no sign of Don. I was beginning to wonder if it might not be best to walk out to Whitegates after all when his taxi passed, rattling up the street and gone before I had a chance to hail him. That at least meant he was around, and I stayed put, now huddled against a surprisingly chilly breeze blowing in off the sea. Inside, the bar was now crowded, safely anonymous, and I went in, hoping Frank would come back and buy me another drink.

He didn't, and nobody else offered either, their attention now on the area around the pole, where a plump, mousy girl was doing what was presumably supposed to be a pole dance. She was obviously drunk, and couldn't stop giggling, while her poses were more comic than erotic. She didn't even take her top off. Yet when she finished the audience clapped enthusiastically and called for more, leaving me shaking my head in despair. Penny had said rustic, but Andy's was positively bucolic, and could have given an Alabama red-neck bar a run for its money for sheer vulgarity and lack of refinement.

With nothing better to do than keep a half-eye out for Don and his cab, I settled down to watch as the DJ thanked the girl for her efforts and called for the next performer. She was better than the first, at least in that she knew how to move and was quite pretty, but she was dressed as if she'd just come back from a fishing trip and hadn't bothered to change. Nor did she strip.

The thought of competing alongside such hopeless cases was at once ridiculous and deeply humiliating, and yet it was impossible not to think about it. After all, if the standard didn't improve markedly I would have been able to win it easily, without even having to endure the embarrassment of exposing myself in front of a bunch of hayseeds. After all, to them I no doubt looked impossibly glamorous and utterly un-touchable, hence their attitude before.

After watching two more girls, both worse than the others in so far as that was possible, I was beginning to feel tempted. I was hungry, for one thing, and the money would presumably pay for some dinner and a half-decent hotel room if I didn't manage to find Fat Don. It might even be quite fun, teasing the yokels and showing their girlfriends how it ought to be done, and while I'm no professional I knew I could do better with ease. The fifth girl looked like she might have been Womble's big sister, which made me more confident still, and as the sixth stepped forward and promptly tripped over her heels, I'd decided.

The DJ was a middle-aged man in a blue velvet jacket, shades and the decaying and greasy remains of a teddy-boy haircut. He seemed to be in charge, so I pushed my way around the room until I was next to his turntable. He favoured me with a leer.

'Is it too late to put my name down for the competition?' I asked, shouting above the strains of Abba's 'Mama Mia', to which the girl on the floor appeared to be having apoplexy.

'For you, darling, it's already done,' he answered. 'What's your handle?'

'I beg your pardon?'

'Your name, darling, your name.'

'Natasha.'

'And where are you from, Natasha?'

'I live here.'

'Incomer, huh? If only they all looked like you. I'm Steve. What music do you want? I've got McFly, or maybe Black Lace is more you . . .'

'No thanks. Do you have any Velvet Under-ground?'

'Not here, no. How about a nice Britney track?'

'Rolling Stones, "Brown Sugar" maybe?'

'Yeah, I can do that.'

He began to dig into the dusty space beneath his deck, first removing a crate of beer, the chilled bottles speckled with condensation, a sight too tempting to resist.

'Could you spare me a cold beer?'

'I'll spare you two for a blow-job.'

'Who the hell do you –'

'Hey, hey, hey, don't get your knickers in a twist. I was only joking.'

He gave me a beer, even opening it. I knew full well his dirty offer had been made to test my reaction and get me thinking about sex, so I deliberately moved away, drinking my beer as I watched the show and waited to be announced. He had got to me though, the sheer outrage of his suggestion bringing out my sense of erotic humiliation. I mean, imagine *me* sucking some ageing rocker's cock in return for a couple of bottles of beer!

It was really just as well, because with contestant number eight there was a marked improvement in the quality of the striptease. She was a blonde girl, obviously a tourist, willowy and pretty in a loose red dress, also younger than most. The crowd loved her, and she knew how to tease, swinging herself around the pole to make her dress lift and show off her knickers, pushing out her bottom to make an enticing ball beneath the thin scarlet material, and repeatedly pulling the front low as if she was going to flash her breasts. When she took it off I knew I had serious competition, but that was as far as she went, parading up and down in her bra and panties to the eager applause of the crowd.

I could still do better, but my bra was going to have to come off if I wanted to be sure of beating her.

16

For the first time I began to feel nervous, and I was very glad indeed I'd be keeping my knickers. There was something almost feral about the crowd, at least the locals, and I knew from Penny that once drunk and horny they could behave with no more restraint than dogs or Tom cats. The thought of showing my pussy to them made my stomach weak, because they were simply not the sort of men it is sensible to tease. Not too much anyway.

The ninth girl was another tourist, but somebody's girlfriend who'd been pushed into doing it, and less than enthusiastic. Again she declined to strip off, leaving the crowd feeling cheated and a perfect opening for me as Steve the DJ announced me and I swallowed the last of my beer. As the opening notes of 'Brown Sugar' rang out, I strutted out into the clear space, trying to ignore the knot in my stomach and remember my friend Cheryl's advice – forget there's an audience; get the timing right; men like bums, tits and pussy, so be rude, not artistic.

I tried, but I couldn't shut out the ring of laughing, leering faces as I danced, thinking of what they'd want to do to me for the way I was flaunting my bottom in my tight business skirt, and knowing that in just three minutes I had to be down to my panties. Three verses and four articles of clothing, or was it four verses? I couldn't remember, but shrugged my jacket off quickly, too quickly, not suggestive, just clumsy. I had to do better, ruder, and tugged up my skirt to rub myself on the pole as I spread my thighs across the hard, warm metal.

That was better. There was cheering and clapping for the sight of my knickers, rude gestures and ruder suggestions shouted above the music, making me scared and excited all at once. I was losing time, but was determined not to rush it as I wriggled my skirt up, just to flash my panties before my fingers went to my blouse and my back to the pole, rubbing my bottom on the hard iron as I flicked my buttons open, one by one.

My blouse was loose, open, and off, leaving my breasts feeling big and exposed in the lacy cups of my bra. I bounced them in my hands, took a spin around the pole and threw myself back, pulling my hair out to let it hang to the floor. Now I was doing it right, the crowd just a blur, the noise no more than a lustful growl behind the music. Once more I took the pole between my thighs, rubbing myself before quickly jerking upright, my fingers on the catch of my skirt. I pushed out my hips as my skirt came loose, peeling it open to show the front of my panties, then jerking quickly away, to kick it free and strut once around the pole, now in nothing but knickers and bra as the third verse kicked off.

There was no way of being coy, the crowd in a full circle, and I knew that if I was to beat the young blonde girl my bra had to come right off. Still I was shaking as I turned to tease them, my fingers on the underwire, ready to jerk it up. Then I did it, my boobs bouncing free to cheers and catcalls. A quick tug and I was properly topless, making one more proud circle of the pole, my knees high with every step.

I hooked my thumbs into the waistband of my panties in a final taunting gesture as the verse finished, but the music didn't. Suddenly I was stuck, about to bare my bum and unable to finish cleanly. I let go of my panties and wagged a finger at the crowd, smiling and winking to tease them. Right in front of me was a skinny, bespectacled tourist in an 'I ♥ New York' T-shirt, a nerd if ever there was one, and I'd made my gesture right at him.

Bitter shame hit me at the thought of showing off to a man like him, but now it really was the last line, it had to be. My thumbs went back into my knickers and on the words 'just like a black girl should' I eased them ever so slightly down, only to jerk them back up as the song began to fade.

Only it didn't, the same lines repeated again, and as I once more stuck my bottom out I was wondering if Mick Jagger would ever shut up. This time my knickers had to come down further, all the way maybe. No, not that, it was too shameful . . .

Yes, I had to, and on the same line down came my panties and I gave them my full bare moon. The crowd was yelling with appreciation as my cheeks came on show, full and pale and nude, right in their faces. I held the pose, with the image of how rude and foolish I looked burning in my mind, posing my bare bum for a bunch of drooling yobs, tits out and panties held down . . . tits out and panties held down . . .

Finally, my courage broke, but, just as I was pulling my panties back up, a great spray of beer caught me, all over my bottom, wetting me, wetting my knickers, and leaving my bum a fat ball encased in soggy cotton as the song finally faded out.

I turned, furious, and intent on giving whichever oaf had sprayed me a piece of my mind, sure it would be the ghastly little nerd, only to stop dead. He was gone, and right in the front of the crowd was Womble, the beer bottle still in his hand, standing among the others like some grotesque troll, and with no shirt on, displaying more muscle and blubber than any three ordinary men. I changed my mind about confronting him, quickly gathered up my clothes as Steve called for a round of applause and ran for the loo.

19

My heart was beating furiously as I leant a hand against the wall in the Ladies. I'd stripped for them, nearly all the way, showing my breasts and bottom, flaunting myself and ending up covered in beer, running away in my wet panties, no doubt looking every bit as vulnerable and as foolish as I felt. Yet at least I could console myself with the fact that I'd almost certainly won.

I'd been better than the blonde girl, and far better than the others, while surely there couldn't be many more girls prepared to dance in front of that crowd, let alone strip? Fortunately, I had some spare knickers in my bag, a three pack of the white cotton spanking panties Percy likes me to wear and makes sure I always have in supply. I dabbed the beer off my bottom and back with loo paper and pulled a pair on, with my dress on top as the rest of my clothes had been on the floor, which was none too clean.

As I stepped out of the loos, Steve was making another announcement, as corny as ever. '. . . and last but not least, another summer swallow, the gorgeous Tanya from Manchester!'

I climbed on a chair to see, just as Destiny's Child started up and a girl stepped up to the pole. She was small, and pretty, worryingly pretty, in a loose black dress with nothing but panties underneath, smart high heels too. I immediately found myself torn between the hope that she'd be prissy about stripping and the desire to see her naked. She was a good dancer, following every move of the song and using the pole in a way that had the boys gaping, one instant with her body held close against it, the next with her toes touching the base, her hands gripped to it and her bottom stuck well out as she pushed it up.

With the first chorus her dress came up, first for a teasing glimpse of her thighs, then higher, letting them have a peep of silky black panties. By then, I was biting my lip and wishing I'd gone after her, because she was easily as good as me and surely would win if she was just a little bit dirtier. I crossed my fingers, praying she'd keep her dress on despite a rising urge to see her stripped, and preferably spanked pink as well.

Again she lifted her dress, teasing, and suddenly she'd jerked it high and off, to stand proud in nothing but panties and heels, her small high breasts flaunted for the crowd as she made a single strutting circuit of the pole, just as I had done. I willed her to slip in the beer Womble had spilt on the floor, but as she repeated the move with her feet together and her bottom stuck out and lifted I felt my pussy tighten for her.

The crowd were clapping wildly and yelling for more, and my heart sank as she reached back to hook her thumbs into her panties, looking over her shoulder with big brown eyes, taunting them. Suddenly she'd done it, her panties not just down, but off, her bottom pushed out bare, her pussy on show, her cheeks just far enough open to hint at the dark spot of her bumhole. Her knickers went into the crowd, thrown casually aside as if being naked but for a pair of black high heels in front of a hundred or more rough-looking men didn't matter in the slightest, and as she went into a final, frantic dance, now fully nude, I knew I'd lost.

Steve the DJ was whooping with joy as the music finished and Tanya came off, running into the Ladies with her bag just as I had done. He began to tell stupid jokes as he waited for her and the other girls gathered around the pole, myself included. I had no idea how the competition was going to be judged, and found myself smiling at the crowd, even the grotesque

21

Womble, in the vain hope that they might pick me after all. When Tanya came back, Steve raised his hands for silence but didn't get it, and was shouting into his microphone to make himself heard as he spoke. 'OK! OK! Simmer down, boys! Now the dancing's done, it's time to vote, so let's have a show of hands for girl number one, Harriet Simms!'

The plump girl who'd been up first stepped forwards, yelling for approval. She got it too, plenty of it; as hands began to go up for her, I realised I'd made an awful mistake. It didn't matter who was the best dancer. It didn't matter how sexy I was or how far I'd gone. All that mattered was who you knew, who you were fucking, whose sister you were. I scored a big zero on all counts.

It was a farce anyway, with half the audience raising their hands more than once, and Womble lifting both huge arms every single time, including for the girl who looked like his sister. Steve barely made a pretence of trying to be fair, and by the time he got to me everybody had voted at least twice. I still got a fair few hands, but by then it was obvious who was going to win, the only islander who'd got her tits out, and who had presumably managed to shag her way through the entire male population. Sure enough, the vote went to her. Another island girl placed second. Tanya, who should have won, came nowhere. I got third prize, a can of supermarket-brand baked beans.

I was left looking mournfully at my can as the rest of the bar began to get down to some serious drinking. Not having eaten since I snatched a sandwich at the airport, I took it into the corner, feeling sorry for myself because I was grateful for the pathetic prize. I ate the beans with my fingers, too far gone to care any more. It was a great start to my new life, doing a striptease for a can of beans.

To make things even more humiliating, I was turned on by what I'd done, unable to stop thinking of how I'd had to show my bare bottom because the song had continued longer than I'd remembered. Now the islanders would think of me as a slut, a girl prepared to take down her panties in the hope of winning a pathetic sum of money. No doubt they wouldn't let me forget it, teasing me, coming on to me because they thought I was cheap, maybe pinching my bottom or tweaking my nipples, maybe trying to push me into blow-jobs.

I'd do it too, if they caught me in the right mood. Despite the fact that becoming the local tart had been no part of my plans, the thought was irresistibly humiliating, and all the more so because they wouldn't understand my feelings. Maybe I could spare myself by accepting one of them as my boyfriend, one of the less awful ones, perhaps Frank? He was a bucolic like the rest of them, but he was handsome in a rough-edged way. No doubt he'd be the same in bed, my body bare, his cock in my mouth, then up my pussy for a brief, hard fucking, two minutes maybe, before he'd spunked in me or on me and climbed off, full of himself because he imagined he'd satisfied me. He'd probably wipe his cock on the curtains.

Then again, maybe I could teach him a little? No doubt he'd regard spanking as perverted, but with luck he'd be prepared to do it. His derision would make my feelings stronger still as he put me over his knee, laughing at the way I wriggled and squirmed, hooting with coarse joy as I begged him to make a big deal out of taking my panties down . . .

I had to get a grip on myself. It was getting late and if I didn't find Fat Don soon I was going to be spending the night on the street, or in bed with whichever yokel got to fuck me in return for a night's lodging. That would be the bargain, I was sure of it. Altruism was not likely to be a popular local concept. In fact, they probably didn't even know what the word meant.

Maybe that was what I wanted, to be taken back to some pigsty of a flat and stripped and fucked, to be put to my knees and made to suck some big ugly cock hard before it was shoved rudely up my pussy, to be mounted and pounded into the bed, my thighs spread wide, to be put on my knees and done doggy style with my bumhole on show between my spread cheeks as I was used, to be fucked up my bottom and made to suck his cock afterwards, to be . . .

No, I had to try to preserve at least a little dignity. As I'd let my erotic fantasy run, my eyes had been half-closed and I'd been drifting towards much-needed sleep. I could still feel the tiredness in my body as I forced myself to stand up, but I pushed it down and made for the door. Inside, it had been hot, adding to my drowsiness. Outside, it had grown not just cool, but cold, with a sea fog blowing up the street to fill the air with scattered orange and blue light from the streetlamps and the sign above Andy's.

I hugged myself, feeling suddenly lonely, only to brighten up as a yellow cab sign emerged from the gloom – Val Cars – Don's firm. Not Don's Cortina though, but an equally battered Vauxhall driven by a man with preposterous sideburns, a moth-eaten moustache and a badly chewed cigar hanging from one side of his mouth. I put my hand out anyway, catching a whiff of hot strong tobacco smell as I leant forwards to speak in at his window.

'Hi. I don't suppose Don's likely to be along?'

'Don? Nah, wouldn't think so. He's been doing the airport all day. Probably knocked off.'

'Oh. I don't supposed you'd drive me out to Whitegates?'

'Driving's what I do.'

'Thank you, but I'll have to pay you when we get there. I left my purse in Don's cab, you see.'

He hesitated, no doubt wondering if I was trying to steal a free ride.

'I assure you I can pay,' I told him, pulling open his door to make sure there was no further argument. 'I'm the new owner of *Les Hommeaux Florains*.'

'I'd heard someone had bought it,' he answered as he let the clutch in. 'About time too. Shame to see a place like that go to waste. I'm Mick, by the way. Used to be lovely when old Mrs Moate had it, *Les Hommeaux Florains*. Velvet curtains she had . . .'

He continued to talk as we bumped over the cobbles, but I was no longer paying attention, too tired to make conversation, while the warmth of the cab was once more making me feel drowsy, and dirty. Soon we were out of the town, the fog now broken only by the occasional dim light, making me very glad indeed I wasn't walking. It seemed to be a long way too, and I was soon on the edge of sleep, his voice now a dull background noise, oddly soothing. I let my mind drift again, thinking how dirty it would feel to have to go with Mick in exchange for a bed for the night, how he'd really get his money's worth out of me, a thought so enticing I nearly spoke out, only to be brought sharply back to reality as the cab jerked to a stop.

'Here we are,' Mick announced. 'Don White's place. I'll wait.'

'Thank you,' I answered him, relief flooding through me as I climbed out of the car. I'd held back from disgracing myself.

We were outside a row of whitewashed cottages, mere dim bulks in the fog save where the occasional light illuminated a door or a patch of wall. The nearest house had no lights on all, and everything seemed ominously quiet, until a great low moan sounded from out of the fog, followed by a dull thump.

'What was that?' I demanded.

'Foghorn at the lighthouse,' he answered casually.

It was obviously the right explanation, and a perfectly reasonable one, yet as the sound came a second time it left me with an unpleasant hollow feeling in my stomach and an urge to be in a warm, dry and well-lit room. There was no sign of Don's battered Cortina. I went to the door and knocked anyway, waiting with my hopes fading further still as nobody responded.

At last Mick spoke up from behind me. 'I don't think he's in, love.'

I bit back my caustic response and turned to him with a helpless shrug. He had put the interior light on, illuminating his face to exaggerate the wrinkles in his skin and the dull-yellow tobacco stains. The damp of the fog had begun to turn into a thin drizzle.

'Do you mind waiting?' I asked, knowing full well he would.

He glanced at his watch before replying. I couldn't pay, and I had a horrible suspicion I knew what he'd want instead. It was going to happen, and I couldn't resist it.

'I've got work, love. It's chucking-out time soon.'

'OK, but I'll have to pay you tomorrow then,' I told him, with a sense of rising panic because it was not what I wanted to say at all. 'Do you mind giving me a lift back into town?'

A look of annoyance crossed his face, quickly replaced by just the sort of shifty expression I'd been dreading and praying for all at once. I could wait in the cold and wet until Don White returned home. I could walk back to town through the dark and fog. I could even shame him into behaving decently towards me if I tried, but a treacherous little voice in the back of my head was telling me to give in, to let him make me do it, and to revel in my own humiliation as I pulled at his cock, or let him grope my breasts, or took him in my mouth, whatever he demanded of me.

'I think you'd better get back in the car,' he said.

I nodded, shame-faced as I stepped towards him. He had me, helpless to the dirty feelings I'd had growing inside me ever since Percy smacked my bottom that morning. I was going to do it, my excuse too perfect, a blow-job in return for my lift, then more, much more. My eyes were downcast as I settled myself into the front seat of the cab, and my hands were reaching for his fly even before he could find the courage to ask for what he wanted.

'OK,' I told him, my voice cracking. 'I'll do it, you bastard.'

The expression on his face as I peeled down his fly was of astonishment, but I pushed back the uncomfortable possibility that he might not have been intending to force me into sex at all. He was a dirty old man, after all. Sure enough, he made no effort to stop me, merely blowing his breath out as my hand burrowed into his fly to pull out a wrinkled brown cock and a bulging scrotum.

He turned off the interior light as I went down, maybe to spare my blushes, maybe to make sure nobody saw. I didn't care, so far gone I quite liked the idea of people watching as I was forced to suck cock to pay my cab fare. Not that it was quite dark anyway, with the few lights from the houses illuminating his thick fleshy cock dull orange and dirty brown where I was now holding it in my hand. Maybe if I was caught they'd join in, and as I took him into my mouth I was imagining the shame of having Fat Don come out and catch me sucking Mick off, laughing together at my humiliation, agreeing to take turns with me . . .

A powerful shiver ran through me at the thought, and I took his cock deeper into my mouth, gulping on the fat wrinkly stem, not even bothering to feign reluctance. It felt too good, the taste of man and the feel of him swelling as the blood pumped in to make him grow in my mouth. Soon he was long enough for me to hold him as I sucked, stroked his balls and masturbated him into my mouth. At that, he gave a pleased grunt, then spoke, his voice still edged with doubt for all my eagerness. 'How about – how about pulling out your tits. I bet you've got lovely tits.'

I didn't hesitate. Out they came, flopped into my hands and held up for his inspection, my nipples straining to erection. His eyes popped as he watched, and I bounced them in my hands to show him how willing I was, and how dirty, before going back down on his cock. Now he was fully erect, a hard bar of flesh in my mouth, surely ready to come, so I slowed down, wanting my own orgasm as I did it. I stuck a hand back, finding my panties wet over my pussy and my flesh swollen and sensitive.

He was still smoking his cigar, but too excited to think of flicking the ash away, so that bits began to fall on my back, still warm. I knew it would be in my hair too, bringing me a powerful image of how I'd look, bent over into his lap, my dress up to show my breasts, my hair and skin speckled with ash, dirty and dishevelled, and sucking cock. The sheer humiliation of it made my pussy twitch, my orgasm rising, threatening to burst, even as he grunted, jerked his cock free and came.

It went right in my face, a thick jet of hot semen landing in my hair and across my forehead and one eye. The second spurt closed my eye completely, his mess squashing out from beneath the lid as I quickly closed it, another bit dangling from my nose. More went in my mouth, and I went down on him once more, sucking and swallowing as my senses filled with the slimy salty semen.

I was still rubbing, my orgasm broken as he spunked over me, but rising again as he jerked my head back by my hair and milked out the last of his sperm over my lips and cheeks. The moment he let go I sat up, my thighs spread and my head thrown back in ecstasy, rubbing urgently with my bare tits bouncing on my chest and my panties pulled aside to let me get at my pussy, the thought of bringing myself to orgasm in front of him adding the final perfect touch to my pleasure.

There I was, among the wealthiest residents of the island, and I'd ended up going down on a cab driver's cock to pay for my fare. Bad enough, but now I was masturbating, masturbating with a cab driver's spunk running slow and slimy down my face, my titties bouncing bare for his amusement, just as I'd had them bouncing in the bar, showing off like a dirty little tart in front of a hundred men, showing off my tits and bum, sucking cock, like a dirty little tart ... like the dirty little tart I am.

My orgasm turned my vision red and made my head swim, so strong I wasn't aware of Mick's warning, or of anything much else until I'd finally come down and opened my eyes to the light in Fat Don's house and the man himself at the front door, staring at me in astonishment.

Two

It was not exactly the start I'd imagined for my new life, but the next morning I found it hard to be upset about what had happened. The day was simply too glorious, as bright as the night had been dull, with a fresh westerly breeze and the sky flecked with tiny clouds. The sea shone, a bright grey-blue flecked with spots where white horses were breaking out in the Channel and around the rocks and islets surrounding the main island. I couldn't think of anywhere else so beautiful. Even the odd mixture of architecture seemed in keeping with the wild surroundings, from the rough stone of the older buildings, through the decaying thirties grandeur of my hotel to the stark concrete of the long-abandoned German fortifications. The air was wonderfully fresh too, exhilarating, and suddenly I couldn't wait to go and see my new home.

I'd booked in at the best hotel on the island, The Royal, and my room overlooked the harbour and a good deal of the island, including Whitegates, now visible as a row of tiny boxes in the distance, sparkling white in the bright sunshine. My emotions swung between embarrassment and amusement for what I'd done, while there was no denying the sexual thrill of having had so little choice. I'd been growing used to the power of being financially secure, and having that taken away had provoked a sense of helplessness that appealed straight to my sexuality. It had been real too, although mercifully temporary, because I can't imagine that sort of feeling as much fun normally.

Not that my problems were necessarily over, but they proved to have faded like the fog. Linda White at the estate agents had already been on the phone to Penny, and was full of apology as she gave me the keys. Getting a cab was a little embarrassing, but there proved to be other firms and my driver hadn't even been in Andy's the night before. He showed a touch of deference when I told him where I wanted to go, which left me feeling rather pleased with myself as I stepped out, and more so as I took my first look at my new home.

Les Hommeaux Florains was at the extreme eastern tip of the island, a square Victorian fort of yellowish stone with rounded turrets at each corner, built on an islet of jagged slopes and ledges, all set against the grey-blue sea, with the rugged French coast far beyond. A broken causeway led out to it, across jumbled boulders and seaweed-clad rocks to a gateway closed off by huge wooden doors. Penny hadn't been exaggerating when she said it was isolated. The nearest habitation of any sort was the lighthouse, while the only piece of land that overlooked me at all was a small but bleak hill, one side half cut away by a quarry and with a German observation tower at the summit, grey and huge with three great slits looking out over the panorama. Even that was far enough away not to be a real problem, while I could see that the interior was completely hidden save from the air, and the waters around the islet were so full of jagged rocks that it was hard to imagine a boat being able to land at all. In places, pink or orange buoys had been put out, perhaps to mark underwater hazards. Once the tide was up, I would be completely alone.

I was full of excitement as I walked across, thinking of all my childhood dreams of being a princess in a castle. *Les Hommeaux Florains* wasn't quite what I'd imagined, but it was close, and it was mine, all mine. As I pushed my key into the wicket gate, my fingers were shaking, my rapture growing as it swung wide. Inside was a courtyard, surrounded by arches leading in under the massive walls, with windows opposite me and in the turrets at either side. I began to explore, breathless with delight.

For the first time in my life I had somewhere I could really call my own. Even with my flat there had always been the background knowledge that Daddy had bought it for me, but *Les Hommeaux Florains* was truly mine, bought with my money, earned with the sweat of my brow – well, not exactly sweat, but it came to the same thing. Better, in fact, because, as stolen fruit is always sweeter, so were the fruits of stolen money.

I'd known it had been uninhabited for some time, but I hadn't expected it to be so far gone. There was no sign of the velvet curtains Mick had mentioned, nor any other furnishings, merely bare boards, grey with age, rotten in places and warped in others. I was going to have to rebuild from scratch, and yet I didn't mind. The walls themselves were solid stone, and thick enough to keep out cannonballs. A little repointing would be needed here and there, perhaps, but otherwise they were sound.

The towers were the best part, two completely abandoned, two divided into three levels. I quickly decided to make the central part my public home, with the long hall serving as kitchen, dining space and living room, the upper floor space for guests, the bathroom and so forth. The towers would be mine, private save for those who really knew me. In one would be my main bedroom, looking out towards France, and on the lower floor perhaps a personal bathroom, with a huge round bath. The other would be where I was punished, with a simple bed and every conceivable device and accessory for attention to my bottom and for my private humiliation.

I could have anything, even a cannon on the gun emplacements at the top of each tower, to which I could be securely lashed, my clothes cut away to strip me behind and my bottom soundly thrashed. There would be a great iron frame on to which I could be tied into a dozen awkward and vulnerable positions, a big cage in which I could be kept at the mercy of my tormentors, a bathroom area too, with a tiled floor I could be made to scrub in the nude.

Setting it all up was going to be tricky, and would probably mean hiring somebody I could trust from the mainland. Not that my acquaintances include any builders or decorators, so I'd have to get locals to do the main accommodation first, then bring men in from outside and make them stay on, buying their silence with my mouth and pussy, even my bottom. At the thought of being taken three ways by a trio of builders, my hand had gone to my sex, pushing through the brand-new jeans I'd bought that morning. My flesh felt puffy and sensitive, making me wonder if I dare just strip off and play with myself, then and there.

It was tempting, and I climbed to the top of one of the towers for a look round, to discover I was cut off. I knew it happened, but I hadn't expected the tide to come in so fast, and now water was rushing across the causeway, sucking and pulling at the rocks. The current was making little whirlpools in places, oddly smooth areas in others, and as a piece of driftwood swept by I realised it was dangerously fast. I was genuinely cut off, the jagged rocks and treacherous current surely far too dangerous for any boat, alone on my island, a wonderful feeling unlike anything I'd experienced since I was a little girl, slightly frightening, but very exciting.

Down in the courtyard I would be invisible, unreachable. I could do anything, go naked in the sun, crawl in the nude with my pussy and bumhole flaunted behind, roll on my back and spread myself wide, deliciously naughty, and too good to resist. Climbing down the stone steps to the courtyard, my tummy was fluttering with tension, which grew as I undressed, fumbling my clothes off in my urgency, then leaving them where they dropped. Only when I was down to my panties did I hesitate, but only so that I could enjoy the final intimate exposure, my last vestige of protection stripped away to leave me stark naked.

It felt so good, just to stretch in the warm air, fully nude and completely safe. I could do anything, no matter how naughty, and nobody would ever know. My eyes were closed and my mouth fixed into a happy smile as I took my breasts in my hands, feeling their weight and stroking my nipples with slow deliberate motions until they had both popped out and I could stand it no more. My hands went behind me, to touch the meaty eggs of my bottom cheeks, rude and bare, and ruder still as I pushed it out and spread my cheeks, showing off my bumhole and the rear lips of my pussy in an ecstatic trance. I pushed a finger between, to tickle the tiny bumps and crevices of my anus and tease the fleshy folds of my sex.

I began to run, dance, do handstands, pose as if for punishment or entry, squat as if I was going to pee.

The grass was thick and fine, but coarse, tickling my feet and my bottom as I sat down in it. I was going to do it, my excitement too high to hold off any longer, but even as my fingers went to the sopping crease of my pussy I caught the distant drone of an engine. Immediately, I ran in under one of the arches, giggling with my hand over my mouth as I watched the little yellow aeroplane fly overhead. The moment it was gone I stepped out again, feeling even naughtier than before.

Immediately, I was down on my knees in the warm ticklish grass, all at once revelling in my loneliness and wishing there was somebody there to take advantage of me, most of all to spank my bottom for being such a bad girl, but to fuck me too, down on my knees in the prickly grass, masturbating with my bum stuck in the air as his long thick cock moved in and out of my body.

My eyes closed as I rocked forwards, on to all fours, pushing my bottom out to make sure my cheeks spread well and leaving my bumhole on full view between, a puckered brown ring, ruder even than the mushy pink flesh of my pussy with my fingers working in among the folds. It was a great position, vulnerable to spanking, vulnerable to fucking, vulnerable to having a cock rammed up my slippery little bumhole, to be mounted and used while my tits swung to the rhythm of my buggering.

I cried out, almost there, only for the fantasy to slip away, unneeded. It was enough, just to be kneeling there in the nude, utterly without inhibition, everything showing as I brought myself to a long shivering orgasm, my whole body in contraction until at last I could take no more and collapsed on to the grass, spent.

*　*　*

After I'd come, I went to sleep in the shade, still nude, with a sense of security I'd never known before. Only when I woke up did I allow the practical things of life to intrude; not least, my thirst. A pipe had been laid into the causeway, but it was off, while I had no fuel either, or even anywhere to sleep. Obviously, a lot of work had to be done before I could move in, and I began to make a list of priorities in my head as I waited for the tide to go down.

First and foremost, I needed the services of a competent builder and other assorted workmen. With luck, my little striptease of the night before would help, in that hopefully I would no longer be seen as some snotty rich bitch to be exploited, but as a girl prepared to join in at their level, and maybe more. Men always work so much harder if they think there's a chance of having their cocks sucked at the end of the day.

I also needed a car, or some sort of vehicle, otherwise I'd be spending forever waiting for cabs. Given the state of the causeway and the track down to it from the road, that was probably best ordered from the mainland, but I could hire for the time being. Then there was the matter of provisions, which hopefully could be delivered to save me time and trouble. I also needed to explore the town for a hair stylist, a doctor and other such essentials.

Then there was shopping, as I had to wait for Penny and Cheryl to get everything together and bring it over. We'd agreed it would be best to wait a couple of weeks, and to take as much care as I had myself, if not more. Nothing would be under my name, and Penny was to travel to Paris, transfer everything to Cheryl, who would then come over with it on the weekly boat from Cherbourg. Elaborate maybe, but I wasn't taking any chances.

As soon as the tide was down, I went across, with the concrete still wet, and having to dodge the occasional splash from a wave. I'd called my cab beforehand, and only had to wait a few minutes before it came. In town, I first went to the estate agent to ask Linda's advice and discovered that not only was Frank a builder, but also her cousin. That seemed promising, and I set off up the High Street to find his premises, only to pause as I neared Andy's.

I recognised one of the men seated on the outside tables, the nerd who'd watched my striptease. He'd seen me, and gave an excited wave, to which I responded with what I hoped was a polite but cool smile, hoping the hot flush that had risen to my face wasn't too obvious. To my irritation, he immediately got up, hurrying after me, and I braced myself to turn down whatever proposal he intended to make.

'Er . . . hi,' he stammered. 'Hi . . . could I have your autograph please?'

It was not what I'd been expecting, and it must have shown in my face, because there was uncertainty in his words as he went on. 'You're Aisha Tyler, aren't you? From *Girls Gone Wild* and that? Sure you are, I saw you in *Stripped*, just the other day.'

Suddenly, I was on the edge of panic, swallowing hard as I struggled for a suitable response. I might not be Aisha Tyler, whoever she was, but I had been in *Stripped*, a magazine that specialised in catching girls in candid poses, pictured being spanked. He'd obviously mixed me up, but if my whereabouts got back to the press I was in trouble. I had to make a snap decision, and I was sure that if I told him I wasn't Aisha Tyler he would carry on searching his brain cell and realise who I really was. He was obviously a tourist, so would soon be gone, and I decided to be her, smiling as sweetly as I could manage as I took the pen he was prodding at me, my positive response unleashing a barrage of words.

'I think you're great, the best. Not that Sammie and Latisha aren't sexy, but you're better, real better, especially on the new cover, with the three of you on the Vegas Strip, well cool! The police had to clear the road for you, didn't they? I know that, 'cause I read everything I can about you . . . Yes, to Aaron Pensler, please. That's me. Could you put "with love to a cool dude"?'

'Of course,' I promised, praying he didn't know what the real Aisha Tyler's signature looked like, because I hadn't the faintest idea, or even how to spell her name properly.

To judge by what he was saying, she was some minor pop star, one who looked something like me, although what he thought she'd be doing stripping in a seedy bar in the Channel Islands was beyond me. I didn't care, keen only to get away as I made an elaborate but more or less unintelligible scrawl in his autograph book. He watched open mouthed, quickly sucking up a piece of drool that was threatening to escape over his lower lip as he took the book back.

'Thanks!' he breathed. 'Wow, Aisha Tyler! So, what, you on holiday here?'

'Yes,' I lied, 'but I'd be grateful if you didn't tell anybody. I've come here to get some peace and quiet.'

'Yeah, right. I won't tell nobody, I swear it. Not 'til I get home.'

I nodded and smiled. He was American, to judge by his accent, and so safe enough once he was gone. For the moment, I only had to hope he wouldn't tip off the press. It didn't seem likely, but at the thought an idea came unbidden into my mind, of whether it would be a good idea to take him somewhere quiet and wank him off to ensure his co-operation. No, it

39

was too gross to contemplate, despite a horrid compulsion to do exactly that, and not really necessary or, at least, I hoped not.

He stayed where he was as I continued up the street, watching, and it was as if I could feel his stare lingering on my bottom. The incident had left a bad taste in my mouth, making me feel vulnerable, despite trying to tell myself that he was just a harmless idiot and of no importance at all. No doubt he would go back to the States and tell his friends he'd seen this pop star strip on holiday, to their disbelief and amusement, and that would be that.

I tried to put him out of my mind as I continued up the High Street, following Linda's instructions to where a squat stone-built house stood in a yard. The bright-blue paint didn't speak much for Frank's taste, and the place was cluttered with wood, machinery and every type of junk. There wasn't even a sign, but I went in anyway, to find a stocky, tawny-haired woman chopping wood with a hand-axe and two small children playing near by. She looked up as I approached, none too friendly.

'Hi,' I ventured, 'is Frank about, Frank White?'

'Who wants him?'

'I'm Natasha Linnet. I've bought *Les Hommeaux Florains*. I was hoping Frank might be able to do some work for me. His cousin Linda recommended him.'

Her response was to bellow his name in the direction of a great black shed in one corner of the yard, but her initial unfriendliness had vanished as she spoke to me again. 'He'll be right out. Would you like a cup of tea?'

I accepted, and as she waddled off towards the door I was wondering if she was his wife. She wasn't old enough to be his mother, so it was presumably that or his sister, which rather called into question the way he had behaved towards me the night before. Not that it was my problem.

He emerged from the shed, as handsome as I remembered him, although the sloppy casuals he'd been in the night before were obviously his idea of smart clothes. Now he was in oil-smeared overalls, and what wasn't on his overalls seemed to be on his hands, including the one he held out to me. I declined with something between a smile and a grimace, making him laugh.

'Yeah, sorry. So you want some work done?'

'Yes, rather a lot. First of all . . .'

I began to explain what I wanted, and to my relief he not only took it in but also quickly began to make suggestions. Before long, he'd accepted the job and promised to deal with sub-contractors as well, and to come down with me the following morning. He even told me the best place to hire a car, from Don White, which was embarrassing, but I could hardly explain why, and he'd soon made a phone call to say I'd be down at Whitegates later in the afternoon.

My first glance at the High Street hadn't been exactly inspiring when it came to shopping, because what few clothes shops there were either seemed to go for rustic, cheap or expensive but far too old for me. No doubt the selection reflected the needs of the locals, but they weren't much use to me. I could at least buy panties and bras, also plain cotton summer dresses which I always like, but even that was spoilt by the constant attention of Aaron Pensler, who was still sitting outside Andy's, his eyes following my every move and grinning at me every time I passed.

Keen to get out of town and with nothing better to do, I decided to explore the western end of the island, which I'd seen from the air as a vista of massive cliffs

41

and rough ground, but hadn't visited at all. An uneven, sandy track led me out towards the cliffs, which were magnificent, great buttresses of broken rock thrusting out into a blue sea flecked with whitecaps and studded with tidal rocks and great lonely stacks, some close to shore, others far, far out, including one with a distant, lonely lighthouse. Further still, I could see the other Channel Islands, low grey masses on the horizon, save for the occasional twinkle where the sunlight caught on glass.

For a long while, I just stood and stared, soaking up the atmosphere, then walked on, following the cliff path up and down a series of little overgrown valleys, eating blackberries and scuffing my feet in the dust until I looked a complete ragamuffin, with dirty legs and purple stains around my mouth and down my front. Not that I cared, because, although people might criticise, it didn't matter any more.

I thought of Penny, and how she would no doubt have walked the same path and eaten from the same blackberry bushes as a child, and as a teenager. She'd told me about her first sexual experience, when she'd let a local boy toss off over her bottom in one of the old German pillboxes. So far as I could remember he'd been called Ryan, and for all I knew he'd watched my striptease in Andy's.

It was just the sort of thing she would have done first, not a grope in the back of a car or being fumbled with against the wall of some alley like most girls, but holding her panties down to let some dirty bastard get his rocks off over her bum. She was far too nice, always letting herself get talked into sympathy sex. In my shoes, she'd have already been had by Womble, no question, maybe even Pensler. She was too timid to say no, but then she'd have probably found somebody to spank her too; she usually seemed to.

I wondered which pillbox it had been, but there were dozens of the things, dotting the cliffs and in clumps around great concrete circles that had presumably been gun emplacements. Most were completely overgrown, but I managed to get into one of the bigger ones, climbing down a rusting ladder to a dank underground chamber, but it scared me, making me think of German skeletons in the decaying rags of their uniforms. Maybe Penny wasn't so timid after all.

The cliffs reached their highest point at the gun emplacements, with a view even more magnificent than before. Now I could see north, with England somewhere over the horizon, which gave me a brief pang of homesickness, but no more than that. I was also near the airport, as I discovered when one of the little yellow aeroplanes came over so low it made me duck. A few paces further on, I stopped to watch it taxi to a halt and discharge its cargo of tourists. Beside the control tower a group of men were working on some sort of mast, perhaps for mobile phones, which immediately made me feel resentful, then smile at my own reaction. I'd barely arrived, and already I was becoming possessive over the island.

At length it was time to go down to Whitegates, which I'd been rather dreading, but with Pensler around it was a relief. Don White might have been fat and getting on a bit, but at least he was a man. Besides, there's something about older men that appeals to my sexuality, and they're certainly the best when I need a spanking. Pensler was just plain creepy.

The afternoon was pleasantly cool, so I decided to walk down to Whitegates and get to know the island a little better. Beyond the eastern edge of the town, the road led out between high stone walls, obviously old, with weeds growing in the cracks, again reminding me of the Med. There were occasional houses set back from the road and, rather incongruously, German pillboxes at most of the corners.

As I walked, I was wondering if I could strike a deal with Don White. He knew what I'd done with Mick, and so might well expect the same treatment. Maybe, even if he wasn't into spanking girls, he could be persuaded to do me when I needed it in return for his blow-jobs. It was either that or wait for Percy to visit, and Don was big enough and old enough to do it, even if he would almost certainly need to be taught the subtleties, such as how to bring home my shame to me as my panties were taken down.

Maybe it would be possible, although I was determined to be cautious. After all, like Frank, he might be married and, while I didn't give a damn for his fidelity, the last thing I wanted was irate women chasing me around the island. Unless they were going to spank my bottom for me when they caught me, of course, but that was probably asking a bit much. It was a pity really and, after all, what better way to punish some dirty little tart than to whip her panties down and give her a thorough spanking, preferably in front of a good-sized audience. That's what happens to bad girls, isn't it? If not, it should be, me at least.

I could imagine the scene all too easily. She would catch me in the High Street, perhaps outside Andy's, with lots of people to watch. I'd fight like anything, but only succeed in drawing attention to myself as I was dragged across the street by my ear. She'd sit down at one of the outside tables and over I'd go, kicking and squealing and begging as my skirt was turned up and my panties taken down. It would be done in a no-nonsense manner, to get me bare for action as much as to humiliate me, and as soon as I was stripped the spanking would begin. She'd do it hard, making my bottom wobble and bounce, with my legs kicking stupidly in the air to show off my pussy, my hair tossing in every direction, my face tear-streaked and snotty. A crowd would gather, standing in a ring around us and laughing at my plight, and as a final humiliation I'd be left draped across the table with a beer bottle stuck up my bumhole and the half-finished contents gurgling slowly inside me.

As I came into Whitegates, I was smiling at my own dirty mind. Just a couple of days without and already I was itching for a spanking. Unfortunately, I could see it being a real problem. Percy had promised to be there to take care of me as often as he could, but we'd both agreed that actually living together would be a mistake. I needed my own space. More than that, I *craved* my own space, and I was determined not to get into a situation where any other person felt they had a right to come and go from *Les Hommeaux Florains* as they pleased.

That meant striking a deal with a man, or possibly a woman, who would be grateful for what he got and respectful of my space, yet spank me when I needed it, preferably humiliating me too. He or she also needed to be discreet and not grow possessive, or arrogant about the way our relationship worked. As I knew from bitter experience, it was something of a tall order, but Don White had to be a possible candidate. Any man that old, fat and ugly had to be grovellingly grateful for the chance to do rude things to me, and I didn't need to tell him that it was precisely because he was so unattractive that the idea of him spanking me appealed. Punishment from him was going to be strong, however bad he was at it, but on everything else I'd have to take a chance. Possibly it would be better if he was married, as that would assure his discretion. It made sense, and the thought of giving myself into the hands of a man like him was enough to set my tummy fluttering, so I decided to investigate further, at the very least.

He was working, but the bony, peevish woman who answered his door introduced herself as his wife and rather grudgingly allowed me to inspect the cars they had for hire. There was a choice of three: an original-style Mini Traveller so old the wooden trim was grey and cracking, a Ford Cortina I'd first assumed was there to provide spare parts for his taxi, and a huge and rusting 3.5-litre Rover. Percy had once owned a near-identical Rover, so I chose that, reasoning that I'd have at least some idea of its faults.

She wanted an outrageous amount of money and refused to haggle or even sell the thing to me outright, so by the time I left whatever qualms I might have had about seducing her husband had vanished. Instead, I was wondering if it might be satisfying to let him fuck me, and determined to get myself across his knee as soon as the chance presented itself.

My chance with Don did not present itself in the following week, nor with anyone else. Stuck in The Royal while Frank made *Les Hommeaux Florains* habitable again, I had little to do but twiddle my thumbs and explore. The island was everything Penny had led me to expect, beautiful and isolated with a rough edge more or less unknown on the mainland, and in places frankly dangerous. On the south coast, the cliffs rose to two hundred and more feet of crumbling rock, while the landscape was littered with the debris of the German occupation, including truly vicious barbed wire and unexpected holes as much as ten feet deep.

The locals were also much as she had led me to expect, a pretty rustic crew of fishermen and labourers contrasting with rich and retired incomers. Half of the locals seemed to be called White, a family I learnt had originally come over as labour to build the Victorian forts and the huge Admiralty breakwater and which seemed to have been breeding like rabbits ever since. The older families mostly had French names and were if anything even more inbred, a process that seemed to have culminated in the monstrous Womble, whose real name proved to be Paul Renouf. He was also related to the Whites.

It was all very strange and unfamiliar, but exciting, and the only real fly in the ointment was Aaron Pensler, who dogged my steps at every turn, until I was seriously considering making a pass at Womble or one of his marginally less Neanderthal colleagues in the hope that having a gorilla for a boyfriend would ward off the little squirt. Unfortunately, it would mean risking my precious privacy, while I had a nasty suspicion that it would make no difference anyway or, worse, turn him against me so that he got his revenge by contacting the press. Worse still, knowing that I'd stripped for him spoke to something deep within me, a tiny spark that made my determination to have nothing to do with him even stronger.

When Frank finally turned up at The Royal one morning to tell me I had a working bedroom and bathroom, my relief was immense. I drove straight down, only to have to wait in frustration for the tide to go out. When I did get across, I found myself well pleased with his work. As directed, he had set up a plain bedroom in the central section, with a bathroom next door. Eventually, both would be for guests, but they would do for my use while my tower rooms were given the attention they deserved.

Frank was flirting with me, as usual, and after a week of abstinence I was tempted, but held back from returning his attention. The fact that he had young children pricked what moral conscience I have, while I was fairly sure that if I let myself go the facts would have been explained in detail to his mates within hours. Instead, I waited until he'd gone before locking shut the gates and stripping nude as I had done before, although the presence of all the building material in my sanctuary spoilt something of the atmosphere.

Not quite fully relaxed, I changed into a rather cute bikini I'd picked up in one of the local shops. It was bright yellow, which works with my brown hair, and tiny, barely covering my pussy and leaving most of my bottom and boobs spilling out at the sides, while it fastened with bows tied at either hip and behind my back. Just wearing it felt pleasantly naughty, and after giving myself a liberal coating of sun block I went out with a towel and a smutty novel, intending to doze in the sun and, if I felt like it, to strip off for another orgasm.

The tops of the turrets were ideal for sunbathing. A walkway ran around the inside of the wall and above the living space, leading into each of the turrets. These had once been gun emplacements, and two retained the original cobbles and rusting iron fittings for the Victorian cannon. The other two had been adapted by the Germans, and were topped with a grainy asphalt, presumably where gun mountings had been removed. Standing, I could see all around me, including anyone who might be approaching, but when I lay down the wall hid me completely, leaving just a circle of blue sky.

I sat on the wall, which sloped gently down for some six feet before the edge, and admired the view, allowing my tensions and the frustrations of the week to fade slowly away. Soon, I was wondering if it would be nice to take off my top, knowing that from the shore I would be providing a tantalising glimpse of my bare breasts, but no more. It would feel nice too, not to mention rubbing in the sun block, and my hands had already gone behind my back to tug open the bow when I caught a movement among the tangle of scrubby vegetation where the hill rose beside the lighthouse to the old German observation post. It was a man.

My first instinct was to pretend I hadn't noticed anything and treat him to a show of me creaming my boobs. He was a long way away, so far his view would be more tantalising than satisfying, an amusing thought. As I let the weight of my breasts spill forwards I was smiling to myself, only to freeze in shock as he moved between two bushes.

There was something uncomfortably furtive about his movements, and something uncomfortably familiar about his figure. I couldn't be certain, but the skinny undersized body and the stooping walk was surely that of Aaron Pensler. He was also carrying binoculars, large ones. Irritated, I hastily refastened my bikini top, and was about to climb down to the main courtyard for some privacy when I stopped. Why should he make me change my behaviour in any way at all?

Yet I certainly wasn't giving him a strip show. I'd rather have touched my toes in front of Womble, bare behind. Obviously, he wasn't going to go away, whatever I did, and he hadn't emerged from behind the bush, so was presumably watching. Whatever I did, I wanted the experience to be frustrating for him, and if I knew that would only encourage him, well, he had to go home eventually.

No bare naughty bits seemed a good rule, but plenty of hint that they might be bared. I stood, stretching in the sunlight, put my hands to one of the bows at my hips, facing towards him, as if to open it, but didn't. My hands went to my breasts again, first to adjust the cups of my bikini top, then behind my back as if to undo the bow, only to pretend to think better of it. Only then did it occur to me that if he had a camera I might well be providing him with some prime shots, either for his own masturbatory fantasies or the papers. It would need a high-powered lens, but I wasn't taking any chances.

Quickly, I ducked down beneath the parapet, spread out my towel and lay down. Two quick tugs and I was out of my bikini, which I tossed up on to the wall, smiling once more. He'd see, and he'd know I was now in the nude, yet he couldn't see me at all and photos of a small yellow bikini lying on a piece of concrete weren't going to have much in the way of market value.

I rolled over on to my tummy, feeling rather pleased with myself as I opened my book. My bottom was bare and showing, something he'd have loved to gawp at, but he could see nothing, only imagine how I would be. I wondered how long it would be before he lost interest and decided he was quite capable of staying there all day. Meanwhile, I could crawl out from the gun emplacement in the shadow of the wall and do whatever I pleased, still in the nude, and leaving him getting in a sweat over nothing more than my bikini. It was only a shame I couldn't leave the fort altogether without him noticing.

The book was just something I'd picked up at the airport, with lots of men striding around in tight jodhpurs and smacking their riding boots with their whips. I kept hoping they'd be smacking some female bottoms instead, but it all seemed a bit PC, with female characters who were supposed to be feisty but just came across as precious. I was soon bored, and wondering if Aaron was still watching, while the very absence of any spanking in my book was making me crave it all the more.

After a while, I lifted my head above the parapet and stole what I hoped would look like a random glance at the hillside. If he was still there, I couldn't see him, but as he seemed to be a skilled and probably experienced Peeping Tom that didn't necessarily mean anything. Not being sure made it feel as if he was getting the better of me, for all that I'd cheated him of what he wanted, and I found myself biting my lip in annoyance. Another attempt to get into my book failed, and I found myself considering the idea of confronting him.

Possibly, if I played my cards right, I could make him feel ashamed of himself without actively turning him against me. Unfortunately, he seemed to be just the sort of obsessive little git who would see things in black and white, so that any overt rejection on my part was likely to mean trouble. Maybe it made more sense to offer him a deal, perhaps a chance to spank me and a pull of his no doubt weedy little cock as long as he understood that there was nothing more on offer and it had to remain between us. It would be unspeakably humiliating too, with his long fidgety fingers on the ties of my bikini as I came bare and loitering over my body as he touched me up before my spanking began . . .

No, I was letting my dirty mind run away with me. He was just too creepy.

I'd been in the sun for well over an hour, and decided I should go in for a bit. Crawling nude out of the emplacement to leave him staring at an unoccupied turret should have been amusing, but was more humiliating. After all, he had essentially got me stripped and put me on my knees, albeit unwittingly. Even indoors, as I tried out the new shower I found myself glancing out of the window, but only the top of the German observation post was visible . . .

. . . with Aaron Pensler standing on top of it.

I swore out loud as I jerked back from the window. He had managed to find the one place from which it was possible to see inside the fort, not much, and he couldn't possibly be able to see me, but it was still annoying. When I looked again, he was gone, but the observation ports in the structure had been built for a purpose, to see out and remain protected. Now they seemed like eyes, evil, slitty eyes watching my every move. I was sure he was behind one, and the fact that he couldn't see me was minimal consolation.

As soon as I was dry, I slipped a pair of panties up my legs and a yellow summer dress over my head. Taking my book as a prop, I went outside. The observation tower was only visible from parts of the walls and the upper windows of my accommodation, not really a problem at all, unless it contained a compulsive and determined stalker with high-powered binoculars, or a paparazzo. Again, I considered the possibility of making a deal with him, just to wank him off, but the thought of taking his horrid little cock in my hand made me shudder. I would wait until he left the island.

Yet, as I walked around the wall to find out exactly what he could and couldn't see, I was boiling with frustration and even more tempted to go and tell the little bastard exactly what I thought of him. He'd invaded my sanctuary, making me cover up when I should have been happily nude and carefree. Maybe he'd seen enough to masturbate over. Maybe he was doing it even now, his skinny little cock jerking in his hand as his dirty mind ran over what he'd seen, my bare tummy and legs, my boobs and bum bursting out of the deliberately inadequate bikini. Maybe he'd already done it.

That gave me pause for thought. Most men, a few dyed-in-the-wool perverts excepted, feel guilty after coming over anything but the most socially acceptable things. What Aaron was doing was far from socially acceptable, and so presumably once he'd come off in his hand he'd slink away, feeling bad about it. Possibly he already had, and the man I'd seen on top of the observation tower hadn't even been him. If not, then perhaps it was worth the sacrifice of going topless for a while, where he could see, just long enough for him to do what he felt he had to do. Then I'd be rid of him, while if he'd already gone it made no difference.

I bit my lip as I considered the possibility. It was a surrender, no question, and intensely shameful, but I was reasonably sure it would work. True, it would also encourage him to come back, but I could be fairly sure he'd do that anyway. Besides, he'd already seen my tits, and my bum, which shouldn't have been important but somehow seemed to make all the difference in the world. I was going to do it.

With a deep and resigned sigh I shrugged off my dress and sat down on the parapet, pretending to read, in nothing but little black knickers and intensely aware of my bare boobs. It felt hideously shameful, so much so that it started the tears in my eyes and I nearly covered up again, but I stopped myself, determined to see it through. He was there, I was sure, not that I could see him, but I felt watched. Yes, there was no doubt. He'd be in behind one of the observation slits, his trousers and pants down around his ankles, his weedy little cock hard in his hand as he wanked himself over my naked breasts. Probably he'd imagine himself coming over them, and watching the disgust on my face as the thick white spunk slithered down over my bare skin, with bits of it hanging from my nipples and more in my face where he'd missed . . .

The bastard! No, he was not going to get me turning myself on over my own humiliation, not Aaron Pensler. I'd come, in my own good time, but when I did it would be over something entirely different. Surely he had to have finished? It was hard to imagine him as anything other than the sort of man who'd come in his hand almost as soon as he was hard, and probably be unable to hold back at all, never mind with a pair of real, flesh-and-blood boobs in view, especially when he was clearly besotted with this Aisha Tyler.

Yes, he'd have come, but putting my dress back on was going to make it look as if I'd been showing off for him, which was not at all what I wanted. For my idea to work he had to think he'd caught me out, otherwise why feel guilty? I lay down on the parapet instead, the asphalt scratchy against the delicate skin of my boobs, my nipples in particular. With one eye trained on the observation tower and the open hillside at its base, I pretended to read my book.

Maybe a minute passed, maybe two, before he emerged from the base of the tower. It was him, no question, a miserable little specimen of humanity, unmistakable even at a distance. I'd guessed right and, if there was a certain satisfaction in the way I'd handled his psychology, then it only went so far in making up for my intense shame for going topless to let him wank over the view. Even telling myself he'd undoubtedly have done the same over my striptease, and after seeing me close up, didn't help.

He was quickly gone from sight, but to my annoyance the episode had broken my mood. I no longer wanted to strip off and play with myself, I wanted to climb up on to the hill and find out how much he would have been able to see and where he'd watched me from. I tried to resist, first making yet another attempt to get into my book and then pulling my panties down in the courtyard and giving myself a few firm smacks as I imagined being taken across Don White's knee.

Not even the spanking worked, because I couldn't stop myself from imagining I was being punished for letting Aaron Pensler come over the sight of my boobs, which was something I felt I deserved. Having given in, I went indoors to change once more, this time into jeans and boots with a long-sleeved top, as the hillside looked extremely scratchy.

It was overgrown with gorse, thistles and various prickly shrubs, so much so that it was impossible not to be impressed, and horrified, at Aaron Pensler's sheer persistence in spying on me. Even dressed as I was, I didn't dare approach the bushes from which he'd watched me sunbathe, and even the track up to the tower was partially overgrown. The structure itself was hardly better, a huge concrete thing, squat and ugly not merely for its shape but for its forbidding Third Reich architecture. Inside, it was a maze of tunnels, half-choked with debris and fetid with aromas I really didn't want to investigate. There was only just enough light to see by as I climbed the interior stair, and the way out on to the roof proved to be via a shaft set with rusting iron rungs, several broken or missing. After a moment of hesitation, I swung myself up, not easily, and again had to admire Pensler's sheer persistence.

From the top I found myself looking down on *Les Hommeaux Florains* as if it were a toy castle, a relief until I thought of his binoculars. To the naked eye, I'd have been just a tiny mannequin, perhaps too distant to distinguish the yellow material of my bikini from flesh. With good binoculars, it would have been a different matter, and something told me his would be the best he could possibly afford. I hid a sigh as I pictured how I'd have looked.

It didn't seem likely he'd watched from the roof itself, so I climbed down to investigate further. There were three main observation slits, one above the other, looking out towards France. A big semicircular room stood behind the uppermost of these, providing almost as good a view of *Les Hommeaux Florains* as from the roof. There, just as I'd been anticipating, spattered down the wall and lying in a sticky pool on the grey concrete floor, was Aaron's Pensler's spunk.

I felt my gorge rise and turned away to look out through the slit. *Les Hommeaux Florains* was as before, a square of stone between the four turrets, the same yellowish beige as the rock from which it had been quarried, save for the pale-grey asphalt topping the broad parapet, where I'd sat, my dress off and my boobs out while he'd tossed his dirty little cock all over the floor. It didn't bear thinking about, but I couldn't help myself. I could even smell his spunk, my head was full of images of how it would have been, with his binoculars focused on my near-naked body, his own weedy frame trembling with excitement and the motion of his arm as he tossed himself towards ecstasy, all the while thinking of how he'd like to do it over my boobs, thoroughly soiling my clean white skin.

Worse, if I'd come up to make a deal it would have been my hand his cock was in, me who was tossing him, with my top pulled up to show him my boobs as I did it. Probably he'd have wanted me to take him in my mouth and suck him hard, or have me show off first, playing with my tits and teasing my nipples hard, pulling down my jeans and even my panties for him. Yes, that would be best ... worst, being made to go nude as he played with his dirty little cock. Then it would go in my mouth, a repulsive thought, before he fucked my spit-wet cleavage and finally came all over me, across my boobs and in my face, splashing my belly and soiling my panties, down which I badly wanted to slip a hand ...

No, I couldn't, I really couldn't, not over him.

Only it wasn't over him, not really, only the way I reacted to him. Yes it was, and I was nothing but a dirty little tart, unable to face the truth, that I wanted him to spunk all over my boobs. No, not really ... Yes, really, wanking his cock over them as I held them up, round and heavy in my hands, showing them off to him, sucking his cock with my panties down behind and letting him titty fuck me ...

Oh, God, I was going to do it, I couldn't stop myself. I cried out loud as I began to fumble with the button of my jeans, popping it open to get at my pussy, my hand pushed down my knickers to find my flesh puffy and hot, my crease sopping with juice, my hole ready for fucking. One touch to my clit and it would be too late, the final surrender, and I pulled back, telling myself I'd go back to the fort and do it there, over something completely different.

I was dizzy with shame and ecstasy as I stood away from the observation slit, willing myself to do my jeans up again and leave. It didn't work, my eyes lighting on the slimy little puddle he'd made on the floor, and I was lost. I would do it, just once, to get it out of my head, and then never again. I was sobbing with shame, but my hand went back down my panties and this time I knew there was no turning back.

57

A biting humiliation as strong as any I'd ever known hit me as I began to rub myself again, now imagining my disgust as he tossed himself over my naked breasts, his little pink penis jerking in his hand, the drool running from the side of his mouth, grunting as he approached orgasm, coming, to send spurt after spurt after spurt of thick white come all over my tits and my turned-up top, in my face and in my mouth, to leave me gagging and spitting on the floor as he wiped himself clean in my hair.

I sank down into a squat, imagining the position he'd put me in, kneeling for him to toss off over me. Maybe I should have offered him a deal after all, and if I had maybe I'd have lost control and done what I was imagining, for real. Maybe I'd have caught him wanking and been made to help, panties down and titties out to let him enjoy my body, just as I was imagining. God, it would have felt good to be spunked on, my clean white skin filthy with his mess, and that was exactly as I should be, tits out and soiled with his spunk.

One firm tug and my top was up, another and my boobs had been spilt out of my bra, lying heavy and bare on my chest, just as he'd seen them. My self-disgust was burning in my head as I dipped my fingers into the little puddle of spunk on the concrete, still warm, and worse as I lifted it, hanging in sticky tendrils from my fingers. A choking sob escaped my lips as I let a piece touch one aching nipple, and I'd lost all control.

I was gasping and crying as I smeared the spunk all over my tits, thoroughly soiling both of them and keeping one hand there to rub it in as I snatched at my pussy. One hard push and my jeans and knickers were down, dirty with the spunk from my hands, my bottom bare. A moment to soil my cheeks, another to spread them and tickle the tight, sweaty little star of my anus with one slimy fingertip and I was masturbating again.

My screams rang loud in the empty room as I began to come, one hand clutching at my aching pussy, the other slapping more of his filth over my tits, in my face, in my open mouth, more on my tits, snatching and slapping at the fat, slippery globes as I imagined his cock exploding all over me, a huge volume of spunk, enough to leave my tits plastered and dripping, my face sticky and foul, my mouth full, bubbling out over my lips to dribble into my cleavage, and at last, squeezing the heavy globes together to make a slide for his cock, kissing the tip as he came slowly down from his orgasm, just as I was doing.

Three

At least I hadn't actually done anything with Aaron Pensler. I had with Mick, and it was soon becoming a problem. He wasn't married, and seemed to regard having squeezed a blow-job out of me as a good way to start a relationship. Maybe it was, by island standards. He even seemed to think I'd been avoiding him, and regarded it as unreasonable, when in fact it was simply that our paths hadn't happened to cross. Given his attention, my first instinct was to make the best of it. After all, I'd enjoyed sucking him off, and perhaps he wouldn't mind taking me across his knee?

I quickly realised it wasn't going to work. After a couple of exploratory outings, the second of which ended up with me back on his cock in his taxi, I found he couldn't keep his mouth shut. If he was going to brag about getting a blow-job, obviously there was no way I could trust him to give me my spankings. He was also much too possessive, calling me his 'babe' and getting aggressive with other men who tried to talk to me after just two rather lacklustre dates.

Obviously it wasn't going to work, and when he asked me to come to Andy's with him on the Saturday I politely but firmly declined. Yet I did need somebody, not only to spank my bottom but also to keep me grounded, because without that I knew I was at risk of slipping completely out of control. Aaron Pensler was still very much around, although cautious after seeing me with Mick. The more of his attention I got, the more ashamed I grew of having masturbated over him coming all over me, and that the spark was still there. Spark or no spark, I certainly wasn't going out with him. There are limits.

Even after he'd peeped on me, I hadn't thought of him as a stalker, but that weekend I began to wonder. Keen to avoid Mick and also Pensler, I'd steered clear of town on the Saturday night and gone to The Barn instead, a restaurant and bar which catered mainly for tourists and was about as close to my tastes as the island could provide. It was also closest to *Les Hommeaux Florains*, and as I'd officially moved in the night before I'd decided on a celebratory meal. I had lobster, caught that afternoon, which was delicious, and washed it down with a bottle of acceptable Viognier.

Afterwards, I felt pleasantly mellow, and more so after drinking a brandy before I started back. It was a beautiful night, with a big moon in a sky full of stars and the beam of the lighthouse sweeping over the landscape to light my way. The tide was falling but still quite high, and I knew my causeway might still be covered, so I walked slowly, enjoying the warm night air and the sense of absolute relaxation I'd come to enjoy, spoilt only by unwanted male attention.

The Barn stood by the main road from town to the east end of the island, which would have taken me more or less straight home. The road came close to the sea by another of the old forts, this one set on a pretty, sandy bay backed by a massive German defence wall, twenty foot high or so and following the full curve of the water. I decided to go via the beach, and kicked my shoes off when I reached the edge, holding them in my hands as I walked, my toes sinking in fine sand still warm from the heat of the day at every step.

I seemed to be quite alone, and it was tempting to peel off my dress and go in just my panties, or even to strip naked, at least until I reached the end of the bay and the road. After all, it was dark, the German wall sheltered me from the left and the sea from the right, while I would see anyone else on the beach before they realised I was nude. It was too naughty to resist, and to think was to act, my dress peeled up over my head on the spot. A few steps later, my panties came down and off, to leave me deliciously nude.

My clothes went into my bag, adding to my sense of nakedness. Slightly drunk and pleasantly mellow, I walked on, enjoying the cool night air on my body and the naughty feeling of being in the nude out-doors, yet quite safe. I told myself I wouldn't put my dress on until I reached the end of the wall, and that even then I'd leave my knickers off, adding to my sense of daring. It felt so nice I was even starting to wonder if I might not be cheekier still and sit down against the wall to bring myself to orgasm under my fingers.

I decided to do it, but not immediately. There was another pleasantly naughty possibility I wanted to try first – skinny dipping. After piling my clothes at the top of the beach, I ran down to the edge of the sea, the water so smooth it seemed like a sheet of dull metal in the moonlight, with the high wall cutting off the lighthouse beam so that it merely flickered across the hillside to the west. I dipped my toe in, to find it surprisingly warm, but still cold enough to make me hesitate, standing at the edge before telling myself not to be pathetic and rushing forward, to stumble and fall full length into the water.

When I came up, I was gasping and giggling together, and spent a moment fighting for breath, sat on the sand in the shallows. I was in, stark naked in the sea on a lovely starry night, completely relaxed, my only concern what I would think about as I masturbated after finishing my swim. There was really only one option, because my need for a spanking had risen to a physical ache. I knew I'd get it from Cheryl when she arrived on the Monday, but it was still a real and urgent need.

I had spoken to Don White that morning, supposedly in an effort to persuade him to sell me the old Rover, but in practice to sound him out as a possible spanker. From the way his eyes had moved over my chest and followed my bum as I walked, I was sure he fancied me, and was very likely thinking of how I'd looked with Mick's spunk plastered over my face. He was Mick's friend, unfortunately, to say nothing of being married, yet I was sure something might have happened if his wife hadn't come out in the middle of negotiations. The result was I now owned a large and ancient car but my bottom was still unsmacked.

As I waded deeper into the sea, I was smiling to myself at my own behaviour, and imagining how things might have been. Probably it would have been best to suck his cock first, just until he was hard, then to demand my spanking if he wanted me to finish him off. A man with an erection will do virtually anything he's asked, in my experience, so, however perverted he felt my demand to be, he would do it. Over I'd go, my bum stripped and smacked, his disgust at my behaviour adding to the humiliation of my spanking.

Only when I was up to my neck did I start to swim, just a few strokes, before rolling on my back to float, staring up at the stars. My nipples had gone hard and felt delightfully sensitive, while my need to come was rising with my fantasy. I promised myself I'd hold off, keeping my hands away from my pussy until I could bear it no more. Until then I'd just think, driving myself gradually mad with desire over the thought of being taken down across Fat Don's lap, my dress lifted to show my legs, my panties eased slowly down until my bottom was bare and ready, maybe my cheeks hauled apart so that he could inspect my bumhole and pussy, then spanked, spanked until I cried, spanked until I howled and blubbered and wet myself all over the ground behind me . . .

I cut off my train of thought, deliberately, twisting in the water then striking out as fast as I could, until I began to worry about getting too far from the shore. There didn't seem to be any current, and the bay was enclosed on three sides, but it was best to be safe and I started back, now at a leisurely pace, until at last my feet touched the sandy bottom. I was beginning to get cold, and hauled myself out, to stand shivering in the moonlight.

Ahead of me the beach ran grey and pale up to the shadow of the wall. The lighthouse beam came across, flickering over the landscape, cut off by the hill and tower for a moment, sweeping the top of the wall, and briefly illuminating a figure in silhouette. I knew who it was immediately, the skinny body too distinctive to be anyone but Aaron Pensler. I felt a stab of anger for his intrusion, then fear, wonder at how he'd managed to follow me, and concern for how much he'd seen.

When the beam passed again he'd gone, the wall now empty, but I was very sure of what I'd seen. As

I ran up the beach I was telling myself he wouldn't dare accost me, but underneath I wasn't so sure, and I wanted to get back in my clothes very badly indeed. Fortunately, he had to go right around the wall to get to me, unless he jumped, in which case with luck he'd break a leg, better still his scrawny neck. I had time, and whichever way he came I could go the other.

It was still frightening, and I was angry too, as I slipped on my panties and pulled on my dress over my wet body. He had no right to follow me about, let alone to peep at me, and I was close to tears as I scanned the beach in either direction. There was no sign of him there, or on the wall above me, just a car moving down the distant hill to turn in at the barn. I moved in that direction, telling myself I could handle the little squirt even if he did try anything, but still scared.

The beach was open until the point at which the wall joined on to the fort, where a heavy bank of foliage hung low over the sand, creating black shadows. My heart was in my mouth as I approached, imagining him crouched there, watching, although I knew he could have hardly got there in time. Nothing happened, and I reached the slipway from the car park to the beach, safe, but still with my heart in my mouth and expecting to run into him at any moment. He wasn't there, but as I hurried across down the track another car approached, this time passing the barn to turn directly in front of me.

I stopped, full of relief, deciding to speak to them whoever they were, just as a head emerged from the driver's window, huge, egg-shaped and topped by a tangle of pale hair, Womble. He was leering at me, and I realised my dress was plastered against my wet skin, making my breasts show and my nipples embarrassingly prominent. I didn't care, just grateful for the company. The car stopped and Womble climbed out, briefly illuminated by the lighthouse beam, his babyish face split by a huge and dirty grin. Another man followed, almost as tall, and well built although looking slight beside Womble's imposing bulk. He spoke first.

'You're Tasha, ain't you? Mick's girl.'

'Not any more,' I pointed out, and as the light swept over us again I recognised him as Liam, the barman from Andy's.

'You're all wet,' Womble pointed out unnecessarily.

'I've been swimming,' I admitted.

'What, in your gear?'

'No, I . . .'

'Skinny dipping? Nice.'

The light flicked over them again, at the exact moment Womble extruded a fat pink tongue to moisten his lips at the thought of me swimming nude. I found myself blushing, but their company was still an immeasurable improvement on being alone with Aaron Pensler somewhere out there in the darkness.

'Would one of you mind walking me home?' I asked. 'I live out at *Les Hommeaux Florains*.'

'We know, love,' Womble answered. 'You rich, or what?'

'I'll drive you back,' Liam offered.

Womble hesitated, perhaps wishing he'd made the offer first. 'What? I can't do the nets on my own, mate. Takes two.'

'I wouldn't ask,' I went on quickly, 'only there's this creep following me around. He was peeping on me swimming, and –'

'You want we should fuck him over?' Womble suggested, bunching a pair of fists like cobblestones.

'No, no, nothing like that,' I said quickly, despite a surge of gratitude that threatened to bring the tears to my eyes once more. 'I'd just like somebody to take me home. Please, it won't take a moment.'

'You stick around, love, I'll walk you back after,' Liam offered.

I nodded after only an instant's hesitation, far preferring to suffer my damp dress than walk back with Aaron Pensler lurking around. Liam and Womble got on with their work, each trying to flirt in his own way as they unloaded crates and various bits of what I took to be fishing equipment from the car. I followed them down to the water's edge, keeping close to the pools of light spread out by their flashlights' beams, which made it impossible to see anything beyond. They had fixed a net below the low cliff fringing the western shore of the bay, among huge sea-worn boulders, one of which I sat on as they worked.

It was an odd sensation, confined in an oasis of flickering light from the torches and lighthouse, my safety guaranteed by my proximity to the two men. For once I was glad of their raw masculinity. They were rustic, even primitive in Womble's case, but in the circumstances that was just what I needed. They had shown an instinctive urge to protect me, as demonstrated by Womble's immediate, unthinking offer of violence on my behalf, and it was impossible not to feel grateful.

My reaction wasn't rational, because from the way they'd looked at me their intentions obviously weren't so very different from Pensler's, but that didn't matter. I could probably have coped with Pensler too, assuming he'd even dared accost me, but Liam or Womble, let alone together, could, if they wanted, simply use me as they pleased. The difference was that, while the thought of touching Pensler even in my own defence made my stomach turn, the idea of being manhandled by Liam was intriguing, and by Womble frightening, but in a not entirely unpleasant way.

It took them maybe half-an-hour to sort themselves out, placing a large flatfish and two more ordinary-looking ones in a crate before resetting the net. They were pleased with the night's work, although it seemed to be an awful lot of effort for three fish. As we walked back, they were laughing and chatting, with Womble adding the occasional snigger, but only when I was a little way away.

They reached the car first, as I'd paused to wait for the lighthouse beam to illuminate the top of the wall, half-expecting to see Pensler outlined against the glare. There was no sign of him, but as I climbed up to the car park I saw Liam and Womble standing close together. Liam had one hand on top of the other, and as he lifted it Womble peered close, then gave a grunt of irritation. Liam laughed. They'd tossed a coin, and I could guess what for.

'I'll walk you back, love,' Liam announced as I reached them. 'See you tomorrow, yeah, Paul, and don't let that flatty go for less than thirty.'

'Easy money,' Womble answered, and swung himself into the car.

He barely seemed to fit, and had to slam the door hard to get the bits of him that bulged out at the sides in at all. We waited for him to go, my eyes gradually growing accustomed to the moonlight as we watched his headlights disappear up the hill towards town, Liam only speaking when they'd vanished.

'So who's this bloke who's been following you?'

'Some American tourist. Aaron Pensler, he's called. Maybe I'm being silly, but he won't leave me alone, and there's something creepy about him.'

'Yeah?'

'Yes. I made a stupid mistake, you see. He thought I was some pop princess, Aisha Tyler, and he wanted my autograph. I just thought it was funny, but he's been following me around ever since, and spying on me.'

It was easy to talk, my words spilling out quickly in my fear and a loneliness I hadn't entirely realised was there. As we reached the road and turned east towards *Les Hommeaux Florains*, I reached out to pull Liam's arm around me, really just for comfort.

'What happened tonight?' he asked.

'I was at The Barn,' I told him, 'and I thought I'd go along the beach on the way back. It was such a lovely night I decided to have a swim . . . maybe I was a bit drunk too, not much. I saw him on the wall, in the lighthouse beam, definitely him, and he was watching. I got dressed quickly and I was going back towards The Barn when I met you and Wom – Paul. That probably sounds really silly to you, but . . .'

'No, I get it.'

'Thanks. What's really scary is that he knew I was there. He must have been watching me all evening, or how would he have known I was in The Barn? He must have been watching while I had dinner, maybe before as well, and I never even knew he was there. If the lighthouse beam hadn't caught him standing up on the wall, I'd probably never have seen him at all.'

A shiver ran through me at the thought of what I'd been planning, to masturbate on the beach, although that was not something I was going to admit to Liam. I'd have been in bright moonlight, indistinct, but clear enough for Pensler to see what I was up to if he was looking down from the top of the wall. As I imagined looking up to find his gargoyle face staring down at me as I lay with my thighs cocked wide and caressing my boobs and pussy, another shiver ran through me, stronger than before.

'It's OK, I'm here,' Liam assured me, his arm tightening around my waist.

I let him hold me as we walked on. Pensler would still be there, I was sure, hidden somewhere out in the night, perhaps up by the observation tower, perhaps closer, if he dared. He wouldn't approach, I felt certain of that much, but he would watch, his horrid little brain flickering with envy and lust, and all sorts of emotions I couldn't begin to guess at. Maybe he'd be angry with himself because I'd spotted him? Maybe not. Maybe he'd be pleased with himself for scaring me. Yes, that was more likely, the smug little bastard.

Suddenly I was angry, and wishing I'd set Womble on to him. Even if we'd failed to catch him, he'd have known how I'd felt, alone and hunted, almost anyway, because, while Womble was pretty terrifying, there'd have been no sexual element to Pensler's fear. I knew I'd been sensible, avoiding the risk of Pensler contacting the paparazzi, but I was now treading close to the edge anyway.

Liam was still talking, explaining how he and Womble sold their fish direct to retired incomers at high prices, but I wasn't really listening. After what had happened the only way I could be sure Pensler wouldn't start to make life difficult for me was by giving him what he obviously wanted. I really couldn't face it, a surrender too extreme and growing worse with each new indignity he visited on me. Sensible or not, what I wanted was to get him back, to make him feel as I did, or at least fill him with bad emotions.

Soon, we'd reached the junction of the track leading down towards *Les Hommeaux Florains*. The tide was all the way out, my causeway a pale ribbon leading away to the dark bulk of the fort, with the parapet oddly bright, brighter still as the beam from the lighthouse swept across it, suddenly dark, and growing bright once more as my eyes adapted. We stopped, one of those moments when you wonder if you should invite somebody in, Liam perhaps wondering if he should push it or not, trying to judge my mood. I wasn't sure myself, still uneasy, yet warm from my earlier dirty thoughts, while I was tempted by the thought of how angry Pensler would be to see me go into the fort alone with Liam so late at night.

'You all right, Tasha?' Liam asked suddenly, his voice now a trifle uncertain. 'You want me to fuck off, or what?'

It wasn't the most elegant proposition I'd ever heard, but it was sweet, giving me a plain choice instead of pushing me or trying to be sneaky. Still I hesitated, my emotions too conflicted for easy resolution, only to think of how I'd feel alone in the fort, not knowing if Pensler was still out there somewhere, maybe lurking around the walls.

'Come in, if you like,' I offered. 'I'd like the company.'

He put his arm around me again as we started down the track, his hand now a trifle lower, on the swell of my hip. I was imagining Pensler watching, burning with jealousy, which was immensely satisfying. As the lighthouse beam swept over us again, I put my arm out in turn, hooking a thumb into Liam's belt to leave my fingers lying gently over one hard buttock. Maybe it was a risk, but I was taking a risk anyway.

Indoors, I gave Liam a brief tour of the habitable part of the accommodation before opening a bottle of a strong Chilean Merlot I'd picked up in town. It was hot indoors, and I suggested taking our glasses up on to the wall. I chose the same turret where Pensler had peeped on me sunbathing, only now with Liam and I seated side by side on the parapet, sipping wine and talking.

It was romantic but weird, drinking wine with a handsome young man in my fairytale castle while a monster lurked outside, yet not unlike so many scenes I'd pictured in my mind as an adolescent. Before we were halfway down the bottle, I was ready, and when Liam bent to kiss me I melted straight away, letting my mouth open under his and giving no resistance as one hand moved to my breasts.

He was as I'd expected, ardent, virile, unrefined. In moments I'd had my dress pulled up over my head and he was squeezing and kissing my naked breasts. I let him enjoy himself, thinking of what a fine show we'd be making, fully illuminated each time the lighthouse beam swept over us, with Pensler seething with jealousy and frustrated lust as he watched. Yet I wanted to deny him anything too intimate, to let him know, but not see too much.

When the time came for my panties to come down I slipped out of Liam's grasp and below the parapet, kneeling with my bottom bare behind as my hands went to his zip. He gave a grunt of appreciation as I pulled him out, his cock already close to hard, big and white and thick in my hand, then in my mouth as I took him in and begun to suck.

Pensler would know what I was doing, but all he could see was Liam's back and perhaps a little of my hair when the beam caught us. It was perfect, to have him know I was on my knees, willingly sucking cock for a real man, nothing the obnoxious little squirt could ever, ever have, which he couldn't even see properly. He'd be furious, burning with jealousy, knowledge that helped my excitement grow as I kissed and licked and sucked at Liam's glorious erection, wanking him too, and teasing his balls from his pants.

To make it better still, Liam wasn't even my boyfriend. He was my rescuer, maybe, but had no more claim to me than Pensler himself. Maybe Pensler had seen Liam toss the coin. With luck, he had, because if so he'd know how casually I'd been given away, made the fuck toy of a man I barely knew on the toss of a coin. For that tiny thing, Liam had me near nude at his feet, sucking cock and available for whatever else took his fancy, while Pensler had nothing but a view of my man's back.

I took Liam's balls in my mouth, rolling them over my tongue and tugging at his cock as I let my dirty thoughts run wild. So many times I'd imagined myself as a princess staked out for a dragon, rescued by a knight in shining armour only to be tossed on the ground and soundly fucked the moment I was free from my chains, sometimes before. It was like that now, on my knees to Liam as I gave him his reward, the full use of my mouth and the offer of more.

He was moaning with pleasure, his body shivering as I sucked, making me worry that he would come in my mouth. Not that I minded, but it was far too soon, and I wanted Pensler to know that Liam and I had gone all the way. I let Liam's balls slip from my mouth and ran my tongue the full length of his now straining shaft, finishing with a kiss on the tip.

'You are fucking magic!' he sighed. 'So good!'

'I can be better,' I promised, taking hold of the sides of his jeans and tugging at them.

As he lifted himself up to let his jeans come down, I was thinking of how the scene would look to Pensler, his view now of Liam's naked arse, hardly what he'd want, although I was sure he'd be unable to take his eyes away. I put my arms out, drawing

74

Liam a little forward and squeezing at his hard buttocks as I went back to work, now licking not just at his cock and balls, but lower, running my tongue up the crease of his bottom. A moment to gather my courage and my dirty feelings and I'd burrowed my tongue deeper, licking at his anus to make him gasp and shiver.

His balls were in my face, fat and soft, his cock a tower reaching up between my eyes, my tongue working in his bumhole, such a dirty thing to do for a man, yet a fitting reward. I could only wish Pensler could have seen, knowing just how dirty I could be for another man, a real man, but never for him. A new fantasy entered my head, the thought of Liam and Womble catching Pensler and making him watch as I gave them their pleasure. It was good, too good not to come over, but even as my hand slid down between my thighs Liam spoke.

'I have to fuck you, Natasha!'

Even as I pulled back, he'd taken me under my arms, and before I could do more than squeak in surprise and alarm I'd been hauled up and draped across the parapet. I tried to protest, not because I mind being fucked from behind, but because Pensler now had a fine view, far ruder and more intimate than I'd intended to allow him. My bum was stuck high, round and white, my boobs squashed out on the asphalt, all on plain view every time the lighthouse beam caught us, and I stayed that way, my words breaking to a grunt as the full length of Liam's cock was jammed up me with one hard push.

His hands found my hips, gripping tight, and I was truly helpless, held and fucked in nothing but my shoes and my lowered panties, grunting and gasping to his thrusts as he used me, my bottom squashing to every push, my boobs slapping and bouncing on the asphalt as I struggled to rise, still resisting, then breaking completely as his pace picked up inside me. All I could do was swallow my humiliation at being done in front of Pensler and make the best of it, going back to my fantasy.

It would be best, really, because the more he saw the more jealous he would be. Yes, they should have caught him and tied his hands to the steering wheel of the car, making him watch as they had me in the back. I'd go all the way, stripped nude, sucking cock like a willing little slut, licking their arseholes, letting them rub my breasts and rut in my bottom crease, fucking in full view of him, on Liam's lap, spread wide with his big cock in my pussy and my cheeks open to show off my bumhole as Pensler stared, wishing it was him, wishing I would so much as kiss him on the cheek.

Liam was getting frantic, pumping into me so hard I was losing my breath, gasping and clutching at the asphalt as he fucked me, my pleasure rising closer and closer to orgasm. His balls were slapping my pussy lips, and I forced my bum higher still to get the friction I needed, spreading myself against him as my fucking rose to a furious crescendo.

Pensler wouldn't get his peck. He'd get nothing. We'd even strip him and tie him up so that he couldn't wank his dirty little cock over what he'd seen, and when we were finished we'd leave him like that in the car park. That would be perfect, utterly humiliated and unable to touch himself, his mind burning with images of me being dirty, pleasuring Liam and Womble too, in my mouth and between my tits, in my pussy, and at last, a final torment, allowing Liam to fuck my bottom.

On that thought I came, screaming out my ecstasy into the night as Liam's balls banged on my sex. My whole body was jerking to his thrusts as he fucked me, but just as I was reaching the very peak of my orgasm he whipped his cock free, jerking it over my upturned bottom. I felt the hot spunk spatter on my cheeks and back, soiling my body, a glorious way to finish me off, and I turned immediately, to take him in my mouth and suck down what remained as I rubbed myself back up to finish my own orgasm, all the while imagining the unseen watcher on the hill.

Four

I spent the night with Liam, and the next. Maybe I
was taking a risk that he would grow possessive, but
with Pensler around I couldn't bear to be alone, and
despite his rough and ready attitude the sex was
good.

Cheryl was coming on the Monday, so I drove
down to the harbour in the late morning. It was a
peculiar place, a little square of quays with a few
fishing boats bobbing on the tide, like something
from a Cornish picture postcard, but behind it a large
fortress and the breakwater, which was out of all
proportion to everything else and created a sheltered
area big enough for several good-sized ships. There
was another, more modern quay at which the ships
presumably docked, so I found myself a seat in a bar
looking out over the sea, where I sipped orange juice
and nibbled cashew nuts while I watched for the
Cherbourg boat.

What I expected was the sort of huge white-painted
monster you get at Dover, so that the small dirty blue
vessel that looked as if it might have been operating
since the war or even beforehand was almost at the
quay before I realised it was what I was waiting for.
I finished my drink and hurried down to greet Cheryl,
who was immediately recognisable, her bright-green

afro standing out from among the group of French tourists and returning islanders, even if it hadn't been for her black skin. Her outfit was typical too, tiny shorts and a crop top in banana yellow with heels and a bag to match, and she was looking around her as if she'd just landed on Mars. I ran over to her, greeting her with a kiss and a hug, the tension I'd never managed to get rid of even with Liam draining away as I held her.

'It is so good to see you,' I told her, kissing her again before I let go. 'You wouldn't believe the time I've had! Did everything go all right?'

'Sweet,' she answered me. 'Penny says hi, and she'll be over in two weeks.'

'Good, and all my stuff's here OK?'

'Every bit.'

I had booked some of the open vans the islanders used for deliveries, and we spent a while making sure all my things came off the boat in one piece and were loaded properly. Cheryl talked constantly, describing her trip to Paris and through France to Cherbourg, and what had been happening in London. My absence had been noticed, apparently, but the press seemed to have lost interest, moving on to easier targets rather than troubling to go after me. She hadn't seen my name once in the past two weeks. It was exactly the news I'd been hoping for, despite what I suppose was an inevitable chagrin at being forgotten so quickly, and I was on top of the world as we made for where I'd parked my car on some open land behind the main harbour buildings.

Aaron Pensler had already come into the conversation, although Cheryl hadn't been able to tell me any more about Aisha Tyler, who was presumably in some very new group or just a local phenomenon wherever Pensler came from. If so, I couldn't help but wonder what he made of my accent, but I was just making a joke of his mistake to Cheryl when who should appear but the man himself, walking towards us between the double row of houses that fringed the harbour's only real street, as usual as if he was there entirely by accident. He gave his normal greeting.

'Hi Aisha, looking good!'

'Hi, Aaron,' I replied. 'Aaron, this is my friend Cheryl. Cheryl, this is Aaron Pensler, my stalker.'

I walked on, feeling well pleased with myself. As I'd spoken, Cheryl had glanced at him as if he'd just crawled out from under a stone, leaving him looking so miserable that for a moment I actually felt sorry for him. He didn't even follow at a distance, for once, but was still standing rooted to the stop when we reached my car.

'What a worm!' Cheryl commented. 'You ought to just kick him in the 'nads.'

'I don't want to antagonise him,' I explained. 'If he starts telling the press Aisha Tyler's here, there has to be a chance somebody will come over to investigate.'

'No way,' she answered me. 'Like I said, if she's getting big, they're going to know where she is, and they're going to know he's a nut. If she's too small, they won't bother chasing her.'

I nodded, still not convinced despite the fact that what she said made perfect sense. Besides, the way I'd been behaving with Liam was hardly designed to placate Pensler, never mind what I'd just said, and he hadn't done anything yet. At least, I didn't think he had. Maybe he'd tried and, as Cheryl had, said they'd known where the real Aisha Tyler was and decided he was a nut.

'The local guys any better?' Cheryl asked as I pulled out after the first of the lorries laden with my belongings.

'Cave men, most of them,' I told her. 'There's one guy called Liam I've been seeing. He's cute, but a bit rough.'

'Yeah? Does he spank good?'

'I don't know. I haven't asked him yet. You know some guys are funny about kinky things, and I'd hate him to turn me down.'

'No guy is going to turn you down!'

'You'd be surprised. A lot of men see spanking as abusive.'

'Yeah, sure, some pussywhipped dickweed, not your piece of rough, no way.'

'I hope so. I'm going to ask him, because I've really missed it.'

She laughed. 'Don't you worry, girl, just you wait until we're alone and Auntie Cheryl'll have that big white bootie bare and smacked, well smacked.'

I hadn't asked, but it was an offer too good to resist. She loved to punish me, not so much for the sexual pleasure but because she got a kick out of spanking a white girl, which I found irresistibly humiliating. Yet more of my tension drained away at the thought of the spanking she'd give me back at *Les Hommeaux Florains*, and the way she did it, telling me what she was doing and what she could see, laughing at me . . .

'Please, that would be nice,' I answered her and she laughed again.

Pensler was forgotten, Liam just about, all my frustration of the last weeks coming to the surface and starting to melt away at the thought of Cheryl spanking me. Along with Percy, her treatment of me was one of the things which had kept me sane since the pressure came on from the press, but up until then I'd never realised how dependent I was on it, and how much I needed the little routines they put me through and to be under their command. I now needed it so badly that my temper was rising as the lorry men unloaded and asked what seemed to be an endless string of stupid questions about where things went. Not that there was even very much, as I'd only held on to the things I couldn't bear to part with, but Cheryl found the state I was getting in amusing and chose to use it as an excuse, speaking quietly to me as we watched the men haul the frame of my bed upstairs.

'Best not get too stroppy with them, Miss Tasha, or I'll let them watch while I give you that spanking, huh?'

I coloured at the thought and felt my stomach tighten in anticipation. She gave a light, knowing laugh and walked back out into the courtyard, looking up at the walls. I followed, already imagining myself being given a brat spanking in front of the workmen, which was making me more urgent than ever.

'Great place,' she said.

'You can go naked all day,' I told her, 'and when the tide's in nobody can get here at all.'

She smiled and started up the stairs to the top of the wall. I came behind, admiring the way her neat, firm bottom cheeks moved in her tight shorts and remembering how good it felt to kiss her after punishment, right between her pretty black bum cheeks, before sticking my tongue well up her anus. At the top she turned to look out across the sea, then back towards the island.

'That's where Pensler watches me from,' I told her, pointing out the hill and the observation tower.

'You got to tell that guy to fuck off,' she insisted, 'or I will.'

'Don't,' I insisted. 'He's only a tourist, and he has

to go back eventually, that or realise I'm not really Aisha Tyler.'

'Why not tell him?'

'I don't think he'd believe me. How long can you stay, a week?'

'I've got a shoot on Thursday, darling. We're not all ladies of leisure.'

'That's a shame, but you'll come back soon, won't you? It's great here, but I do need my friends.'

'I'll be back,' she promised, and put her arm around me, once more making me feel secure and wanted, also more in need of her attention than ever.

Below us the men had emerged from the house, and the older of the two called up. 'That's the lot, Miss Linnet.'

'Thank you,' I answered, but he didn't leave immediately, obviously hoping for a tip.

I went down and gave them a twenty-pound note each, leaving them looking well pleased with themselves as they left. They were barely on the causeway before I had the gates shut and the bar in place, leaving me alone with Cheryl. She'd come down, and stood in the middle of the courtyard, her hands on her hips as she spoke to me. 'Now, what did I say I was going to do about that temper?'

'Spank me,' I answered, now with a huge lump in my throat, 'spank me in front of the men.'

'But you sent them away, didn't you? Now that's a shame, 'cause I'm going to have to make up for it, ain't I?'

I nodded dumbly, no longer able to speak as she sat down on the steps, making a lap with her long dark legs. She beckoned, crooking her finger and smiling, her eyes full of wicked laughter for what she was about to do to me. I came forward, shaking badly as I draped myself across her knee, into spanking position for the first time in weeks, a feeling so intense I was already close to tears as her hand found the hem of my dress.

'Let's get that big white bootie bare, yeah?' she purred, and my dress was coming up, baring my thighs and the seat of my panties, taut and white around my cheeks, which suddenly felt huge. 'All the way, I reckon, best to let those fat white titties swing free, yeah?'

She tugged my dress higher as I lifted my upper body, over my breasts but not off, so that my position was as undignified as possible, or would be shortly. I held myself in place, shaking badly as she reached underneath me to tug up the cups of my bra, flopping out my boobs and briefly catching each to grope me and bring my nipples erect with a couple of deft touches.

'Dirty little bitch, ain't you?' She chuckled in response to my sigh of pleasure. 'Now, down with the panties.'

Her voice was full of relish as she said it, and she already had hold of my waistband. I closed my eyes, utterly helpless to my own need as my panties were peeled down off my bottom and settled around my thighs, well down to leave me showing behind, my aching pussy open to her, the wet between my lips and my sopping panty crotch betraying my excitement. Her knee came up and my exposure was complete, my cheeks open to show off the puckered brown star of my bottom hole, which she had so often teased me about, saying my colouring made me look as if I didn't wipe properly.

This time she simply chuckled and brought her knee up higher still, lifting my bottom into a wonderfully ridiculous position, much the highest part of my body and completely spread, to leave everything showing behind and completely vulnerable.

'I've got a little present for you, darling,' she said.

I tried to peer back between my dangling boobs as she reached down into her bag, but all I could see was her legs and the edge of the steps.

'What is it?' I asked, wondering fearfully why she needed me in spanking position before I was given it.

'Shut up and stick it up,' she told me.

I obeyed meekly, lifting my bottom into full prominence by rising up on my toes. The sight made her chuckle, and I felt her fingers touch, pressing down between my cheeks to stretch my already flaunted bumhole wide. Something was going up my bottom, maybe a dildo, maybe anal beads, something to enhance the shame of my spanking, and it was impossible not to purr at the thought of my own degradation.

'Right up the bootie,' Cheryl said cheerfully, 'right in, Miss Tasha . . . shit, what do they want now, huh?'

Somebody was knocking on the gates, presumably the lorry men. I scrambled quickly up, making myself decent as quickly as possible as Cheryl returned whatever she'd been about to stick up my bum to her bag. I was blushing as I went to the gates, but also cursing under my breath, with my sense of frustration almost unbearably strong, so strong I was seriously considering asking for Cheryl to carry out her threat and spank me in front of the men.

It wasn't them at all, but Frank, whom I'd asked to come over when I had my things and was being unreasonably efficient. There was nothing I could do but introduce him to Cheryl and start going around the house, all the while dreading and at the same time hoping that she'd carry out her threat and punish me in front of him. She didn't, but was constantly bossy, telling me to fetch beers and generally wait on both her and Frank, an attitude I found impossible to resent. One thing I'd always imagined doing when I had my safe home was giving myself over completely into somebody else's charge. Now I had the opportunity to spend two blissful nights as Cheryl's plaything, and it could start just as soon as Frank left, or even before.

I was quickly coming to realise that I'd been wrong to think that having friends to stay would keep me grounded. In Cheryl's case she was bringing the possibility of my losing control completely ever closer. She just didn't care, and responded to my urgent gestures by wagging a threatening finger at me, which made my feelings more ambivalent still. Only when she needed to go to the loo did I manage to get her alone, leaving Frank measuring one of the tower rooms.

'I really need to keep at least a veneer of respectability, Cheryl,' I explained as she casually pushed her shorts down to sit on the loo.

'Sounds like it,' she answered me, as her pee began to trickle into the pan. 'How many guys have you been with since you got here?'

'One,' I responded, 'well, two if you count Mick, I suppose, but I only sucked him off . . .'

'Yeah, right,' she said, laughing, 'and that's how respectable ladies behave, sucking cabbies' dicks? Sure it is!'

'Yes, but that's *sex*,' I insisted. 'I'm not sure how they'd react to spanking, badly probably.'

'You said you were looking for a spanking partner,' she pointed out.

'Yes, but I want to take it carefully, and be discreet. Frank's married for one thing, and I'm sure if you did me in front of him it would be right round the island by tomorrow. Anyway, you know I need to be cautious.'

'I don't know so much,' she answered. 'Frank's a good-looking guy, and if he's married then maybe he won't shoot his mouth off.'

'I had thought of that, but with another man, Don White. He's a cabbie who works with Mick.'

'And he's better looking than Frank?'

'No. He's a lot older, and fat, but that makes him perfect to spank me.'

She shook her head. 'I will never understand you, Natasha, not if I live to be a hundred. Frank's got to be the better deal, yeah? I'll take you back and we'll have those panties down in a minute, right in front of him.'

'I'm really not sure, Cheryl . . .'

She shrugged. 'OK, your call, but you know you'd like it.'

'Of course I'd like it, Cheryl, you know I love to be spanked by you. As soon as Frank's gone, you can do anything you want to me, I promise. I'll be your plaything for as long as you're here, OK, but only when we're alone.'

'OK, then dry me, a kiss first.'

As she spoke she had stood up, and now pushed out her belly. She was shaved, her neat black pussy lips quite bare, and parted a little to show the pink flesh between, wet with the last of her urine. I nodded and got down on my knees, crawling quickly across the bathroom floor until I was at her feet, my face just inches from her pussy. A moment of hesitation and I'd done it, reaching out my tongue to lap up the drops of pee from her pussy, and to make her groan in pleasure as I touched her clitoris. I'd have licked happily, and masturbated as I did it, with the taste of her pee in my mouth, but she pulled my head back, laughing.

'Later, slut,' she told me, 'no, not slut – well, you are, but for now you're what? My maid? My slave?'

'Your floor mop?' I suggested as I dabbed a piece of loo paper to her pussy.

'You are too bad!' She laughed. 'Yeah, if that's how you want to play it, I'll treat you like a floor mop, better, a piss mop. First off, you can eat that.'

She pointed to the piece of loo paper I was about to drop into the bowl, the centre soggy with her pee. I hesitated only a moment as a sharp stab of humiliation caught me, and then I'd done it, pushing the used loo paper into my mouth and looking up into her eyes as I ate it.

She held my gaze, watching until I'd swallowed before giving a chuckle of pleasure, and surprise. 'Now *that* I didn't expect even you to do. Come on, piss mop, after me, and stay on your knees 'til we get near Frank.'

I waited as she wiggled her bottom back into her thong and shorts, then crawled out of the bathroom behind her. I only stood up when we reached the passage and there was a danger of Frank seeing us. He was still working happily away, whistling to himself, oblivious to how close he'd come to seeing me given an ignominious bare-bottom spanking in front of him. The thought had me tingling and clumsy with excitement, so that when I spilt a coffee Cheryl had ordered me to make I was sure she was going to forget what she'd said and put me across her knee then and there.

She didn't, but the incident left me trembling and barely in control. My release would come soon too, as the tide was high in the late afternoon, so Frank had to go before the causeway was covered. He still seemed to take forever, not leaving until the first wavelets had begun to lap across the concrete. I stayed at the gate as I watched him drive away; a few more minutes and I'd be cut off, completely at

Cheryl's mercy, and isolated until shortly before dark.

Only when the current had begun to run across the causeway and nobody in their right mind would have attempted to reach me did I turn away and shut the gate. As I did so, I caught a movement up on the hillside, bringing the thought of Pensler back, but only for a moment. Maybe he was out there, maybe not, but he would see nothing. I told Cheryl when I got back inside and she nodded before taking another sip of her beer. She was seated in the cheap armchair I'd bought in town, her feet up and her shoes kicked off. I went to stand in front of her, my head hung down, hoping to be ordered across her knee for the spanking I so desperately needed.

She clicked her fingers at me, pointing to the floor. 'Strip. Naked.'

I hurried to obey, peeling my clothes off to go naked in front of her; I put my hands on my head to display my body.

She gave a nod of satisfaction as her eyes moved slowly down from my face to my toes before moving back up as far as my breasts. 'How come a skinny piece like you gets to have such big fat titties?' she demanded. 'And a big arse.'

'I – I don't, not really,' I answered, stung despite my chosen role.

'Turn around,' she ordered and I promptly obeyed, showing her my bottom. 'Sure you have a big arse, a big fat white bootie. Now get that big fat white bootie in the bathroom and clean it up, piss mop. Move!'

She shouted the last word and I ran, resentment mingling with my arousal at being made to clean up instead of being spanked. My punishment would come though, I knew, maybe not until I was grovelling at her feet in my need, but it would come.

Meanwhile, I'd been told to clean my own bathroom in the nude, and that was what I had to do.

Not much needed doing, as it was brand new, but I did what I knew she'd expect, crawling naked as I scrubbed the floor and kneeling over the toilet bowl with bleach and a brush until the china was gleaming and completely spotless. Cheryl took no notice whatsoever, drinking beers and reading a magazine, until at last I'd finished and felt ready for inspection. By then I was hot and prickly with sweat, my knees sore and my arms aching, but more in need of punishment than ever.

I stayed kneeling as Cheryl came in, my head hung in submission as before. She stopped at the door, tilting her bottle to her mouth as she ran her eyes over the spotless tiles and china and chrome, then spoke. 'Filthy, fucking filthy!'

'It – it is not!' I protested.

'Yeah?'

As she spoke she had pulled the crotch of her shorts aside, her panties with them, spreading her pussy as she thrust out her hips. I realised what she was going to do almost immediately, but still too late as she let go. The stream of pee caught me across my chest, splashing over my boobs and into my face, to run down my cleavage and over my tummy on to the floor. She was laughing as she urinated on me, and I didn't even try to get away, but let her do it, thoroughly soiling me and my clean floor together. When she'd finished, I crawled meekly forwards through the puddle she'd made and kissed the last few drops from her sex.

'Filthy, like I said,' she told me. 'Now mop it up, with your hair, and it had better be clean when I get back, or you're going to get that fat bootie smacked.'

That was exactly what I wanted, and she knew it, but that didn't stop me carrying out the humiliating task I'd been set, crawling on the floor with my hair trailing in her pee in a vain effort to soak it up. She really had made me her piss mop, and as I rubbed my pee-soaked hair over the floor it was all I could do to keep my hands off my pussy. She'd been so mean to me, and so dirty, but I was due to be spanked and determined to hold off.

By the time I'd finished, I was slippery with pee as well as sweat, with my hair a sodden mess, but the floor was immaculate, save only for a couple of smudges where I'd been kneeling. I was just trying to work out how to get rid of these when Cheryl returned, standing over me as before, shaking her head and tutting in dissatisfaction as she inspected the smudges.

'I'm sorry, Cheryl, I –' I began, only to be cut off.

'Shut up! You can't do anything right, can you, you dirty little tramp? And you're filthy. Get in the bath.'

As I climbed in, she stepped forwards and immediately twisted the shower tap on full, and to cold, deluging me with freezing water, so that all I managed was a squeak of shock. I was still gasping as she stood back, chuckling to herself before snapping another command. 'Five minutes, outside, and you'd better be clean and dry, or else.'

It was impossible, obviously, but that didn't stop me trying desperately to obey her, with a sense of rising panic as I towelled myself off and tugged on fresh panties and another dress over my still damp skin. She already had me in that awful, delightful state of grovelling obedience and fear, and it was going to get worse before I was allowed to come.

She was waiting for me when I ran outside, seated on the steps as before and tapping her wrist in disapproval because I was late. My hair was still wet too, and she gave a sigh of disappointment as I reached her.

'You are useless, Natasha. What are you?'

'Useless, Cheryl . . . sorry.'

'You don't even make a decent piss mop, I mean, how pathetic is that?'

'Very,' I admitted, glancing to her big yellow handbag, which she'd brought out as if she intended to go somewhere. I had an immediate vision of being left tied up on the grass or some similar torment, but there was nowhere to go. 'The tide's up –' I began.

'Shut up, and get over my knee.'

I obeyed, quickly arranging myself in the same humiliating position I'd been in when Frank interrupted us, and even more emotional than I'd been then. As before, she put me through the shameful little ritual of having my bottom prepared for spanking, and as before she pulled my dress right up to leave my tits hanging bare from my chest and took my panties well down to make sure my pussy and bumhole showed from behind.

'Now for your present,' she remarked as her fingers pushed between my cheeks to spread out my bumhole. 'Keep that arse up.'

'What is it, please?' I managed, craning back in an effort to see what she was doing.

'Something I saw a girl get on a shoot,' she said, her voice calm but full of amusement as she dipped into her bag. 'They say it stops a girl from tightening her cheeks when she's spanked, not that I'd know myself . . .'

She trailed off, just as I felt something touch my bottom hole, something round and slippery. I already knew what it was. I was being figged, a piece of ginger root inserted in my anus to keep my cheeks apart during punishment, one of the most painful and humiliating things you can do to a spanked girl. It was a big one too, yet as my bottom hole spread to the pressure I couldn't help but sigh in pleasure.

'Slut,' she said as she wedged it in, and my bumhole closed on the neck of the plug, 'but let's see how you get off when it starts to burn.'

My answer was a sob, because I could already feel the warmth starting to build in my ring, making the little muscle twitch and Cheryl laugh to see. Her hand found my bottom, cupping one cheek, before lifting it and bringing it down again with a loud smack, and my spanking had begun. My bottom hole was already burning as she found her rhythm, smacking one cheek at a time, quite calm, just enjoying herself with my bum as the stinging grew and my emotions began to spill over.

'I love smacking you!' she said happily as she began to spank across my cheeks so that each one pushed the fig in up my burning bumhole. 'Lord, how I missed taking those panties down and slapping your fat white bootie, Miss Tasha, so you'd better be good, 'cause this is going to be a long one!'

She tightened her grip, laying into my wobbling bottom harder still, to set me kicking and shaking my head, with my boobs bouncing under my chest. My bumhole felt as if it was on fire, forcing me to keep my bottom loose and open to the smacks, so that they hurt even more while I was quickly losing all sense of control. I could feel my ring tightening on the fig, and knew just how silly I'd look from the rear with my bottom stuck up, fat and pink with the ginger root plug in my gaping bumhole.

My tears began to come, trickling down my face and splashing on the dusty stone beneath me, and faster as Cheryl once more began to concentrate on the tuck of my cheeks, jamming the fig deep, until suddenly I felt my bumhole close and knew that she'd pushed it right up inside me.

'Oops!' She laughed. 'Guess I forgot how much you like a guy's cock up your arsehole, huh! Huh, bitch?'

I tried to answer, but my words came out as a broken sob. My bumhole was still burning, as hot as ever, but now loose too, with the fig up my bottom and Cheryl's words filling my head with burning shame. She never stopped spanking, now laughing openly at the state I was in, as I began to try to get my legs open across her thigh to come off on her leg. I couldn't do it, my thighs trapped in my lowered panties, while she had quickly wrapped a foot around my leg to stop me, leaving me blubbering with frustration as the spanking went on.

'Oh no you don't, Miss Tasha!' she said, laughing. 'I know your dirty tricks, bitch, rubbing off on my leg like that. You come when I say you come, bitch girl, and that's after you've given me mine.'

'Please then, do it!' I managed. 'Make me lick you, Cheryl, please make me lick you . . . please . . . I'll lick your bottom, anything . . . please . . .'

'You will,' she assured me, 'when I'm good and ready, now shut up!'

I tried, my whole bottom now a huge burning ball behind me as the spanking continued, now harder than ever, with me blubbering freely, my hair every-where, my titties bouncing wildly and dripping sweat from my nipples, my pussy dribbling juice into my panties, my bumhole pulsing and oozing with the fig still burning inside my ring. She began to slap my cheeks, making them wobble, laughing as she watched, then to do my thighs, sharp, stinging blows that brought fresh tears to my eyes and wails of distress to my throat; then she cupped her hand between my thighs and pussy-smacked me.

Even as I began to gasp in shock and pain, I knew I was going to come, each smack sending a jolt of ecstasy right through me. I pushed up my bottom, spreading myself for her attention, wide open to her slaps as I thought of how I was, stripped off in the open air, figged and spanked long and hard, and what I'd have to do afterwards, lick my friend's bottom hole until she too came. I screamed, right on the edge, and it had stopped, Cheryl laughing at me as she got up, to tumble me off her lap and on to the grass. I rolled over, to sit splay-legged, my hot bottom in the ticklish grass, my pussy open to the air, red with spanking.

'What did I say, bitch?' Cheryl taunted. 'I said I get it first, didn't I?'

All I could do was nod feebly as she stretched out one bright-yellow heel and pushed me down into the grass. A flick of her toes and my dress was back up over my titties, a quick tug and my panties were off, leaving me naked from the tangle of cloth around my shoulders and neck to my feet. She straddled my body, looking down on me with her eyes glittering with pleasure and not a little contempt. I opened my mouth, eager to lick, both to serve her and so that I'd be allowed to touch myself.

Her response was a small cruel smile as she squatted down over my face, pressing the crotch of her shorts to my mouth. I could smell her musk, and feel the shape of her pussy lips through the cotton, making me want to nuzzle. She let me, for just a moment, before once more rising, and turning, to present me with her bottom, her cheeks spilling out where she'd pulled her shorts tight. As she looked down at me, I stuck my tongue out, begging to be allowed to push it in up her bottom hole. She chuckled and stuck her thumbs into the waistband of her shorts as she spoke.

'Oh yeah, you'd like that, wouldn't you? Look at this, Miss Tasha, look at what you want to lick, you dirty little bitch, my bootie, my bare black bootie.'

She'd begun to push her shorts down, and the thong beneath with them, slowly exposing herself even as she sank down. I was staring, wide-eyed and wide-mouthed, as her neat black bum came bare, the trim, muscular cheeks, the crease between, and the jet-black wrinkle of her bumhole, a moment before she had dropped a curtsey into my face. I was licking immediately, wriggling my tongue up into the tight, musky crevice of her bumhole, tasting her in wanton delight as she laughed at my eagerness and my dirtiness.

I took hold of her hips, my tongue well in up her bottom, as she settled herself down on my face for her licking. Her hands caught my legs, pulling them up and wide, to spread my pussy and roll me up high enough to leave my smacked bottom showing, and my still burning anus. For a moment I thought she was going to forget herself and go down on me in turn, but as the flat of her hand found my pussy in a firm pat I realised that I still had some spanking to come.

She began to smack, right across my aching sex, to make me jerk and writhe beneath her, while I was still licking at her now open anus. A small movement and she'd slithered back, pressing her pussy to my mouth as the tip of my nose went in up her bumhole. Her hand slapped down hard on my pussy and I jerked beneath her. She wriggled, sighing with pleasure as she used my face, smacking harder to urge me on, talking too, her voice now hoarse with excitement. 'Lick it, you lily-white bitch, lick Auntie Cheryl's cute little cunt. You like that, don't you, your big white bootie smacked and putting your tongue up my arse. Oh yeah, you love it, don't you, to taste my shit –'

Her words broke off in a cry of ecstasy and she was coming, writhing her bottom in my face and smacking hard on my pussy. I was wriggling beneath her, squirming my hips and drumming my feet on the ground, in so much pain but not wanting it to stop for a moment. She'd stripped me down and figged my bumhole. She'd spanked my bottom and she'd smacked my pussy . . . my cunt. She'd sat on my face and made me lick her anus . . . taste her anus . . . taste her shit . . .

On that awful thought I started to come, her hand still smacking down on my spread pussy, over and over as she rode her own orgasm, with me twitching pathetically between her, utterly abandoned, my legs held up and wide, my smacked cunt on show to her, my burning bumhole in spasm, opening and closing, to squeeze out the fig at the very peak of my orgasm.

Cheryl stayed on my face until she'd quite finished, rising only when she felt like it, to leave me gasping for breath, my face smeared with her juices, lying sweaty and dishevelled on the ground. I managed a weak smile and she reached down, helping me to my feet before putting an arm around my waist to guide me back into the house.

Cheryl kept me firmly under her thumb for the next two days. While other people were around, she was relatively well behaved, content with having me fetch and carry for them and for herself, but the moment we were alone I'd be back on my knees, or stripped, or turned over for a spanking, or made to lick her to ecstasy.

Most of the time she kept me nude, with my bottom spanked more often than not, while my mouth was forever full of the taste of pussy, or worse. By the time she left on the Tuesday I'd been wondering if I could take any more, but no sooner had I watched the little yellow aeroplane disappear into the haze of distance, with the glow of my goodbye spanking slowly fading from my cheeks, than I'd begun to feel I wanted more.

For a while I tried to resist it, about as long as it took me to walk to my car. I knew it was hopeless, and that the only way out was to find a local to give me regular spankings. After all, I'd been the same ever since I began to crave punishment, but when I'd been working at least there had always been something to distract me, a looming deadline or the need to get ready for an event. Now I was my own mistress, and ironically that left me needing to be smacked and humiliated more than ever before.

The only question was: who should do it? Liam was the obvious choice, although his reaction to Cheryl's behaviour had been protective, so that I'd had to tell him she was only mucking around. Yet he was definitely masculine and might well be prepared to take me in hand, while I was also happy to go to bed with him. On the down side, I didn't want him thinking of me as his exclusively, and I could see him being confused between having the right to dominate me and having me genuinely under his command.

Don White still appealed, older and bigger, altogether a better man to spank me. His being married was an advantage, and yet, if we did set up an arrangement and things got out, there would be all sorts of trouble. The island was, by definition, insular, and I already knew how quickly gossip and rumours could spread. Yet the thought of those big, red hands fumbling at my panties and groping at my bottom cheeks held a definite appeal.

Womble just wasn't going to work. Even if the concept managed to filter into his brain he was sure to be too harsh and too clumsy. I like it quite hard, but I could imagine a smack from him would be like the kick of a horse. He'd think it was funny too, which would be thoroughly humiliating for me, but also meant he was sure to tell his friends. Womble was out.

Mick might have been an option if he hadn't proved so possessive, and that was the main problem with locals in general, or the 'genuine' locals anyway. Some of the incomers might prove worthwhile, but other than passing the occasional polite comment about my new home I'd yet to meet any. Tourists had the disadvantage that they went away, which rather defeated my purpose, while they also included Aaron Pensler among their number.

He was out of the question, obviously, although no doubt he'd have loved to do it and possibly even kept it to himself. I hadn't seen him for a while anyway, in fact, not since I'd introduced him to Cheryl as my stalker, making me wonder if he'd finally left, or at least been successfully put off. Alternatively, he might simply have refined his stalking techniques, and I promised myself I'd keep my eyes open.

By the time I got back to *Les Hommeaux Florains* I'd made my decision. I would test Liam, carefully, so that I could pull back if he reacted badly. It seemed the most sensible option, but if I wanted to get it that evening I would have to work quickly. Besides, the house seemed oddly empty without Cheryl, and the tide was coming up, so I showered and snatched a bite to eat, slipped into a pair of plain white spanking panties under my dress, just in case, and drove back up to town.

Liam worked shifts, in the bar in Andy's most evenings and free during the day. I knew he'd be starting in a couple of hours, so drove to the flat in which he lived, one of just six in a block set in one of the valleys running down towards the harbour. He was in, as I'd hoped, sitting at his computer, and as I tapped on the glass of his back door he started, looking distinctly guilty.

I was hoping I'd caught him surfing porn, but he was only playing a computer game, possibly not a very macho thing to do, because I couldn't think why else he was embarrassed. Having let me in, he exited the site hastily, but he had already given me an idea, the perfect test.

'Has Cheryl gone?' he asked as I sat down.

'Yes, just now,' I told him. 'You have internet on that thing, don't you?'

'Yeah, broadband.'

'Do you ever surf for porn?'

He looked surprised, even guiltier than before, and had opened his mouth to deny it before he fully caught on to the tone in my voice. Still unsure of himself, he gave a reserved shrug. 'Yeah, now and then, just for a laugh.'

'What's your favourite site?'

Again he shrugged. 'Don't have one, not really. I don't do it much . . .'

'I do,' I told him, which was a lie because, while I had occasionally, and brought myself off over stories, it was very much something I did when bored, and my recent life had been anything but boring.

Percy had shown me enough to know what I was doing at any rate, especially when it came to searching for spanking pictures, for which he had an insatiable appetite. Liam gave me an odd look as I took the mouse from his hand, but made no objection. I needed to gauge his reaction, but without giving myself away, so made a quick search for listings sites in the hope of finding one with everything neatly set out in categories. Liam seemed more than a little taken aback to find me so unabashed by pornography and said nothing as I quickly dismissed the first two sites, neither of which worked the way I wanted. The third was better, listing galleries by category, and there, near the bottom of a long list, was that crucial word – spanking.

I deliberately avoided it, instead trying something I was sure he would like, a category simply listed as 'Young Ladies'. What I got was a series of pictures showing a pretty girl stripping out of a cheerleader's outfit. She was cute, with a slim waist, firm high breasts and a cheeky bottom, surely a turn on for any man.

I smiled at Liam and he returned a distinctly nervous glance before speaking, his voice highly defensive. 'Are you testing me or something, Natasha? Guys get turned on by this stuff, you know, it's just the way we are.'

'Relax, will you,' I told him. 'I'm just having some fun.'

Not wanting to get into a discussion on my bisexuality, I quickly moved back from the girls' gallery and clicked on another, this one entitled 'Big Cock'. They weren't joking either, because the pictures that came up showed a middle-aged black man with a cock so large I was wondering if the pictures were faked, although the worried-looking blonde girl who was sucking him off seemed to be having very real trouble opening her mouth wide enough to take him in. It was alarming, but intriguing too, for the man's sheer monstrous virility, but Liam was far from impressed.

'Gross!'

'What's the matter, don't you like images of other people having sex?'

'Yeah, but not like that, not close up on some bastard's cock!'

'You are fussy, aren't you? OK, no cocks, how about girls having rude things done to them, you must like that?'

Now was my chance, and I made the cursor skitter across the screen as if choosing at random before clicking on the spanking link. It was a beauty, a series showing not one girl but three, supposedly friends having a sleepover and the mother of one catching them drinking. They were made to kneel on their beds with their pyjamas and panties turned down behind, then spanked, one at a time across the mother's knees while the others looked on with expressions of rueful anticipation or rubbed at already sore bottoms. The quality was high too, and the cameraman had made sure there was plenty of exposure of the girls' pussies and bottom holes, always important for a girl being punished. My heart was already beating fast as I awaited Liam's reaction.

'Fucking hell, weird or what!'

I bit my lip, wondering how any red-blooded male could possibly be unaffected by the sight of three pretty girls having their bare bottoms smacked. Even if he didn't like the cruelty of it, there was no denying that they were beautiful, and their exposure was absolute, and just the way he liked to fuck me, with my bottom on show behind. It was not the reaction I'd been hoping for, but I wasn't giving in, not that easily.

'I suppose it's a bit weird pretending two of them are mother and daughter,' I said, despite the fact that the two women obviously weren't really related at all, 'but don't you like the way they're showing their bums? You like me like that.'

I scrolled down and clicked on another spanking link as I spoke, praying that it was just the implication of finding a mother spanking her daughter erotic that he objected to. The gallery that came up wasn't as elaborate, but it was very good, a beautiful young girl in a pleated tartan tunic turned across the knee of a dirty old man. There was no story, no explanation, just the classic sequence of a girl turned across a man's knee, her dress lifted up, her panties pulled down and her bottom smacked. She was a great actress too, her face full of consternation and pain and all the right emotions, while she ended up on her knees with her hot red bottom stuck out towards the camera, cheeks spread wide, sucking on the old bastard's cock, just the way I like to be made to do it myself.

'You like me like that,' I repeated, indicating the last picture.

'Yeah, but I don't beat you, do I?'

'No,' I replied, and would have gone on to defend my right to have my bottom smacked, but stopped. There had been real disgust in his voice, and it was plainly hopeless. 'You choose,' I suggested, passing him the mouse.

As he took it, I stifled a sigh. Obviously, he felt spanking was abusive, and I'd met men like that before, full of machismo and gallantry, but without the guts to put a naughty girl in her place with a good spanking when she's begging for it. He would never understand that I wanted to be the girl in the second set of pictures I'd seen, turned over a dirty old man's knee for no better reason than him getting off on it, and so there was no point in trying to explain.

He was taking his time, running the cursor up and down the links, obviously nervous. I began to wonder what my own reaction would be if he chose to click on a transsexual site or maybe something involving midgets or amputees. I was telling myself that at the least I'd try to be more tolerant than he was, but as he made his choice I saw that I needn't have worried.

It was a typical American porn site, the worst sort, with silicone-breasted dolls having predictable sex with muscle men and about as erotic to me when compared with spanking as a fridge-freezer to a Ferrari. I was hoping he didn't see dyed-blonde hair and fake tits as the ideal of femininity, and was going to say something when to my relief he clicked on another link, too quickly to let me see what it was.

The pictures that came up seemed very ordinary at first, a threesome with two men and a woman, although they at least looked reasonably natural, she pretty and slightly plump with a mass of curly black hair and big heavy breasts, one of them tall and thin, the other compact and muscular with a nice thick cock. They were sharing her, but it was plain from the sequence of pictures that the girl and the skinny man were together, perhaps married even, and the stocky man a lucky friend.

Liam seemed more nervous than ever as he sat back, and threw me a glance as if daring my disapproval before he spoke. 'That's what I like, a girl who'll do anything her man wants.'

I nodded, refraining from pointing out that he wouldn't do what I wanted, because it was no time for an argument. 'Including go with another man?' I asked after a while. 'Is that what you'd like me to do?'

I was praying his answer would be yes, because while I might be missing out on my spanking it was an intriguing suggestion, and something not many men are prepared to do, or even capable of. It also meant he was less possessive than I'd expected, although the implication that I was now his girl was clear. I decided not to challenge it, more interested in what he had in mind for me in the way of threesomes.

'Well?' I demanded, when he hadn't answered for a while.

'There was this girl,' he said, his voice thick and hesitant, 'two girls . . . years ago. My brother Saul and some mates took them down the quarry near your place and they had them, together, all at once. It really stuck in my head . . .'

He trailed off, glancing at me once again as if expecting disapproval. I merely nodded, because I was thinking of what Penny had said about the local men behaving like wild animals, and where the worst, or best, incident had taken place, in a quarry. Presumably he was thinking of the same incident, and I found myself biting a nail, thinking of how it would feel to be taken and really used by three or four of the biggest, roughest locals. I'd told myself I wouldn't, that I'd be discreet and not do anything to attract unwanted attention, but it had to be tempting.

'I – I wouldn't mind, if you like?' I suggested. 'But not just anyone. I'd have to choose, and it would have to be on *Les Hommeaux Florains*, with the tide in so nobody could catch us, but yes, once I'd given you the green light, you could do whatever you liked, and I do mean that.'

'Really?' he asked, now staring at me as if he wasn't sure I was real.

'Yes,' I confirmed, 'just let me choose, that's all I ask, and now I'm going to suck your cock before you go to work.'

Five

Despite the fact that I didn't seem likely to be getting a spanking, I was feeling more than a little pleased with myself over the next few days. At least, I wasn't likely to be getting a spanking from Liam, but if he was prepared to share me with his mates then surely he could hardly object if I found myself a spanking partner. Not that he needed to know anyway.

The process of choosing the men occupied me for most of the week, and kept me more or less permanently excited, despite being on my period for most of the time. We'd agreed on four, and Liam himself was obviously one of them, which left three choices. Most of them had seen me strip, and I was pleased to discover that the general opinion was that I was one of the sexiest girls on the island, maybe even the sexiest of all. There was no shortage of men who would have liked to fuck me, but there were other difficulties, lots of them.

As I was to be fucked rather than have anything kinky done to me, I wanted good-looking, virile men, but inevitably these tended to have girlfriends who were not going to be happy about their partners making a slut of me. Those without girlfriends tended to be the ugly or awkward ones, who didn't appeal. After some argument, I agreed to include Liam's brother Saul, a heftier, rougher version of him, who was married but apparently no longer had sex with his wife. That left two, and as we sat in Andy's one hot afternoon with just a couple of tourists drinking coffee outside we were debating who'd get third place. I'd explained a lot of how I felt to Liam, and he was catching on or, at least, beginning to.

'Yeah, but if you don't want any say in what happens, shouldn't I get to choose the blokes?'

'No. I have to find the men attractive, but once it's started you should all do as you like or, better still, you should make me do things for them, that, or take me by surprise and just go for it. Maybe it would be nice to be gagged first, so I can't even protest, and you're not to stop no matter how much I struggle, because struggling is part of the thrill, and knowing it's going to happen anyway. Yes, that would be nice . . . but only when I'm ready.'

'How am I supposed to know that?' he demanded, frowning.

'Use your intuition,' I told him. 'OK, you don't have any. Look, if I'm in the mood I'll wear something red . . . no, yellow. That way you'll know it's OK, but I won't know it's coming. How's that?'

'That's clever. So how about Steve?'

'The DJ? Too smarmy.'

'Gary White?'

'Linda's brother? Hmm . . . no, not really.'

'Carl. All the girls go for Carl.'

'With that bald spot coming? No thank you.'

'Dave White?'

'Too fat.'

'Dan Reynaud?'

'Too thin.'

'Paul?'

'Too wombley.'

'Come on, Tasha –'

'No way!'

'There must be somebody!'

'How about Frank, the builder? I know he's married, but he is dishy.'

'No way.'

'Why not?'

'Paul's after him.'

'So what? Anyway, why is Womble – Paul after him?'

'He made up that nickname. Paul hates it.'

'Oh. Anyway, why should that stop him joining in? You're OK with him, aren't you, and he's doing work at my place, so he could pick the time. He's ideal, I just need to chat him up a bit and, believe me, that won't be hard.'

Liam was looking shifty and turning his bottle of beer with his fingers, something I'd come to recognise as a sign that he was nervous.

'What's the matter?' I demanded.

'We really ought to have Paul,' he replied after a pause.

'I said no.'

'Yeah, I know, but . . . he's my best mate and that, so . . .'

'I said no, Liam.'

'Why? What's the matter with Paul?'

'What's the matter with Paul? Where do you want me to start? He's . . . he's like some huge overgrown baby. He must weigh over twenty stone anyway, which I wouldn't mind, only he's . . . he's just too wombley, like I said.'

'Come on, Tasha.'

'No!'

He was moving his bottle even faster, and a horrible possibility struck me.

'You've told him, haven't you?'

'No.'

'Yes you have.'

'No I haven't ... not really anyway, but I did mention something was going on, and he's well into you, Tasha.'

'Liam! He's a complete thug ... a monster, and he sprayed beer all over me when I did my striptease.'

'That was just a laugh.'

'Oh very funny! I'm not having Womble, and that's that. You shouldn't have told him anyway.'

'Yeah, but I did.'

'Then tell him it's all off.'

'And when he finds out?'

'Why should he find out? This is supposed to stay between ourselves, remember? I don't want a reputation as the local tart.'

He didn't answer immediately and I found myself colouring. The island was a typical old-fashioned community, where any girl who dares to be open about her sexuality is immediately branded a slut, usually by the very men who want her. It was not an attitude I was ever going to give in to and alter my behaviour, but it was impossible to stop my reaction.

'So how about John Martell from down the harbour?' he said, changing the subject.

I gave a vague wave of my hand, no longer really in the mood for discussing who could have me.

I was furious with Liam for telling Womble, and seriously considered calling the whole thing off. The prospect of being had by four locals was exciting, but I could see the way it would go. They'd arrange it between themselves, come down to *Les Hommeaux Florains* and enjoy themselves with me, then go around boasting about it to all their friends. Inevitably, the women would find out, and make my life unbearable out of jealousy and spite, while every man on the island would assume he could fuck me in return for a couple of drinks, if that.

On the other hand, I didn't see why I should allow myself to have my behaviour curtailed by local pettiness. I didn't need their approval. Who were they, a bunch of rustics living on an island so backward they caught and killed their own food, to set my moral boundaries? If I wanted to be fucked by four men, then I would be fucked by four men, and that was that.

I was still so angry the next day that I managed to miss the tide and found myself stranded. Not that I minded, particularly, because it was best to cool off a little before speaking to Liam again, and I did want my group fucking. Despite my ill feeling, I had masturbated over it the night before, partly remembering how it felt to take a man in my mouth and up my pussy at the same time, partly imagining how it might be again. That had fixed the idea in my mind, and I decided to let it build up as I did things around the house, then play with myself again before the tide fell and I could get off.

The work was coming on, with all the new floors laid and the walls plastered. I'd had the window in what was to be my bedroom reglazed as well, so that it was full of light and at last gave some idea of how it would be when finished. Frank had also fitted my washing machine and dryer, which meant no more trips to the laundry in town. After admiring my property, which always improved my mood, I slipped into my bikini and went outdoors to sunbathe.

I climbed up to my favourite turret, where there was a cool breeze, while down in the courtyard it was too hot and still. As usual, I scanned the hillside before settling down on the parapet, which provided the perfect place to spread my towel. One person was visible, a man walking his dog on the track up to the observation tower, but once again there was no sign of Pensler. Evidently, he really had gone home, and I was able to relax properly as I began to rub my sun block in.

My head was still full of dirty thoughts, undercut by annoyance at the likely reaction of the locals, and as I lay down I was wondering if there was anywhere in the entire world where I would be able to truly do as I pleased without having to endure the interference of prudes and snobs and Peeping Toms and men who saw me only as a nicely shaped piece of meat with no regard for my psyche. Even Liam fell into the last category, with his negative attitude to spanking, his friends too.

I put them out of my mind, instead thinking of how nice it was to be cut off for the next few hours. Once down in the courtyard, I could strip and masturbate as I had before, although after a dozen or so sessions the thrill was beginning to pale. Alternatively, there was the rear of the fort, the high wall completely blocking the view from the land, save for the French coast a safe seven or eight miles across the sea. Thanks to the offshore reefs, no yacht could get close either, which left only the aeroplanes, but unfortunately there was nowhere to duck to safety outside the walls.

Then again, what could they see? A girl in the nude? Big deal, although it still felt intrusive. A girl in a bikini? That wasn't intrusive, but it wasn't naughty either, and if I was going to play with myself I wanted that delicious feeling of being bare outdoors and just not caring. Unless, of course, I made use of the very fact that I was in a bikini . . .

112

I was smiling as I walked back to the house. It was a great idea, naughty and defiant at the same time, indulging myself in something that would undoubtedly shock the locals, even Liam, if only they knew. They wouldn't, not ever, and I didn't even need to worry about being seen from the land because, even if Pensler, ten paparazzi and a hundred locals were watching me, all armed with powerful telephoto lenses, they wouldn't realise what I was doing.

Back indoors I drank a large glass of orange juice and took out one of the two-litre bottles of cold spring water I'd taken to keeping in the fridge. I was already well creamed, so took just my towel and a pair of flip-flops, left the fort and started around the side of the walls. It was harder going than I'd expected, with great slants of rock and in one place a deep gully running almost to the wall. I couldn't jump it and I didn't dare try to climb around the end in case I fell, which left the option of going down to the water, swimming across and climbing out on the smooth rocks at the far side.

I really didn't want to get wet, not in the sea, so I tried the other way, which proved easier, with the rocks falling away to a tiny boulder-choked cove and easy to climb on the far side. It was still tricky, and I had to take off my flip-flops and throw them down first, leaving me barefoot on the smooth wave-worn boulders when I'd got down. They were hot under my feet, while my exertion had left me prickly with sweat under the brilliant sun. I was completely hidden too, save for directly out to sea and the air.

Eager to bring my sense of naughtiness a little higher, I pushed my thumbs into the sides of my bikini and eased it down a little way, just enough to show my bum at the back and a little of my pussy. It felt nice, rude and slightly silly, childish almost. I left it like that, posing in the hot sun, first with my bottom pushed out, then touching my toes as if awaiting the cane. That made me think of how Cheryl had pulled my breasts out when she spanked me, and I quickly tugged my bikini top up to get them bare, remembering how she'd made me strip and kept me in the nude to clean and serve her.

I was grinning as I straightened up, now feeling thoroughly naughty. A good swig of water and I covered up, but I was still thinking how bad I'd been as I climbed up the other side, and how much worse I was going to be. Beyond the little cove it was easy going, with three great flat expanses of rock in turn, separated by ledges like enormous steps. Any one would have been good enough, and the third, where the tower I was going to live in rose, was largely invisible from the land. That ended in another ledge, taller, so that I had to scramble up. Beyond was another area of smooth rock, bigger still, sloping gently from the wall all the way down to the water, and extending halfway across the rear of the fort. A few patches of coarse grass and tiny hardy flowers clung to the very top, but otherwise the rock was so smooth I could lie down in comfort, which I did, not bothering to spread my towel.

Once again I pulled up my bikini top, closing my eyes as I stroked my breasts, bumping my fingers over my nipples until they had grown erect and repeating the motion until I was wriggling with pleasure and could bear it no more. I was almost ready, but wanted to leave it until I had no choice, and stripped instead, peeling off my bikini completely to walk nude on the smooth warm rock, pausing occasionally to touch my breasts, pat my bottom and tickle my bumhole and pussy, or to take another swallow from my water bottle.

My tummy had begun to feel heavy and round, but I made a point of finishing the bottle, every last drop. With the full two litres inside me I felt like a water balloon, wobbling as I walked, still nude with my bikini, towel and flip-flops in my hands, across the flat to where a series of more broken ledges rose to the next corner of the fort. Beyond was the area across from the gully which had first blocked my path, quite high, with grass growing in the cracks and a fine view across to the next fort and the one beyond, also a good deal of the main island. It was perfect, visible from afar yet absolutely unreachable, except maybe by paraglider, which seemed unlikely.

I pulled my bikini back on and climbed up, now feeling naughtier dressed than nude. My tummy was a little less bloated, but my bladder had begun to ache, not yet painful, but enough to make me want to wriggle my toes as I folded my towel on a ledge and sat down. I could see the hill, now completely empty, a few houses, a couple of cars, one parked, one moving, humans too, but only as tiny stick figures, far too distant to make out in detail. Even if Pensler was up in the tower with his binoculars, he'd only see me as an unsteady doll-like figure, a girl in a bikini, quite respectable . . .

. . . except that I was about to wet myself, to deliberately pee in my bikini pants, a thoroughly dirty thing to do.

With that thought I could hold it no longer. I let go, tugging my towel out from under my bottom at the last second before my pee squirted out into my gusset, instantly soaking through the material to erupt in a little yellow fountain, pattering on the ground between my feet. I was giggling as I watched, with my belly pushed out a little to show off as the wet patch spread quickly up the front of my bikini pants and down between my legs.

There was a little fat bulge over my pussy where some of the pee was trapped, which suddenly burst, squirting out around the sides and up between my bottom cheeks to wet my bumhole. I stopped for a second, then let go again, once more enjoying that first burst and the exquisite sensation of pissing in my clothes on purpose. Pee began to run down my thighs and up under my cheeks, quickly leaving me sitting in a warm squashy puddle, into which I wriggled my bottom in sheer delight.

Already I wanted to come, but I was determined to get the most out of what I'd done. With gushes of pee still squirting into my bikini pants, I stood up, letting it run down my legs until I was standing in my own puddle. I began to tread in it, enjoying the wet on my feet, and as the pee finally dried to a trickle I sat down in it again, rubbing my bottom in the wet. My bikini pants were sodden, right up the front and over most of the back, so that the material clung to the contours of my bottom. I moved forwards, into a crawling position, imagining how I'd look from behind, my bottom stuck up, round and cheeky in my pee-soaked pants.

Close up, it would be quite obvious what I'd done, wet myself, peed my pants, disgraced myself – all those lovely shameful words that go with a girl who has pissed in her clothes. A last glance at the land to make sure nobody was too close and my hand went back, rubbing at my pussy through my soggy gusset, revelling in what I'd done, on purpose too. I closed my eyes, now masturbating freely, with the piss-wet bikini material pushed deep into the groove of my pussy to let me get at my clit as I played the scene over in my mind.

I'd been so naughty, so, so wonderfully naughty, showing off my bottom and boobs outdoors, stripping bare on the rocks to rub my tits and smack my bare bum, and lastly ... lastly, deliberately putting my bikini back on so that I could pee in it, utterly disgracing myself, and, worse, masturbating in it, on my knees with my bottom straining out my soggy bikini pants behind. That was enough, just the knowledge of what I'd done and the way I felt, with my pants clinging warm and wet to my skin, my peed-in bikini pants, and lifted in blatant show as I masturbated.

My thighs went tight around my hand and I'd started to come, my pussy in contraction, my bottom cheeks squeezing in the wet material, my knees splashing in my pee puddle, gasping and shaking in my ecstasy as shock after shock ran through me, until I was finally spent.

My little session out on the rocks did a great deal to help me calm down and think more rationally about what Liam was planning for me. For all my defiance, it really was important that it didn't become common knowledge, but it seemed inevitable that it would. After all, Penny had done it and they were still talking about it over a decade later.

I considered my options for the rest of the afternoon, wavering between the ideal of doing exactly as I pleased and the reality of having to accept the consequences. If I went ahead, I could expect to be followed by vicious whispers and sneering looks and, unlike in London, I had little or no choice as to where I went. I had to shop at the main store. I had to have my hair done at the salon run by Steve's sister Teresa. I had to deal with Frank's wife Paula over the invoices for my building work. The island, I now realised, was isolated only in a geographical sense. Socially, it was the exact opposite.

Various compromises ran through my mind, such as chatting up a few tourists, but I knew there would be severe problems. For a start, Liam wouldn't like it, because the locals had a bizarre attitude to male tourists, who they resented having any intimate contact with the local girls, although they were quite happy to get off with female tourists. Perhaps more importantly, not that many men would be willing to do as I wanted, or even capable, and I'd feel pretty silly expecting to be fucked senseless only to find myself surrounded by limp cocks.

A better choice was to invite some friends over from the mainland, perhaps Monty, Fat Jeff and the boys from Razorback paintball. They would deal with me, thoroughly. Unfortunately, they all had jobs and couldn't simply drop everything on demand, while again Liam wouldn't be happy about it. Worse, when Liam saw Monty and Fat Jeff, he would immediately want to know why I wouldn't go with Womble, because he just couldn't understand that it was all in the mind.

Finally, with a great deal of regret, I decided to abandon the idea of being had by four men, but to tell Liam that if I was wearing yellow he was welcome to do as he pleased with me, and not bother about asking. It was a poor compromise, and I was feeling more than a little bitter about it as I walked across the causeway and towards town, but it really was the only sensible option.

I hadn't taken the car because I felt I needed a drink and it was such a beautiful day. Keen to walk, and in no hurry to confront Liam, I didn't follow the road, but struck off into the quarry where Penny had had her own adventure so many years ago. It was bigger than I'd expected, and more complex, really several quarries linked together by broad ways blasted from the rock, along which an old railway ran. I'd seen the other end of the railway down by the harbour, and decided to follow it, past rusting trucks and bits of industrial debris, among tangles of bramble and areas of flat soft grass on which it was all too easy to imagine Penny being laid out and soundly fucked by five men.

The route was longer than I'd anticipated, curving around the hill and past yet another quarry, this one full of water, alongside a road with a large campsite and a beach beyond, before passing close to White-gates. By then I was wavering in my resolve, thinking of how good it had felt to be made to get down on Mick's cock and suck him off in return for my cab ride, and to be seen by Don White with spunk all over my face. I wanted the same treatment again, or worse, if only I could avoid the consequences.

I left the railway where it curved down towards the harbour and started up the hill towards town. One of the men who'd delivered my stuff to *Les Hommeaux Florains* happened to be passing and gave me a lift in his lorry, asking questions about Cheryl as we went. I'd known he was called John, but it was only when I saw the work sheets in his cab that I realised he was John Martell, the man Liam had suggested should be one of those to fuck me. Like most of the locals he was rough and ready, but not bad-looking and also friendly, making it harder still to stick to my decision as I walked into Andy's.

Liam had just come on and was polishing glasses behind the bar, already with an open beer at his elbow. Womble was also there, playing pool with some other locals, and gave me a greasy leer as I approached the bar.

'All right?' Liam greeted me, and bent forwards across the bar, first to kiss me, then to whisper into my ear. 'I've got it sorted, everything. You just have to say OK to John and –'

'John's fine,' I cut him off, 'but I'm not happy about it at all, the whole thing.'

'Why not?' he demanded, his face dropping in disappointment.

'I'm sorry,' I told him, 'it's just that I know what's going to happen. We'll do it, and I'm sure it will be great, but then it's going to get out and everyone's going to be calling me a slut, and –'

'No, no. I've sorted all that. It's cool.'

'How?'

'Easy. We make it a regular thing, right? That way, the lads know they have to keep quiet, or there'll be no rumpy-pumpy. Good, huh?'

I bit my lip, still doubtful, but he did have a point. So long as I made it abundantly clear that if the secret got out there would be no more sex, then they probably would be able to keep it to themselves. I'd have to agree how often it could happen too, and put a few restrictions on where they could do it, but that was all.

'How often were you thinking of?' I asked cautiously.

'Don't know. What suits you?'

'Once a month maybe? Or it'll get stale, and I have to choose the time.'

'Sure, just wear yellow when you're ready.'

'OK, and it's not to happen anywhere we might get caught.'

'No problem. So what, you're up for it?'

I nodded, already with a huge knot in my stomach. Liam grinned and kissed me again, then turned and gave a thumbs-up sign and a wink. I followed his gaze, to find myself staring into Womble's huge blubbery face, the little pursey mouth now turned up in a knowing smile. For a moment I couldn't even speak, my mouth hanging slack as the implications sank in, before I rounded on Liam, speaking in an urgent hiss. 'I said not Wom – Paul!'

'Sh!' he urged. 'I had to, didn't I. I'd already told him, remember?'

'Yes, but –'

'What else could I do? If I turned him down, he'd fucking kill me, and tell everyone.'

'Couldn't you just say I didn't fancy him? Or I was cross with him because of the beer thing?'

'He'd still tell everyone. Anyway, Paul's not so bad, and he is my best mate.'

'Maybe, but he isn't going to fuck you, is he!? Go on, think about it, how would you like him humping away up your arse?'

His face twisted into the horrified reaction I'd wanted, but only for a moment. 'Yeah, sure,' he said, 'but I'm not a poof. If I was a poof –'

'If you were the biggest screaming queen on earth I bet you'd still run a mile!' I broke in.

He shrugged and made a face, evidently not convinced, then spoke again. 'He's not really that different from any other bloke.'

'He's barely human,' I pointed out, my voice sulky in my own ears. 'I wouldn't mind so much if – if . . .'

I'd been going to point out that my real objection to Womble was that he was on the edge of being mentally subnormal, only to feel suddenly guilty. After all, he couldn't help being the way he was, and he obviously had a healthy sex drive, whatever else he lacked. He wasn't completely stupid anyway, because he made a living as a fisherman and was sensitive enough to resent his nickname. Also, he'd stuck up for me when Pensler was stalking me. On the other hand, that didn't oblige me to let him fuck me, let alone the way Liam and I had been planning.

'What?' Liam demanded, and there was a touch of aggression in his voice.

'I don't know ... nothing,' I answered. 'Can I think about this, please?'

'You'll be OK,' he urged. 'Come on, Tasha, you know you want it!' He was grinning, full of eagerness, for me, and to give me, his girlfriend, over to another three men.

I found myself smiling back, but still confused as I answered. 'Maybe ... I don't know, Liam. Let's play it by ear, OK?'

'Sure. If we see you wearing yellow, then?'

I made to qualify his statement, but stayed silent. It was simple enough, after all. If I felt ready, I would wear something yellow and it would happen. If I didn't, it wouldn't. Maybe if I quickly sucked Womble to make him come, it wouldn't be so bad.

The prospect was still putting my stomach in knots, and I ordered a bottle of Aussie Shiraz to help calm my nerves. Womble was still at the pool table, and I sat down near by to watch him play, which was atrocious. I was hoping he would improve with closer acquaintance, but it didn't really work. Every grotesque face he pulled, his emotions showing larger than life at each triumph or set-back of the table, each wobble of his monstrous buttocks or the great reams of compact flesh around his torso, his habit of adjusting his cock and balls within his trousers before every shot – all of it made me shiver.

He was showing off to me too, attempting trick shots to impress me, and when one finally succeeded going into a frenzy of thrusting hips and shaking arms put out as if to clutch a girl by the hips as he fucked her from behind. I knew who he was thinking of, me – bent over with my knickers pulled down and his cock jammed to the hilt up my pussy. With a push like that, any man in my mouth at the time would probably get his cock bitten off by accident, while my bum was going to look as if I'd been spanked with a paddle. I grimaced at the thought, promising myself that if it did happen I would definitely suck him off first.

I'd soon finished my bottle of wine, excepting a fair bit of it which Womble had drunk from the neck in what I supposed had been intended as a show of bonhomie, but I felt more nervous than ever. Telling myself I merely needed to avoid wearing yellow didn't really help, as, while I could hold off for a bit, I knew that eventually I would have to do it.

With a whole bottle of wine on an empty stomach I was feeling really quite drunk, and decided to go and eat, somewhere else, because another of Womble's bad habits was pinching food from other people's plates, and now that he obviously regarded me as one of the gang it seemed likely I'd get the same treatment. There was an Italian restaurant of sorts a little way up the street, and I went to look at the menu to see if they had anything half-edible.

One look in the window and I'd changed my mind. Aaron Pensler was there, eating pizza and talking with a seedy-looking man in a brown suit who had no food in front of him but was fiddling with a glass of what looked like mineral water. I had moved back immediately, but I had seen enough, enough to be seriously worried. The man in the suit was considerably older than Pensler, and had a businesslike look about him. He was no tourist, nor a local, but a man with a job of work to do. Surely he could only be one thing – a journalist.

Another peep as I walked past with mock nonchalance seemed to confirm my worst suspicions. The man was maybe fifty, his suit and tie badly out of place on the island, while his expression as he listened to Pensler talking was one of interest and concentration. It was hard to imagine anyone listening to Pensler talk with interest and concentration, at least unless they had very good reason. If the man was a journalist then there could only be one good reason – me.

I was cursing out loud as I walked on up the street, both at Pensler and myself. It was all too easy to imagine what had happened. He'd have kept his faith at first, perhaps lusting after me hopefully, perhaps merely content to spy, until I'd stupidly put him down in front of Cheryl, a humiliation I knew would cut a man like him to the quick. He'd planned his revenge, and somehow managed to persuade some idiot of a paparazzo that Aisha Tyler really was having a secret holiday break in the Channel Islands.

My first thought was to hide, and I did so, in the Coronation, a pub frequented by elderly incomers and the better class of tourist, the last place I'd usually have gone. Now it was ideal, dim, poky and with plenty of little alcoves, one of which I sat myself in with a large glass of brandy. I ordered a meal to stop myself getting completely wrecked, although that was exactly what I wanted to do, and began to plot with feverish urgency.

The man was going to want photos of me, preferably candid ones. If he got them, and it would be hard to stop him getting something, he would send them to his agency or direct to his paper or magazine if he was in-house. They would then publish them, or at least I had to assume they would. At some point, be it when he first saw me or when some celebrity buff realised, people would find out that I wasn't Aisha Tyler. They then might or might not realise that I was Natasha Linnet. Again, I had to assume they would.

So how to stop it happening? The obvious choice was to get off the island, quickly and anonymously, that or to hole up in *Les Hommeaux Florains* and never show my face outside the gates. Unless of course Pensler had taken pictures of me, in which case I might already be in trouble. Presumably he had, and the journalist had seen them, or why else would the man have bothered to come over? Yet that could only be the case if Aisha Tyler and I were sufficiently close in looks to fool an experienced journalist rather than some celebrity-crazed geek. Unless he'd seen the pictures and recognised me as me, which was worse.

I needed to find out what she looked like, badly. When I'd tried before, it had been half-heartedly flicking through magazines at the hair salon and the doctor's, and I'd had no luck. To be sure of results I needed the internet. Fortunately, I had a set of Liam's keys, and he would be serving behind the bar until closing time. I could get to his house by a roundabout route, very roundabout, because it could be disastrous if Pensler and the journalist saw me.

There was a family near by, a harassed mother trying to deal with a baby in a pram, the father with a pint to his mouth as he gazed wistfully at a picture of a schooner under full sail, and two older children quarrelling, a girl and a boy, with the girl's primrose-coloured sun hat lying on the floor where she'd knocked it off the bench, just inches from my foot. I'd pinched it and stuffed it in my bag before I could think better of the impulse. The rest of my drink went down my throat and I left, my meal forgotten.

As soon as I was in the street I had jammed the hat on my head. It was too small, but the neck protector concealed my hair, which was surely my most distinctive feature, and with the peak pulled low my face would be hard to make out at all clearly. I felt a complete fool as I hurried up the street and around the edge of town, but I arrived at Liam's flat without seeing either Pensler or the journalist, and that was enough for me.

I went straight to his computer, my fists clenched with impatience as I waited for the ancient machine to boot up and load his browser. With a search engine up, I typed in Aisha Tyler, praying I'd got the spelling right as I clicked for an image search. The results were not immediately helpful; a girl in Philadelphia called Aisha Tyler, who was six months old, and so it was hard to see even Pensler mistaking me for her; a Japanese company specialising in bulk haulage who seemed to be very fond of their own logo; a variety of geranium. The second page was more promising, two more of the same company logo, then a picture of a full-chested girl with a head of gloriously curly hair who looked somewhat like me. She was also dressed in a minuscule Union Jack bikini far too small for her breasts, which were surely bigger than mine.

A click for the full-sized image showed that I was right – she was bustier than me, also maybe a bit shorter and less slim, with a little tummy on her, while her hair was dark gold rather than brown and probably dyed rather than natural. Her face did resemble mine, vaguely, but I could never have mistaken a picture of her for myself. Pensler evidently had, but I couldn't see the journalist being fooled. If he had his finger on the pulse, he was sure to recognise me.

I sat back with a long sigh. It all depended on whether Pensler had taken recognisable photos of me. I hadn't seen him with a camera, not close up, and surely he would have asked for a picture, probably with him standing next to me to show his mates. He hadn't, and to photograph me effectively from the hill would have required a powerful lens, a very powerful lens. I let myself relax a little, because while I'd seen his binoculars I was sure he hadn't had anything like the huge lenses people like Pia Santi had been chasing me with.

For a long while, I stayed as I was, staring at the picture of Aisha Tyler on the screen and fiddling with Liam's mouse to make the cursor follow the contours of her body as I tried to decide what to do. If the journalist already had his information I was lost already, so I had to assume he didn't. That meant evading him and Pensler at all costs, and they would no doubt be looking for me. They'd look in town, they'd go down to *Les Hommeaux Florains*, they'd scout Liam's flat, because more than once I'd seen Pensler lurking in the road when I visited.

I left hurriedly, with the sun hat jammed down over my face in case they were near by. Pensler might not have a camera, but the journalist certainly would, and a good one. Going back into town was out of the question, so I turned down the hill and on to the railway track, sure it would be the safest way home. It was also the hardest, with the sleepers difficult to pick out in the dim moonlight. When two figures approached me from the darkness it nearly stopped my heart, but they were only a couple out for an evening walk.

As I approached the quarry, my tension grew greater still. Pensler and the journalist might well be waiting, watching for me, and the tide was coming up. In fact, it *had* come up, the water already rushing over the causeway in a torrent of broken foam I wouldn't have dared try to cross. I was stuck, watching from the shelter of the lighthouse wall, but there was absolutely nothing I could do until well after midnight. Cursing more bitterly than ever, I sat down by the shore, well hidden but able to watch the land with each sweep of the lighthouse beam.

Slowly my adrenaline rush faded. Drunk, mentally and physically exhausted and comfortable against a bank of thick grass, I was soon having trouble keeping my eyes open. There was something hypnotic about the lighthouse beam too, moving over the landscape in utter silence, never varying by so much as the tiniest instant, nor by a millimetre, round and round . . .

A car passing on the road woke me up, making me start in awful disorientation as I wondered where I was. As my memory came back, I sat up, shook myself and glanced at my watch. It was just before midnight, but the tide was still too high for me to get home. It was cold too, and I hugged my knees in dejection as I once more settled down to wait. In Andy's, Liam would be calling last orders, no doubt wondering where I was. So would Pensler, if he wasn't already in bed, no doubt with his dirty little cock in his hand as he fantasised over Aisha Tyler's tits or, rather, mine, although it came to the same thing.

Occasionally, a car would pass, the headlights first appearing as a yellow haze among the scrubby bushes of the hillside, suddenly bright as it came over the rise, then sweeping past me out of sight. Each time my heart gave a little jump, expecting to see it turn off down my track or park near by. It would have been odd, watching my own stalkers from behind, but it was not a pleasant feeling at all. Yet all I could do was wait, with my emotions swinging between dejection and defiance.

I should have been in Liam's arms, or at least walking hand in hand with him through the night in anticipation of sex, no doubt with me bent over to let him enjoy my bottom, or perhaps sucking on his beautiful thick cock as I teased myself to orgasm. Instead, I was crouched in a gully, cold and frightened, with nobody to comfort me. I hugged myself more tightly, wondering if I should masturbate, both to get my blood flowing and as an act of rebellion against the situation Pensler had forced me into.

My hand went to my pussy, stroking myself through the material of my jeans, but it was hard to concentrate with the prospect of Pensler turning up, while the thought of the journalist catching me playing with myself was off-putting to say the least. I stopped, knowing it would be foolish but smiling at the fact that I could still feel naughty even in such an awful situation.

Another car passed, a cab, and a second, presumably taking people home from the pubs and restaurants to the few houses beyond the lighthouse. A third approached, only this time it slowed, paused, started again, and turned in down the track to *Les Hommeaux Florains*. I ducked down, my body shaking, then lifted my head once more, cautiously, to peer out through the grass.

The car had stopped at the beginning of the causeway, a dark, sinister bulk with its headlights making a long pool of yellowish light on the grass at the turn of the track, then all brilliantly illuminated as the lighthouse beam swept across it. It was Liam, and he was just getting out to inspect the causeway. I was up and running immediately, my body seeming to melt as the awful tension of the last hours began to dissolve. He didn't see me at first, but as I called out he turned, just as the beam swept over us again to leave him blinking the light out of his eyes.

I stepped into the pool of light, smiling with relief, my body suddenly limp as my tension faded and I held my arms out for a hug. He looked a little surprised, then he began to grin, and as he stepped around the car both doors on my side opened. Saul climbed out, and John Martell, both grinning like idiots, so that I was wondering what the matter was.

'Hi, guys, what's up?'

'Our cocks,' Saul answered, and only then did I realise what was happening.

'Hey, no, I –'

Liam laughed and grabbed me, pulling my arms behind my back even as John pushed something into my face, a handkerchief or a rag, forcing it between my teeth as I tried to protest. It tasted foul, as if he'd wiped up oil with it, and worse, so that I was struggling to spit it out and lost my balance. They were on top of me immediately, wrenching at my clothes as I kicked and squirmed, still trying to get the rag out of my mouth so I could tell them to stop before it was too late. All I managed was a pathetic burbling noise, drowned out by their own voices.

'I want her naked.'

'I'm going to fuck her doggy style!'

'Tits out, darling!'

'Get her knickers off, John!'

'Oh, yeah!'

'Fuck me, they're big!'

'Yeah, spread 'em wide, doll!'

'Wait your fucking turn!'

As they spoke, they stripped me with brutal efficiency, tearing what wouldn't come easily, my jeans ripped open and hauled off down my legs, my top jerked roughly up and the catch of my bra snapped, the cups jerked up over my boobs. My panties went last, torn off by John Martell, who immediately grabbed my ankles and spread me open. He was already fumbling with his fly as Liam pushed him aside, and a moment later I'd been mounted, Liam rubbing his half-stiff cock in the wet of my pussy with me still squirming feebly underneath him.

I finally managed to get my tongue behind the rag in my mouth, and pushed, spitting it out, still coughing and spluttering as Liam managed to get his cock in. My mouth came wide in a completely involuntary gasp as my pussy filled, and before I could speak Saul had forced the full bulk of his cock into my mouth, gagging me more effectively than the oily rag, with both his hands locked tight in my hair. He began to fuck my mouth as Liam pumped into me, robbing me of all control.

All three of them were laughing at me and calling out in delight at the way I was struggling on the intruding cocks, still fighting, but only managing to encourage them as the two men in my body came rapidly to erection and John Martell groped at my naked breasts and wanked himself to readiness. It had taken moments, to go from perfectly respectable to stripped and double fucked, not even long enough for me to react save in blind panic, and it was only as Liam began to find his rhythm in my pussy that I realised they'd done it because I was in the yellow sun hat.

Now it was too late, their cocks working in me, Saul fully erect as he fucked my head, Liam already close to orgasm, and there, whipping his cock out at the last moment to spunk up all over my belly and breasts, even soiling my ruined bra and my top where they'd been jerked up around my neck. Held firmly in place on Saul's cock and beginning to give in, I managed nothing more than a feeble wriggle of protest before John had hauled my thighs wide once more and pushed his cock in up my now gaping pussy.

He caught my thighs up, rolling me high and holding me open, kneeling so that he could watch his cock slide in and out of my body in the bright-yellow light of the headlamps. As he used me, he was grinning down at me, admiring my tits and watching Saul fuck my mouth. I'd given in, now holding Saul's balls and cock shaft to stop it hurting so much, still in shock, but my pride and resistance gone as I began to gobble on his shaft.

As my body moved on their cocks, I was telling myself it had been what I'd wanted, what I'd asked for, to be entered at either end as if I was on a spit and well and truly fucked. They'd done it right too, catching me unawares and gagging me, stripping me and forcing me as I was still fighting, laughing at me as they used me, a cock in at each end . . . a cock in at each end . . .

I gave in completely, reaching down to touch myself as I was used, to the delight of all three men as they saw what I was doing.

'What a tart!'

'Oh yeah, dirty or what?'

'Turn her over, she likes that.'

John Martell already had a firm grip on me, and at Liam's suggestion immediately turned me, twisting my body on his cock so that Saul's slipped from my mouth. I was left panting into the grass as my fucking began again, only now with my bum in the air. Not that my mouth was left empty for long, Saul quickly pulling back my head and sliding himself deep. I took hold of him, masturbating him into my mouth as my body began to rock between them, moving back and forwards on their erections with my boobs swinging in the ticklish grass.

Liam laughed to see me so dirty, and as I glanced from the corner of my eye I saw that he was tugging at his cock in an effort to get it erect again. I was hoping he would, but I already wanted to come, thinking about what they'd done to me as I rubbed myself, still with their cocks in my body. My hand went back, leaving Saul to fuck my mouth once more as my fingers burrowed in between my pussy lips, briefly touching John's straining shaft where it entered my hole, before finding my clitty as I began to masturbate.

They were right to call me a tart. I had asked for it, three men at once, taking me as they pleased, my body nude, all modesty gone as I sucked cock and presented myself for fucking. Only it hadn't been that way. They'd taken me, for real, catching me by surprise and stripping me down, gagging me with a filthy rag and tearing my clothes, forcing my legs apart and filling my holes as I struggled to stop it.

It had to be the right people, or course, but it was, my boyfriend and two big rough men, stripping me and forcing me, using my mouth and using my pussy, just to fuck in, so good. I felt used, dirty and so, so horny, now on my knees and fucking with willing abandon as I masturbated, but only because they'd taken me high, forced me . . . stripped me and forced me . . .

I wanted to say it, but I couldn't, not even in my head, not even with my fingers working frantically in my pussy and my muscles already tightening, right on the edge of climax. John was pumping into me from behind at a furious pace, his hips smacking on my bottom hard and fast. Saul was wanking into my mouth with his hand twisted tight into my hair, grunting with the approach of orgasm. Liam's cock was hard again, and as he reached down to grab on to my tits I knew it was now or never and tried again.

They'd caught me ... they'd caught me and stripped me ... they'd caught me and stripped me and fucked me, forced me, forced my pussy and mouth ... caught me and stripped me and forced my pussy and mouth ... yes, I was coming and I could say it, if only in my mind, they'd forced me ... forced my pussy ... my cunt ... forced my dirty little cunt as I lay kicking stupidly on the grass ... yes, they'd forced me ... they'd raped me.

On that awful word I came, my body in violent contraction on their cocks as I went into orgasm, rubbing furiously at my sex, with John jamming ever harder up me, and Saul ... Saul, whipping his cock out to spunk in my face, right in my open mouth and all over me, in my hair and across my cheeks, over my nose and in my eyes, before stuffing his cock back in, deep.

I'd have stopped, then, but I couldn't, not with John humping away furiously on my bottom, my body jerking on his cock as if I was a rubber doll. My orgasm began to die, but with a little peak each time he thrust his cock home, and then he'd come, deep up me, filling me with spunk, and as I felt it squash out of my hole on his final hard shove a last peak hit me, making me scream as Saul's now limp cock flopped out of my mouth.

Six

They hadn't really raped me, of course, merely followed the rules in a game of my own devising, which I just hadn't happened to be playing when it came to a climax. I would like to think men should be able to understand the difference between indulging a woman's fantasies of forced sex and actually forcing a woman against her will. Liam did, certainly, not even insisting I cope with his second erection afterwards, but letting me cuddle him and helping me clear up. Saul and John were well pleased with themselves, and maybe a little embarrassed for what we'd done, talking loudly and constantly asking if I was all right even once the four of us were seated around my kitchen table in *Les Hommeaux Florains*.

I explained about the yellow hat, which made them laugh, but also had them in a fine chivalrous fury over Pensler. As before, their typically primitive solution was to offer to beat him to a pulp, and it took me quite a while to explain to them that it would only make things worse. Yet it was a huge relief just being able to talk to somebody about it, even if they didn't have any constructive advice.

We sat up talking and drinking until the early hours of the morning. When Saul and John finally left, I took Liam to bed for straightforward loving sex and, if I knew it would leave him with every right to regard me as his girlfriend, then I was no longer able to resist. The whole night had been too emotional for me, and I needed to be held by somebody, somebody protective, which he was.

Only in the morning did I make an effort to confront my problems. John Martell had come inside me and I was approaching the peak of my cycle, so it was of paramount importance to get a morning-after pill from my GP. His practice was in town, like everything else, which meant braving Pensler and his paparazzo.

The important thing was to make sure neither of them got a clear photo of me, because without that they had nothing to print, while if they already had it I was already in trouble big time. Saul had taken Liam's car back and we drove up to town in mine, with the stolen sun hat pulled low over my face. There was no sign of either Pensler or the journalist, but I found myself jumping at shadows all morning, even expecting them to burst in while I was with the doctor.

It occurred to me that they might have been snooping around, although as everything was still in Penny's name it wasn't going to be as easy as it might have been. I called in at the estate agent to see Linda just in case, but nobody had asked about me or *Les Hommeaux Florains*. Nor did anyone else seem to know anything about it. Evidently, Pensler's paparazzo wasn't trying too hard, or with luck he was simply incompetent.

By lunchtime I was feeling a little more confident, but it was a small island, and Pensler had to be somewhere. I couldn't get back to *Les Hommeaux Florains* until the tide had gone down, something that was beginning to become a nuisance despite the wonderful sense of isolation it provided. The cliff walk seemed the safest place to be, and I struck out from the top of town, with my sun hat pulled well down and glancing repeatedly over my shoulder, but reached the open land without incident.

Once I was beyond the last of the houses, the track led between corn fields dotted with bright-red poppies, lazy in the hot sun, with no sound but birdsong and the chirping of grasshoppers, a scene so pretty and so peaceful it made me more determined than ever not to be driven out. The cliffs had a more majestic beauty, but were every bit as tranquil, and also colourful with flowers, while the sea was as blue as I had ever seen it. As I stood watching I promised myself I would do anything, whatever it took, to make the island a genuine sanctuary.

One or two boats were visible, a ferry in the hazy distance halfway across to France, several yachts with their sails tiny white triangles against the blue, and a stubby red fishing boat in which a man was standing, pulling up lobster pots. He was a long way off, but unmistakable by his shape – Womble. I waved cheerfully, hoping nobody had told him about the night before or, if they had, that he'd accepted not being there as bad luck rather than a deliberate slight. When Liam and the others had come down on the off chance that I might be game, they'd left him deliberately because of what I'd said. For a moment I actually felt sorry for him, and so full of charity I considered asking Liam if I should offer a quiet suck to make up for his exclusion, only to dismiss the idea. It could only lead to trouble.

Womble hadn't seen me, and I realised that to him I would be no more than a colourful dot against the landscape.

I didn't see any sign of Pensler at all that day, nor the next, despite keeping a constant look-out. It was as if he'd vanished, just as he had before. Nor was there any sign of the journalist, although I was sure I'd recognise him, while I kept expecting him to turn up at *Les Hommeaux Florains* and demand an interview. Gradually, I began to relax, even to wonder if I might have misinterpreted what I'd seen, although it was hard to imagine what else Pensler would have been doing.

Penny arrived on the Friday, triggering a scurry of activity, with the deeds to be signed and all sorts of paperwork and messing about. We also had a lot to talk about, swapping stories of the island past and present, and the people we knew. She confirmed what Cheryl had said, that the media had largely lost interest in me as soon as I disappeared, although she felt it was probably because they didn't want to look foolish by admitting they didn't know where I was. Percy had apparently had to turn a couple of them away from his door and put the phone down once or twice, but nothing more. He was still threatening me with a spanking for his trouble, but had given Penny one instead, which made me feel rather less bad about letting my relationship with Liam progress so far.

She found my being with Liam highly amusing because, while he'd been in his late teens the last time she'd seen him, her main memory of him was as Saul's snotty-nosed little brother. My agreement to make myself available by wearing yellow she found fascinating, but again warned me that gossip tended to be irrepressible on the island. She also suggested buying another sun hat, which I did, a blue one, despite having told Liam it would be some time before I was ready again.

I told her about Pensler as we sat down over dinner in The Barn, my outrage rising to her sympathy and as the level in the bottle of Alsace I'd chosen to go with our lobster gradually fell. At first she just nodded and looked suitably horror-stricken at the appropriate moments, until I came to the incident when I'd found the pool of spunk in the observation tower. She made a face and put the mayonnaise-topped cherry tomato she'd been about to eat back on her plate.

'That's disgusting.'

Despite not having told her what I'd done afterwards, I immediately felt defensive. 'Didn't you once do something similar with a boy called Ryan?' I asked.

She made a face. 'Sort of, yes. This Pensler sounds a bit like Ryan, in fact.'

'What? I thought he was just somebody who talked you into showing off for him.'

'Yes he was, but he was the local Peeping Tom too, always watching the girls on the beaches and trying to peer in at windows.'

'That sounds like Pensler. Is Ryan the guy who works on the pumps down by the harbour?'

'I doubt it. I think he left the island after some particularly bad incident.'

'I wish Pensler would leave the island. So what, did you feel sorry for Ryan, or did he push you into it?'

'A bit of both, I suppose, but it wasn't really like that. I caught him wanking in one of the bunkers up on the cliffs. He didn't know I was there, and I wanted to see, but he caught me, and . . .' She trailed off with a shrug.

I continued for her. 'And dropped your knickers so he could toss off all over your bum?'

'No!' she said quickly as she turned a rich shade of pink and glanced back over her shoulder. 'Well, yes, sort of. I put up a bit of a fight but, like you said, I felt sorry for him, and it felt wonderfully rude. Maybe you should do the same for Pensler.'

It was my turn to blush. 'No! Absolutely not! He's a creep, a complete nerd!'

'So was Ryan, but the thing is, after that he never used to bother me. I felt bad about it, as if I'd done something really disgusting –'

'You had.'

'– and ought to be punished for it. That's one of the things that got me into spanking. Ryan was strange ... different. It was as if he respected me because I'd been dirty with him.'

'It's normally the other way around, the more sex they get the less they respect you.'

'Not always.'

'That's true, but I don't see Pensler reacting like that. He'd just want more. Anyway, it's too late. He's already gone to the press. Not that I'd have done it anyway, not ever.'

I shivered and grimaced, forcing the revolting image of myself holding my panties down behind while Pensler tossed his horrid little cock over my bare bottom out of my mind. In the same way I'd imagined him coming over my breasts; it was one of those things that came up unbidden from my subconscious, despite my very real feelings of revulsion, or maybe because of them. There's a fine line between the desirable and the repulsive, at least for me, but actual physical sex with Aaron Pensler was definitely on the far side.

'I love the way you've done the rooms,' Penny remarked. 'How long until it's all finished?'

We fell to discussing *Les Hommeaux Florains*, Pensler thankfully forgotten. She could remember the old woman who'd lived there before me and, although she'd never been inside, she had walked out to the island and around the walls at low tide. I found myself smiling as I remembered how naughty I'd been with myself just a few days before.

'It's great when the tide's up. I can do just what I want.'

Her answer was a quizzical smile, tempting me to go on, despite the blood rising in my cheeks.

'Yes, anything. I can go nude and nobody will know at all, and other things ... play with myself ... even pee, you know, in my panties ... my bikini pants ...'

She nodded and bit her lip gently. It wasn't particularly her thing, except for the sake of humiliation, but I knew she'd appreciate it. More importantly, it had turned her thoughts towards sex, and very kinky sex, which was where my own were beginning to go. When she answered her voice was low and husky. 'I saw Cheryl. She says she spanked you, a lot, and made you go naked around the house.'

'Yes, and scrub and clean. She seems to have a thing about making a slave out of me.'

'I know.'

'What, you too?'

'A little. We shared a room in Paris. We got a bit drunk over dinner and when we got back to the room she made me lick her.'

'That's nothing. She pissed all over me and made me mop it up with my hair.'

'She did? I didn't know she could be that cruel. She made out she spanked you as a favour.'

'I suppose she did, really. God, I needed it so badly. Liam thinks it's weird, and abusive.'

'Welcome to the island. They'll take turns with you but they're too chivalrous to smack your bottom.'

'I know. I've been trying to find a spanking partner, but it's not easy. One man I thought of was Fat Don, the cabbie. I thought he might be up for it, but I've not had a chance to talk to him properly.'

'Don White? I don't suppose he's into it, but I bet

he'd welcome a chance to have sex with you, any sort of sex, if he could get away with it.'

'My thoughts exactly. He'd be discreet, which seems to be a rare quality around here. They all know about what happened to you in the quarry.'

'Surprise, surprise.'

She went back to her lobster, silent for a while as she ate. I was thinking of how it might be later, back at *Les Hommeaux Florains*. We'd played together before, many times, and I knew I only had to ask, yet with both of us always wanting to be on the receiving end it was never fully satisfying. What we needed was somebody to look after us both, as Percy had done occasionally, but again, it wasn't the sort of job just any old man was capable of taking on.

We'd finished our main course, and decided to be good, ordering brandies rather than any of the sticky puddings on their menu. As we sipped our drinks, our conversation was growing increasingly nostalgic, and increasingly dirty, right back to when we'd first met in France and I'd spanked her in front of Percy, among other things.

'You really howled!'

'I usually do, I can't help it.'

'Nor can I, not if it's hard, and it should be. I'd like that right now . . .'

'Perhaps when our dinner's gone down a little, and maybe not in a crowded restaurant.'

'Don't be such a pedant! You know what I mean. I'd like some really big man to come in. Maybe Don White, why not? He'd have some petty quarrel with me, something really trivial, to do with money. When he asked me to pay up, I'd refuse. I'd laugh at him too, and he'd lose his temper. He'd tell me I was a little brat and needed a spanking. He'd pull me up by my ear and flip me over his lap, really easily. He'd pull up my dress before I'd even recovered from the shock, but I'd fight for my panties, really fight –'

'But lose.'

'Of course. They'd rip, and he'd have me bare, completely bare, showing everything to everyone.'

'With your bottom towards all the diners.'

'Yes. Do you see the woman in the corner, with the pearls? She'd be saying how disgusting I looked and complaining about the noise I was making as he spanked me.'

'Not her husband. He'd love it. He'd be squeezing his cock under the table and wishing he could stick it up you, up your bum.'

'Dirty girl. He would too. When Don had finished with me he'd take me out to the back and throw me on the rubbish heap. The man would say he wanted to see if I was all right, and he'd follow, only that wouldn't be what he wanted at all ...'

'No. He'd hold you down in the rubbish and have a good feel of your bum ...'

'And my boobs. He'd pull my dress right up and have a good grope, smearing me with all sorts of muck.'

'Pushing your face in it too.'

'And fingering me.'

'Up your bumhole.'

'You're obsessed with bottoms, Penny Birch. He'd fuck me first ...'

'And you're not? Yes, he'd fuck you, and stick an old black banana up your pussy afterwards –'

'Then squash it up me.'

'And use it to grease your bottom hole. Then he'd bugger you.'

In my mind's eye I was there, face down on the rubbish heap as the man forced my slippery bumhole, wriggling in his grip as I felt my ring stretch, helpless to stop it, and then not wanting to as he wedged his cock deep up inside me. A powerful shiver ran through me, and I was going to speak again, telling her how I'd like him to spunk up my bottom, only to quickly shut my mouth as I realised the waiter was right at my shoulder. Penny was trying desperately not to giggle as he asked us if we'd like anything more, and I was blushing furiously as I declined.

We paid the bill and left, still giggling as we stepped out into the night. It was dark, with a thick bank of clouds to the west obscuring the moon. I could barely make out the road, until the lighthouse beam caught us, to illuminate the landscape for a moment and then leaving me with coloured after-images dancing before my eyes and worse off than before. Penny and I spoke almost at the same moment.

'We could ring for a cab.'

There was no question of which cab we would ring for, only of what might happen once we had. I dialled in the number with all those wonderful feelings of uncertainty and excitement rising inside me, yet still half-hoping that he'd be busy, or simply not answer. He answered, and said he'd come out to us as soon as he'd dropped off a fare at The Royal.

We sat down on one of the benches outside The Barn, lit in colours by the string of rainbow bulbs along the guttering. I glanced across at Penny and she made a wry face, no doubt thinking the same as me, thoroughly ashamed of what we wanted to do, yet wanting it too much to draw back. It was always the same, that terrible contradiction of wanting not only to be smacked and humiliated, but also to have every detail of my ordeal as vivid as was possible. Penny understood, as few others.

Don's cab arrived in just a few minutes, and as I rose from the bench I felt as if I was already

prepared, with my dress pinned up and a pair of
'Spank Me' knickers to make it obvious to all the
world what I wanted. Penny, I was sure, felt the same,
and I found my eyes drawn to the cheeks of her
bottom, prominent in tight blue jeans, as I followed
her to the cab. As I saw Don White's fat red face
beaming at us from the window, I was wondering
what in hell I thought I was doing. That didn't stop
me climbing in behind Penny, with Don already in
full flow, talking to Penny, as I put on my seatbelt.

'. . . must have been eight, ten years since I've seen
you, more maybe. You used to come here every year,
didn't you? I remember you in a pram, I do, and
those cousins of yours, Kate and . . . and her sister.
She was a looker, that Kate. What happened to her
then?'

'She's married,' Penny answered.

'No surprise there,' Don went on. 'All the boys
used to be after her, that Kate. I'd have had a go
myself, I would, if it weren't for the missus. You went
out with Ryan, didn't you?'

'No, not really,' Penny answered, her voice full of
embarrassment.

'No? I could've of sworn. Our Linda told me about
Les Hommeaux Florains and that. So what, you going
to make it into flats?'

'No,' I answered, 'it's just for me.'

'All of it? All right for some, ain't it? Mark you,
old Mrs Moate wouldn't have liked it to be devel-
oped, not that way. Very particular was old Mrs
Moate. I hear you've got Frank doing the work.
Good lad, Frank, he won't let you down. Always
buys the best, he does, and . . .'

We were already crossing the common behind the
defence wall from which Pensler had spied on me,
halfway back, and I was wondering how to interrupt

his flow of prattle long enough to get the conversation around to spanking us, or to do it at all for that matter. The only way seemed to be to make a bold offer, yet I could feel my embarrassment rising even as I considered it, building to a choking lump in my throat as we crossed the rise.

The cab came to a stop, pulled slightly off the road at the top of my track. It was now or never, but it suddenly occurred to me that I was merely assuming that Don White was a dirty old man from the way he looked, and by past experience. He was an islander, and perhaps no more decadent than Liam and the others, for all his appearance. With that it came home to me just what I was asking for, something that had come to seem normal over the years with Percy and Penny and others, but was in fact utterly outrageous, me, a grown woman, wanting to have my panties taken down and my bottom smacked.

Yet I was the bold one, and Penny was looking at me across the car as we got out, and pointing. I pointed back, but I was the one at Don's window, the one he was looking up at, his little piggy eyes almost entirely lost in the fleshy mass of his face, a bead of sweat running down his red skin, the look of a born spanker, surely, of a man who liked nothing better than to whip a young girl down across his knee and strip her bottom, a man who had seen me with my face plastered in spunk, and was surely going to proposition me as he opened his mouth . . .

'That's three-fifty, darling.'

'Fine, no problem . . . um . . .'

I dug my hand in my pocket, wondering if I should pretend I didn't have enough money, but it was only a step to my house. Penny had come around the car, and gave me a meaningful nudge with her foot. I gave her a pleading look, and dropped my coins.

'You all right, love? Need the toilet, do you?' He laughed.

I found myself blushing yet immediately more confident. Surely any man who could make such a crude and intrusive remark to a woman had to have a dirty mind.

'Fine, fine,' I assured him, scrabbling frantically in the dirt for the money. 'Um, I . . .'

'Would you like to come in for a coffee?' Penny asked him, her voice calm, level and above all respectable, exactly what you might have expected from a female academic.

Don glanced at his watch. 'Don't mind if I do, love. Got to keep an eye on the tide though.'

I'd found three of the coins, and glanced out at my islet just as the beam swung across it. He was right, the water was already quite high, with the causeway a narrow band of pale concrete between arcs of still black water to either side. My fingers touched the fourth coin and I quickly gave it to Don. He climbed out, the car creaking in relief as he shifted his weight on to his legs. With him standing right beside me, I realised how tall he was, over six foot, and his legs were like tree-trunks. My tummy gave a flutter as I thought of how easily he'd be able to put me across his lap, and hold me down, and strip me, and spank me.

We set off across the causeway, Don doing most of the talking, with an apparently endless stream of questions for Penny. I glanced at the state of the tide, trying to estimate how long we had. It couldn't be more than half-an-hour, unless he stayed. I glanced at Penny, wondering if that was what she was planning, but her expression gave nothing away.

Indoors, I offered him wine, hoping he'd accept and be unable to drive back, but he refused. Having taken out the bottle, I had little option but to open it and pour for Penny and myself. Don glanced at his watch again as he sat down, obviously happy to chat but thinking about getting back to his wife.

'Don't you usually stop work at about this time?' I asked, again steeling myself to put the crucial question.

'No, no, three, four in the morning, sometimes,' he answered, 'unless I've been on the airport shift. No rest for the wicked.'

'Are you wicked then?' I asked with what I hoped was a suggestive smile.

He merely looked at me blankly. 'It's just a saying,' he stated.

'Yes, I know ... never mind. Look, Don, I was wondering if we could maybe come to some sort of arrangement, you and I. Um ...'

'What about, the car? You bought it, love –'

'No, not the car. You see ...' I stopped, once again horrified by the sheer outrage of what I wanted to say. What if he turned me down? It would be mortifying. I threw Penny a frantic glance.

She gave me a dirty look, then swallowed most of what was in her glass before speaking. 'The thing is, Don, we were hoping you might do us a small favour.'

'Sure, if I can.'

'You can,' I supplied, and Penny went quiet, assuming I would go on.

Neither of us wanted to be the one to say the crucial word, and Don was looking between us in affable puzzlement. I followed Penny's example and swallowed the entire contents of my wineglass, only it went down the wrong way, leaving me coughing. Don reached out to pat me on the back, just gently, but enough to push me forwards. I thought of how it would feel on my bottom, and as soon as I'd got my breath back I was stumbling out the words.

'I – I need . . . I like to – to have discipline in my life, Don, male discipline, and, well, you seem like – like the sort of man who'd be able to do it properly.'

'That's right,' Penny agreed, finally finding her courage. 'It's old-fashioned, I know, but it's something some women need from time to time . . .'

'And it's always better from a mature man . . .'

'Or a woman . . .'

'But in this case a man – you.'

He looked from me to Penny and back, then spoke. 'Sorry, darlings, I don't get you at all.'

My face felt as if it was on fire, and if Penny's was anything to go by my cheeks were beetroot-coloured. Only the fact that I felt I'd already made a complete fool of myself enabled me to go on. 'I'd like to make a deal, Don, for you to discipline me occasionally . . .'

His face squeezed into a huge frown.

I had to say it. 'Yes, to give me discipline, to smack my bottom for me . . . to spank me.'

I'd said it, and if I'd thought my cheeks were hot before I hadn't known the meaning of the word.

He was staring at me, still puzzled, but with the light of comprehension dawning slowly on his face. 'What?' he asked. 'Like you was naughty or something?'

'Exactly,' I answered quickly, 'to spank me as if I'd been naughty. You can do that, can't you?' I was pleading, unable to keep the tone out of my voice, my face and chest burning hot, tears welling in my eyes.

Don nodded slowly, perhaps wondering if I was joking, even trying to trap him into something. Penny was biting her lip and fiddling with her glass. Finally Don spoke. 'But why would you want me to do a thing like that?'

'Because . . . because I need a man to do it for me,' I managed, 'a sensible, mature man who'll do it properly, and be discreet about it. Say you'll do it, please, it takes a lot of courage to ask for this.'

Again he didn't answer immediately. I'd been at the same point before, hoping I'd found a man who understood me, or at least who could cope with me. Sometimes they'd been horrified, even disgusted. I'd been given lectures on women's rights. I'd even been told I should see a psychiatrist. I'd been spanked too.

Don looked to Penny, who returned a shy smile. 'I'm the same,' she said. 'Lots of women are. Would you, please?'

'Both of you? You want me, old Don White, to smack your bottoms?'

'If you don't mind,' she went on. 'I'd like that very much.'

'So would I,' I put in, my hope now rising.

'You're serious, aren't you?' Don queried. 'Nah, you're joking, you're pulling an old man's leg!'

'No, really,' I assured him. 'We want you to, and – and you know what I did for Mick?'

'Yeah.'

'Well, I'd do the same, afterwards.'

He was staring at me, hard, obviously sure I was trying to make a fool of him. 'If this is a joke –'

'It's not! Come on, Don. You can pull our knickers down, everything.'

It was too late to back out. We'd asked, but he simply didn't believe we meant it. As he glanced at his watch again I knew he was going to go, but I'd already stood up, and before he could rise from the sofa I'd draped myself across his lap and pushed my bottom up into spanking position. I was shaking badly and my voice was thick as I spoke.

'Go on, do it, Don. Take down my panties and spank my bottom, just as if I was a naughty girl, a naughty girl you had to punish. Please, I'm begging you.'

As I spoke, I'd reached back to tug up my dress and show my knickers, the plain white spanking panties I usually wore even when I didn't expect to get it. Don blew out his breath, and then he was touching me, ever so gently, still not sure of himself as he laid one huge hand on my leg, just inches from my bum. I stuck my hips up a little more, offering myself in complete surrender.

'If that's the way you want it,' he said doubtfully, but his hand had moved up, touching my bottom. 'So what, you want like I should do you like you were my girl or something?'

'Yes,' I sighed, 'nice and hard, and don't mind if I make a bit of a fuss, OK?'

'If you say so.'

'Pull her knickers down,' Penny urged, her voice as thick with emotion as my own. 'You must pull her knickers down.'

'For real? I should take your knickers down, Natasha?'

'Yes, please, right down.'

'You don't mind what I see then?' he queried. ''Cause I'm going to, love. I'm going to see the lot.'

'Yes, all the way. Get me bare. Make me show behind.'

'Fuck me! You are a little minx, ain't you? Who'd have thought it? Mark you, you know what they say about posh girls.'

I didn't know what they said about posh girls, and I didn't care. He was taking my panties down . . . fat Don White was taking my panties down, slowly, with all the loitering familiarity I'd expected from him, his piggy eyes feasting on my bum as my cheeks came bare, and between, with the brownish-pink star of my bumhole showing to him as he prepared me for spanking. I kept my bottom lifted, choking on my own humiliation at the thought of what he could see and the way he was reacting to us. He knew he was unworthy, somebody young women like us wouldn't normally even glance at, except with disgust, and yet there I was, over his lap with my panties turned down and my little brown bumhole on show, begging to have my bare bottom slapped.

His other arm came around my waist, holding me in place, and it had begun, firm smacks laid full across both my cheeks. I'd done it. I was being spanked, bare and wriggly across Don White's lap. He was being gentle, but it still stung, and worse as he began to realise that I genuinely wanted it. My cheeks began to bounce and I was gasping. My feet began to kick as I started to lose control to the pain. My thighs began to pump in my half-down panties as he finally started to use his weight and strength, and I was there, a squalling, writhing little brat, spanked bare across a big man's lap, burning with the heat of his slaps and the shame of having it done to me.

I was completely in his control, my body locked tight beneath his arm, my involuntary struggles merely making me feel more pathetic. My thighs were cocking wide with every smack, my cheeks spreading too, to show off my pussy and my bumhole, bare and rude in front of him. It hurt so much, so much I couldn't stop it, genuinely unable to prevent the dirty exhibition I was making of myself. I'd asked for it too, asked for my knickers to be taken down, asked to be spanked across his knee, asked to be given my discipline just like the dirty, wanton little brat I am.

Now I'd got it, my bare red bum stuck up in the air as his hand smacked down, so calmly, so casually, as if he was giving me real discipline, as if he was spanking my naughty bottom for being bad, which was what I wanted, exactly what I wanted, so badly. To have a man take my knickers down and spank my bottom, whenever he wanted, whenever I was bad . . . panties down and squealing over his knee, spanked and spanked and spanked and spanked . . .

He nearly made me come, bringing me so close to the edge I was trying to rub myself on his leg, a really disgraceful display, gasping and grunting too, completely unladylike. Maybe that was why he'd stopped, I thought, unable to continue because I was being such a slut about it, but no. He was pushing me off his lap before I could even protest that I hadn't had enough. I landed on the carpet with a squeak, and he was apologising even as he scrabbled for his fly.

'Sorry. I've got to do it, love, or I'll fucking burst, I will. You're so fucking lovely . . . so fucking lovely . . .'

He finished with a gasp as his cock sprang free, a great bulbous thing as red as his face, poking out from under his huge gut. I got to my knees, eager to fulfil my end of the bargain and show him I really meant what I said. As I took him in, he gave a grunt of ecstasy and I was sucking, my mouth full of bloated, straining erection, my face pushed to his belly as I struggled to do him properly, my bottom stuck out behind, red with spanking, my panties still down to show off my bumhole and my sopping eager pussy.

Even as I began to masturbate, he had grabbed the base of his cock, jerking it into my mouth with his massive hips thrust out at me. I rubbed harder, hoping to be given my mouthful while I was coming myself, but he was too quick, his cock erupting to fill my mouth with salty, slimy sperm as he held me down, forcing me to swallow and breaking my concentration on my own pleasure.

I was close though, and being made to let him come first and to swallow his spunk was good too. My mouth was still full of it as I rocked back on my heels, a slimy puddle on my tongue, as I showed him what I was doing, masturbating for him, because he'd spanked me, and because he'd made me suck his cock. He'd been right to do it first, to use my mouth as a spunk bag before I was allowed to come. Now it was my turn, to rub myself as I knelt at his feet, my mouth full of spunk with more of it dribbling down my chin.

My dress came up, and my bra, jerked high to show him my tits, because I wanted him to know me completely, every private inch, nothing hidden, boobs and pussy and bumhole all on show for him, my dignity stripped away, wanking in front of him like the dirty little tart I am . . . a dirty, spanked little tart . . . spanked and spunked over. I was nearly there, rubbing furiously at my spread pussy, clutching at my bouncing titties, squirming my hot bottom against my heels, with his come drooling down my chin and into my cleavage, spunk bubbles blowing from my nose as I gasped in air, and coming.

I screamed the room down, again and again, as wave after wave of ecstasy shot through me, with my whole body in such powerful contractions my bladder gave way and a fountain of pee squirted out into my hand and down into my knickers, splashing in all directions. That was not part of the plan, not pissing in front of him, but I couldn't stop myself, and it merely made the blazing humiliation in my head stronger still, leaving me sobbing and gasping even when my orgasm was over as I emptied the contents of my bladder all over the floor.

For a moment it was bliss, a final glorious touch of degradation to the experience, but as my ecstasy died it was simply too much. I jumped up and ran for the bathroom, unsteady on my aching legs, clutching my soggy panty crotch and bawling with tears. Only when I'd got to the guest bathroom did I stop, and as I climbed into the shower to strip I could hear them talking, Don sounding worried and Penny desperately trying to explain that I was OK and that spanked girls should be expected to be emotional.

Seven

Despite my little accident, I was extremely pleased with myself the next day. I'd been wanting a spanking from Don White since the day I'd arrived and now I'd had it, and in style. He was good too, dishing it out as if he was giving a genuine brat a punishment, which is painful, but good. Penny was less happy about it, as he'd had to leave while I was still in the bathroom, and had only just made it across the causeway. When she came back in, she told me he'd been flustered and full of apology but was definitely willing to do it again. His discretion, I felt, we could take for granted.

She was upset because she hadn't had hers, so I did my best for her, taking her across my lap and making her mop up my pee with her red bum showing behind. Once she was finished I put her in the shower, still in her panties, and soaked her while she masturbated. She came quite quickly, but with none of the power of my own orgasm and she clearly hadn't had the full benefit of the evening.

We spent most of the next day at home, with Frank hard at work, and other men dealing with plumbing and gas-fitting and sewerage and all the other things I prefer simply to work without me having to think about them. Liam was there too, but had quickly been roped in to help, leaving Penny and me to our own devices. I showed her around the fort, inside and out, including where I'd deliberately peed myself, which had her giggling and would probably have led to something if the men hadn't been there.

Even out on the rocks, a good distance from the shore and with my sun hat on for good measure, I still found myself glancing at the hill every few minutes, and not entirely reassured by the absence of Pensler, or anybody else bar the occasional dog walker. After a while we went back inside, but were pushed out again by dust and noise, to take our lunch in the courtyard. The men continued their work as the tide rose and fell once more, leaving the causeway uncovered by early afternoon.

Penny was keen to explore old haunts and I drove her around the island, visiting favourite places from her childhood, the houses her parents had rented, even the bunker where she'd let Ryan come over her bottom. For her it was one long nostalgia trip, but I was constantly jittery, expecting Aaron Pensler and half-a-dozen paparazzi to leap out from the bushes at any moment. She didn't say anything, lost in her memories and rediscovering the atmosphere of the island, until we'd returned to *Les Hommeaux Florains* and seen the men off.

She stayed the whole weekend, introducing me to old acquaintances and showing me every inch of the island, which she knew in amazing detail. I learnt how to climb down to the lonely bays on the south coast, how to tell when the tide was turning by tiny patches of floating sand, along with an immense amount of history, geology and biology, more than I'd have picked up in years if left to my own devices. By her last day I was beginning to realise just how much there was to the island, although she had done nothing to alter my opinion of it as being backward.

On the Saturday night she got the spanking from Don White she had wanted, parked by the lighthouse with her laid across his legs on the back seat of his cab. He'd gained confidence, or else he found her easier to enjoy, taking a good grope of her bottom both before and after her panties came down, then giving her a good telling off as he spanked her. As with me, spanking her had him rock hard in no time, and she was made to suck him off then and there, Don accidentally adding an extra touch of humiliation by telling her she had to swallow properly to make sure there was no mess on his car seats.

We'd seen plenty of Liam, also Saul, who'd been hoping to get Penny involved with our games. I was still too jittery over Pensler to really relax, and put them off, but agreed they could come round to dinner on her last night. Safe within the walls of *Les Hommeaux Florains*, I let myself go, getting thoroughly drunk and taking Liam's cock out in front of them before he swung me over his shoulder and carried me up to bed for a night of rough, urgent sex. In the morning Penny confessed that she'd gone down on her knees for Saul, sucking his cock even as Liam and I christened my new bedroom.

I was feeling a little the worse for wear as I drove her up to the airport, with her sorry to go and promising to be back soon. As with Cheryl, I was left watching the aeroplane out of sight and feeling rather lonely. I felt unprotected too, although it was ridiculous when the thing I was most scared of was having my photograph taken, and as I left the airport I got a nasty shock.

The new mast beside the control tower was almost complete, with the main structure in place and steel cables being fitted to support it. All this was in plain view of the car park, and as I opened the door of the Rover I saw the journalist, unmistakable in his brown suit. He was looking at the mast, with a plastic coffee cup from the dispenser in the departure lounge in one hand, a piece of inattention for which I was extremely grateful as I slipped into my seat.

To make matters worse, I passed Pensler as I was driving into town. He saw the car and immediately looked away, no doubt still piqued at what I'd said to him when Cheryl was there. He had no luggage, so my first wild hope that he might be leaving was evidently false. Nor was he likely to be going beyond the airport, as the road only really led to the cliffs, unless the dirty little bastard was going up for a wank in one of the pillboxes. It was far more likely that he was going to meet the journalist.

Maybe they'd known I was going to be there, but somehow got their timing wrong. It was hard to see what else they could be doing, and their knowledge opened up all sorts of questions. Had they been spying on me? Had they been asking questions about me? Did they know about Penny and, if so, how much?

I drove straight back to *Les Hommeaux Florains*, and didn't feel entirely safe until the tide had risen to cover the causeway and cut me off. Spring tides were approaching, which meant the causeway was covered for longer and that when it was the current absolutely tore through between my islet and the shore. I still found myself up on the battlements, peering cautiously through one of the gun slits above the main gate and scanning the hill. Nobody was visible, and I knew they could hardly have reached me so quickly anyway, not without me noticing, and yet the slits of the great grey observation tower seemed to stare down at me.

For the next couple of days I hardly left the fort. I was forever telling myself it made sense, because Frank and his men were now laying carpets and I needed to be there to make sure they didn't make a complete hash of it. Realistically, I knew that I was only getting in the way, and that effectively I'd allowed Pensler and his journalist to make me a prisoner in my own home. The knowledge fuelled my resentment, making me irritable and increasingly frustrated.

I was sure they were watching my every move, waiting for a chance to get that crucial picture. Even in bed with Liam I didn't feel right, the security of his presence and my own massive walls merely adding to the sense that my freedom was being curtailed. I'd always envied those with fame a little, but I was rapidly coming to feel pity for them, and for myself, wondering how it would feel to go through what I was suffering all the time.

By the end of the week I was climbing the walls, when I hit on an idea so simple and so obvious that I felt like kicking myself for not thinking of it sooner. If Pensler and the man in the brown suit could spy on me, then I could also spy on them. The island was small, and so long as I knew where they were I didn't have to worry. All I needed was a group of people I could rely on to phone me whenever they spotted either man, and that was easy. There are hidden advantages to being a slut.

Liam was in Andy's and around the town, John Martell either at the harbour or out on deliveries, Saul out on call at any one of the island's rented cottages. Even Womble got in on the act, although unless Pensler had fallen into the sea, with luck, it wasn't very likely that he could help. The only place I didn't have covered at all was the airport, but I didn't know anyone who worked there well enough to ask and felt that Don White was probably confused enough by my behaviour as it was.

It worked too. The day after I'd suggested it, John Martell came over in the morning with some curtains I'd ordered from France and told me he'd seen both men that morning, having coffee in the Marais Hotel. There were no more sightings during the day, but when Pensler walked past Andy's later it was immediately reported to me. The following day was Saturday, and by ten o'clock I knew that the journalist was still at the Marais, where he seemed to be staying, and that Pensler was playing arcade games at the harbour.

Suddenly I felt free again, and immediately stripped stark naked to walk around the battlements, which made me feel wonderfully alive if also slightly silly. It wasn't enough though. My sudden release demanded something really naughty, something that the papers would love to get their hands on, and with which I could celebrate my little victory. By the time the tide was high and I was lazing on the parapet in just a pair of panties I had decided what to do.

Peeing my bikini had been rather fun, tempting me to do more. I like secret dirty things, going far beyond anything I'd do with a man, even Percy on some occasions. It makes me feel wonderful, doing something I know the vast majority of people would find improper, even disgusting. Not only does it turn me on physically, but also it fills me with all sorts of powerful and exciting emotions, apprehension, a little fear and, best of all, deep, deep humiliation.

Wetting myself is always good, as it breaks one of the earliest and most heavily reinforced taboos, potty training. It is entirely private, entirely safe and painless, harms nobody, and yet is undoubtedly even less socially acceptable than wanting to be spanked or put in bondage, far less so than lesbianism or adultery or any of the other things the media get so worked up about. After all, over the last decade or so, several advertising companies had used mild sadomasochistic images to push their products, but I'd yet to see a billboard showing a girl who'd pissed her knickers, let alone what I was planning.

I wanted to do it in style, to build myself up slowly over a period of hours, so that when the time finally came for my climax it was as powerful as possible. That meant planning, and privacy, because any interference would ruin my fun, even from Liam. He was behind the bar until one in the morning, at which point I would be cut off anyway, so I came in early, having rung ahead to check that Pensler wasn't there, had a few drinks with him and left, saying I was hungry and was going to get an early night as soon as I'd eaten, which was nothing but the truth.

With my sense of naughtiness already building inside me, I drove down to The Barn and ate as much as I possibly could, and of the best: a thick soup of local crab served with granary rolls, a dish of smoked duck breasts dressed in apricot jelly, a twelve-ounce rib-eye steak smothered in green-peppercorn sauce and accompanied by floury potatoes and green peas, a large slice of double-chocolate pudding liberally topped with cream. By the time I'd finished I could barely stand up, while my tummy was a hard fat ball beneath my dress, so swollen I looked pregnant. I spent nearly half-an-hour lingering over a brandy before starting home, but even then I was clutching my stomach as I went out to the car.

Walking back to *Les Hommeaux Florains* would have been out of the question, and I was glad I'd stuck to a single half-bottle of wine and the one brandy. Even driving the car was uncomfortable, and as soon as I was safely back in the fort I collapsed on to my bed, lying flat on my back and with my hands over my swollen tummy, groaning softly to myself. It was even an effort to undress, and I didn't bother to put any night clothes on, but slumped back on the bed, stark naked but too stuffed even to play with myself.

In the morning I no longer felt bloated, just heavy and uncomfortable, in a way that would not normally be nice at all, but was now. Knowing the causeway would still be uncovered, I threw on a T-shirt and my sun hat and went outside. Just being nude under the thin cotton of my top felt powerfully erotic, especially with a light breeze to make the hem flutter and give the occasional flash of my bare bottom cheeks or my pussy to imaginary watchers.

Nobody was about, and I wandered slowly around the battlements, my sense of apprehension rising with the tide. A little part of me wanted Liam or somebody to come down so that I wouldn't do it, but only a little part. He wasn't going to anyway, not after finishing work in the early hours. I was safe, completely, except from my own filthy imagination and my strong need for erotic humiliation.

Even my bugbears weren't a concern, as with the tide high the rear of the fort would be entirely secure. Still I was grateful when John Martell called to say that both Pensler and the journalist were down at the harbour. High tide was now late morning, and a full spring, one of the biggest of the year, which was ideal. I sat and watched it come in, with the water rising slowly in the two little bays to either side of my causeway, one rock after another vanishing beneath the surface. There was no more than a light breeze, creating ripples on the sheltered water, but beyond my islet the sea was moving in great heavy swirls, the current so fast it was creating white-capped overfalls just a few hundred yards offshore. Out towards France, a pair of yachts were toiling against the current and making no headway whatsoever.

It was only as the water was approaching the surface of the causeway that I realised it was considerably higher on one side than the other. Soon the waves were beginning to splash over, quickly merging into a trickle, then a torrent, which had consequently made the causeway impassable, with my island cut off from the shore by a great roiling mass of water. Once again nobody could get to me, and I was going nowhere for at least a couple of hours.

Now there was no excuse to back out, and my tummy was fluttering urgently as I went back inside. I'd been in my little yellow bikini before and it had been nice, so I got into it, along with a pair of sandals. My T-shirt I abandoned, knowing that to take it with me would provide a sense of security and so spoil some of the fun, and after a moment's hesitation I decided against even a towel.

As I left the fort, it was as if a hundred eyes were on me and every onlooker knew what I was doing, pushing my excitement so high there was a sick feeling in the back of my throat and my fingers were shaking badly as I hid my keys under a rock. My phone was indoors, and I skipped quickly around to the side of the fort, just in case Pensler was headed my way.

Only when I was on the widest of the big slants of rock did I stop, biting my lip as I sat down on a ledge. I could feel the pressure building inside my rectum, already very uncomfortable. I was telling myself not to be so silly, so dirty, that all I needed to do was pop down to the edge of the water and do it there. I mean, what sort of a filthy little bitch deliberately goes to the toilet in her bikini? It's against all decency, all common sense. Nobody would do it, nobody with the slightest shred of self-respect, only a girl so utterly debauched it had become a madness. That was what the world would think of me, if only they knew. I didn't care. I was going to do it.

Not until I had to, I wasn't, not until I really and truly couldn't hold it any more. I wasn't going to let my arousal overcome me, I was determined, not until I'd suffered every pang of anguish and helplessness and disgust. Not that it would be long, because my discomfort was changing to pain, waves of a dull, embarrassing ache that made me clench my thighs and wriggle my toes.

I stood up, my breathing now heavy and urgent, shivering with arousal and humiliation. My hands went back to feel the swell of my hips and the weight of my bottom cheeks, big and fleshy in my hands. I let a finger burrow in under my bikini and into my crease, to tease my bum star, tight and clean, but already pushing out a little from the heavy load inside me. All I needed to do was let go, to let that little ring spread, and out it would all come, into my bikini pants, and I would be well and truly soiled, a dirty little disgrace, with what I'd done on blatant show behind me.

Not yet. I took my hands away from my bottom, to take hold of my breasts instead, cupping them and jiggling them in my hands, rubbing my nipples until they'd grown to two straining points beneath the bright-yellow material. I wondered if I should pull them out, even go topless, because perhaps a dirty little tart like me didn't even deserve the dignity of keeping her breasts covered. No, they were better covered, so that I remained respectable until the last moment.

That was best, to stay as I might have done on the beach, because it made my coming fall from grace all the stronger. As I was, I could have walked down any promenade in the world, one modern young woman among many, inciting a little desire, a little envy perhaps, but none of the shock or disapproval I'd get topless, let alone the disgust and pity and ridicule fit to be directed at a women with a pouting, telltale bulge in the rear of her bikini where she's soiled herself, which was what I was going to do, very shortly.

The waves of pain in my tummy had grown stronger and I was having to hold my bumhole tight to stop it happening. I squeezed my thighs together, trying to make the pain go away, but it wouldn't, not until it faded of its own accord. I closed my eyes as I imagined myself in the same awful situation, only not in the safety of my private little island, but somewhere hideously embarrassing. I remembered a beach in Italy, where to my amusement the local authority had put up notices insisting that people wore tops when off the actual sand.

I'd thought it was ridiculous, having to cover my midriff and back yet leaving my bum cheeks showing beneath the hem of my top, a sight if anything more provocative than being in just a bikini. There had even been some officials to enforce the rules and fine malefactors, little puffed-up men and women in fancy uniforms. I'd enjoyed taunting them, deliberately wiggling my bottom as I walked past, or bending to pretend to adjust my sandals so that I could give them an even ruder show.

In the state I was now in, it would have been a very different matter, with the back of my bright-yellow bikini showing under my top, about to be filled with what was currently up my bottom and nothing I

167

could do about it, no way to escape, no way to hide. It would have been hideously embarrassing, too shameful to even take in, and worse, with a half-dozen of those self-righteous little Hitlers watching me in my desperation, completely unhelpful as I begged for directions to the nearest loo and waiting in amusement for me to fill my pants.

I was now gasping, deep even breaths, with my hands clasped over my tummy as another wave of pain hit me, stronger still, to leave me with my legs crossed and bent low, shivering in reaction. My bumhole began to open despite everything I could do, but I held it, sucking in to leave me wriggling my toes and sobbing with emotion as the pain once more faded. Next time it was going to happen. I knew it.

As I waited I was shaking my head and sobbing, the urge to whip my bikini pants down and save myself from disgrace so strong I could barely keep it in check. My thighs were crossed tight, my toes wiggling, in an agony of shame and embarrassment, but with my arousal soaring to crazy heights at my utter helplessness. I could even feel my bumhole pouting between my clenched cheeks. Again I thought of myself on the promenade in Italy, running frantically backwards and forwards in search of a loo, with people beginning to stare and comment, to snigger and pass disgusted remarks among themselves. I'd be crying, and I was going to be for real, my tears squeezing out to run down my cheeks in burning frustration as the pain began to rise again.

My mouth came wide in a small wordless cry. My bumhole had begun to open immediately, my load pressing out, hard and urgent, too painful to keep in. I tried, my teeth clenched and my hands clutching at my belly as I fought to keep my ring tight, but it was no good. Again my bumhole began to spread, pouting, the head of the first piece of dirt squeezing out between my cheeks as I cried out again, louder. I was in utter despair as I felt the lump between my bum cheeks grow fatter. I was treading my feet on the ground, sobbing brokenly, the tears streaming down my face, and as I fought back a final powerful urge to pull down my pants a new wave of pain caught me.

I screamed as my bumhole opened, properly this time, all the way, gaping wide. Out it came, a thick solid log, pushing between my cheeks, further, to touch the seat of my bikini pants, and it was too late. I was soiled, my dignity utterly destroyed, and I gave in. Resting my hands on my knees, I began to fill my pants, deliberately, no longer gasping in pain and desperation, but sighing in relief, a blissful sensation that can come only to a girl who has completely abandoned all right to the respect of her peers.

Just as I'd intended, there was an immense amount inside me, and I couldn't hold it at all. First I felt my bikini pants begin to push out, then to swell and grow heavy as my bulge began to form, fattening in my pouch as I let piece after piece of dirt squeeze out of my now gaping bumhole. I let it come, my mouth wide and my eyes shut in bliss, completely concentrated on the glorious sensation of filling my bum pouch with shit.

Pleasure had began to take over, a truly wanton, utterly uninhibited ecstasy far, far beyond the reach of normal people. I'd done it, soiled myself on purpose, something so unspeakably improper that just to think about it had me gasping and shivering, never mind the feel of my still-growing bulge as the last few pieces of dirt came out, now pushed hard to join the rest in a fat soft lump beneath my bottom.

When my bumhole finally closed, I felt mainly disappointment. I'd wanted more, so much that my bikini pants fell down under the sheer weight of what I'd done in them. Yet there was plenty down there, and that particular exquisite disgrace couldn't be far off. I opened my eyes again, taking in a deep breath as the hammering of my heart slowly began to subside, although not by much. I'd done it with a vengeance, my bikini pants absolutely bulging, my load making a heavy, squashy ball, sticky against my bum, the ties at my hips just that little bit tighter in response to that awful feeling of weight.

I had to touch, and reached beneath me to place a single tentative finger on the fat rounded bulge hanging beneath my bottom. It felt delightfully, disgustingly squashy, tempting me to do more even as I screwed my face up. Slipping my hand between my legs, I took hold of the whole disgusting mass, big enough to fill the palm, just gently, before once more standing up, smiling at my own filthy behaviour. I already wanted to come, and badly, but I was determined to make the best of it, to prolong the agony. First I would walk a little, which felt exquisite, with so much weight hanging down underneath me, wobbling obscenely as I moved, and dragging my bikini slowly down with each step, so that my bottom was being exposed as I went.

With every pace my emotions rose a little higher, while my face was set in a fixed smile. Occasionally, I would stop to give my bottom a wiggle, or to reach down, back or front and touch my bulge, every shift of the weight in my bikini pants, every touch of that fat soggy lump once more bringing home to me how dirty I was being. To add a fresh touch of daring I went to the corner of the fort, standing where I was in full view of the shore, with only the visor of my sun hat to obscure my features just in case Pensler and his journalist were out there.

I was rather hoping they were, because while they'd have had a fine view of my front, there was no way they could see what was behind me. As I climbed down again, I was smiling more mischievously than ever, and at the very centre of the open area of rock I put my hands on my head, stretching in the sunlight with my mind concentrated firmly on the weight in my bikini pouch and how I would look from behind. It would be truly disgraceful, my body gently tanned, showing no more than is proper for a girl in a bikini, with my brown curls tumbling down my back from beneath my sun hat, my legs bare and long, set slightly apart, my back pulled in a little to show off the curve of my bottom. It was a pose for a holiday brochure or a lads' magazine, wholesome and sexy, except . . . except that the pouch of my bikini bottoms held the most enormous bulge of shit.

A fresh shiver ran through me at the thought, and another strong flush of shame. I thought of myself on the Italian promenade again, only now disgraced, having been forced to stand there with my thighs crossed, one hand on my pussy and one hand on my bum, burning with blushes as my mess squeezed out into my bikini pants with several dozen onlookers to witness my humiliation. That wouldn't have been the worst of it either. One of the nasty little officials would have stepped forwards, all pomp and self-importance, to pull open the back of my bikini and inspect what was inside, first with a sniff of distaste, then with a lecture, telling me I was a disgrace and a dirty girl, but all the while still holding my pants out so he could see what I'd done, and show it to everyone else. Then he'd have fined me fifty Euros for public indecency and marched me off to get the money with my bulge wobbling behind me.

The picture had me purring with delight and one hand on the front of my bikini bottoms, gently stroking the mound of my pussy and exploring the feel of my sex lips through the material. Now I was going to have to come, bringing myself slowly up to what promised to be a truly exceptional peak. First, I no longer deserved my dignity, not a shred of it. I pulled up my cups to flop my boobs out, round and bare in the sunlight. For a while I stroked them, running my fingers over the sensitive skin and teasing my aching nipples, just enjoying the sensation of being topless outdoors, topless in nothing but my soiled bikini pants and a sun hat.

Again I shut my eyes, stroking myself while my breathing grew deeper and heavier, until once again my hand had stolen down to my pussy. I began to tickle in my crease, enjoying the little shivers sparked off by each touch. My bladder was just a little full, and I let go, moaning with pleasure as my pee erupted through the material in a tiny hot fountain, running down over my fingers and pattering on the warm rock at my feet, soaking back too, to wet my bulge and dribble from the lowest part of my sagging pants.

I pushed to get the last of my pee out, and as I did so I realised there was still more dirt in my rectum. Pushing harder, I stuck my bottom out, to make my bikini pants tauter and to feel my bulge swell fatter still as my bumhole opened once again. Out it came, increasing the load in my pants, making my bulge sag lower still as it grew heavier, and heavier, so heavy they suddenly fell down and landed with a heavy plop between my feet. I looked down, giggling.

Now I was all but nude, save for the filthy bikini pants around my ankles and my silly hat. I knew I looked a fine sight, stark naked with my bottom filthy, as lewd as I was ridiculous. I had to come, then and there, standing there in that ludicrous, shameful pose. My hand went to my pussy, rubbing properly now, to send my pleasure soaring instantly. I was going to do it, just as I was, standing naked and open on the rocks, teasing my boobs and rubbing my pussy with my filthy bikini pants around my ankles . . .

No, I needed to feel that horrible, shameful weight as I came, the weight of my load in my tiny yellow bikini pants. They had to come up, and that was that. I bent down and wriggled them back up my legs, sighing deeply as the warm mess pushed against my bottom. It felt better than ever, dirtier, to have had to put them back on after they'd fallen down under their own weight. I retied the knots, tighter, my fingers shaking so badly I could hardly do it, to leave me more aware of my bulge than ever.

For a moment I masturbated, just gently, until I was close to orgasm, but letting myself come back from the edge, feeling ever dirtier, until at last I felt ready for the final humiliation. I walked to the ledge, swinging my hips to make my bulge wobble, laughing with obscene glee. As I reached it I stuck out my bum, reaching back for a last touch of the huge ball of turd in my bikini pants.

Then I sat down, slowly and deliberately, my face screwed up in blissful disgust as my load squashed out over my bum, up between my cheeks and over my pussy. That was it, the final straw. I'd soiled my cunt and I had to come. How dirty could I get, how utterly, unspeakably filthy, to deliberately go to the toilet in my bikini pants, to parade about the place as if having about a kilo of turd down my panties was something to be proud of, and then sit in it.

I was rubbing frantically, revelling in the mess I'd made of myself as I began to circle my clit, faster and faster, all the while wiggling my bottom in the filthy mess beneath me. Even that wasn't enough, and I began to bounce, squashing my bottom in it again and again as I rubbed, until I was panting in ecstasy, clutching at myself and tossing my head about, my control gone save to pleasure myself, as once again I thought of what I'd done, gone to the toilet in my bikini pants, soiled myself, fouled myself, and, yes, paraded around as if having my knickers full of shit was something to be proud of, and lastly ... lastly I'd sat down in it ...

My scream cut the hot still air and I was coming, snatching at my cunt and clawing my breasts as shock after shock of ecstasy tore through me, and all the while wriggling and squirming and bouncing my bottom in the hot soggy mess I was sitting in. My legs came wide and I'd jammed both hands down my into my filthy panty pouch, ramming two fingers well up into my open slippery bumhole and another two into my vagina, to hold them there, deep up as I squirmed in my own filth and came again and again, so strong I was close to fainting before at last it began to fade, and as I came slowly, slowly down from my ecstasy I had slumped forwards, gasping for breath, my head spinning and my vision hazy.

It was time to clean up, and I got to my feet, slightly dizzy and unstable, so that I had to wait for the spots to clear from my eyes before I could see what I was doing. When I could, I trotted quickly down to the sea to wash my hands and sit my bottom in the water. It didn't make a great deal of difference, and when I stood up again it was to find that the sea to the east was no longer empty. A squat red boat was visible, in among the rocks where I'd never imagined anyone would dare to go, and in it a single man, Womble. Seeing him so close after what I'd done gave me a little shock, but he was much too far away to make out any detail.

I still put my top back on, rather amused by the thought of him able to see me in the distance yet blissfully unaware of the state I was in, although I wasn't going to turn around in a hurry. It felt daring, which is always nice, and when he turned in my direction I gave him a cheerful wave. He waved back, briefly, before reaching out with a landing hook to pull in one of the buoys I'd noticed, which proved to mark a lobster pot. I watched, admiring his skill, with the boat held exactly against the current as he checked the pot. The tide was all the way up, my islet smaller than I'd yet seen it, and the current had began to slacken, yet what he was doing couldn't have been easy, and he clearly knew every rock and reef of the island.

Only when he eased the boat between two jagged rocks, just a foot or so on either side, did I begin to wonder if perhaps I wasn't as safe as I'd imagined. He was getting closer too, and one of his pot buoys was no more than fifty yards beyond my islet. I started back, just a little worried, and carefully keeping my front to him so that he couldn't see my dirty bottom. That made it harder to cross the ledges and rocks, while he was using the current to his advantage, quickly drawing closer, only not towards his buoy, but into the little bay full of boulders I had to cross to get back home.

I hesitated, my sense of embarrassment growing rapidly stronger and less pleasant. There was no way out, with the deep gully cutting me off the other way, and absolutely no chance of crossing the boulders without showing him my bum, no, flaunting my bum, because I'd have to scramble over the rocks, making a fine show of my bulging bikini pants and my filthy cheeks. Being caught running around in dirty bikini pants would be unbearable at the best of times, let alone by Womble, but that was exactly what was going to happen, and I could feel panic welling up inside me.

There was only one choice. As I reached the second ledge I ran down it, his boat just thirty yards or so away as I plunged into the sea. As the chilly water hit me I was gasping in shock, but there was no time to fuss over that. Better nude than dirty, and I was immediately peeling my bikini pants off underwater and rubbing frantically at my cheeks and between my thighs. Womble couldn't see, and my awful shame and panic faded a little as I cleaned myself, only to rise again as I realised that I'd got out of one difficulty straight into another.

I was standing chest deep, in a bright-yellow bikini top and no pants. When I came out there was only one possible conclusion for Womble to draw, that I was showing off for him, in yellow. Maybe I could pretend I was just swimming about, but the water was so clear he was sure to see I was bare lower down and, in any case, I didn't dare risk the current. As he nosed the boat into the little bay and threw out two huge stones bound in net to hold it in place, all I could do was stand there grinning stupidly, my face burning crimson and searching my mind for a way out.

There wasn't one. Even by coming out of the water bottomless I was going to look pretty stupid and, if I refused Womble the sex he would undoubtedly expect, even he was sure to wonder what was going on. Maybe he'd even guess, or at least think I'd had an accident, because no girl soils herself on purpose, of course. He'd think it was hilarious, and the way gossip spread around the island, everyone would know by the evening. All I could possibly do was strip off my bikini top to pretend I'd gone nude for him, and then get it over with as quickly as possible.

I had to be sexy about it too, and despite my idiotic calendar-girl smile as I eased one strap down from my shoulder I was burning with chagrin inside. Again I thought of backing out. Maybe I could pretend I'd been teasing him. No, not wise, not with Womble. Maybe I could pretend to stumble on the rocks and hurt my ankle. Yes, that was perfect, a conclusion I reached just as my dirty bikini pants floated to the surface just a few feet away. He'd see them, he had to, unless . . .

One quick tug and I'd undone my bikini top and tugged it away. I threw it at Womble as I took my boobs in my hands. My top fell short, into the water, but I had his full attention, his pursey mouth open and his little piggy eyes fixed on my chest as I bounced my boobs in my hands and rubbed at my nipples. I saw him swallow once, and he had leapt over the side of his boat, vanishing underwater with a colossal splash.

I snatched for my bikini pants, but missed, and they were still floating in plain view as he came up, snorting water and gasping. A few powerful strokes and he'd found the bottom, wading out on to the boulders, his clothes dripping wet. Immediately he'd began to strip off, watching me all the while. His gaze was frightening, a lust-filled animal stare, but all I could do was pout and wiggle in some sort of idiotic parody of flirtation, desperate to keep his attention on my body. It certainly worked, his gaze never leaving my breasts, even as he pushed down his rough trousers to lay bare his massive pasty white legs.

Where he was, down among the boulders below the ledge, nobody could see. I knew I'd have to do him there, or risk being seen from the land. I came out of the water, my apprehension rising as I exposed myself and he did the same. Naked, he was more alarming still, far more alarming, his massive body packed with muscles beneath the fat, his skin pale and unhealthy looking, oddly smooth, with no hair at all save for straggling tufts sticking out from beneath the flabby overhang of either arm and a moth-eaten tuft at his crotch, from which sprouted a huge, pale scrotum and a heavily wrinkled cock, the obscenely fleshy foreskin already peeled back to reveal the bright-red helmet within.

I hurried across and scrambled down to the boulders, knowing that I risked being seen, maybe by Pensler, maybe by Liam or somebody, because this was not part of our deal. Not that Womble cared, grinning lecherously and pulling at his cock as he admired my body. I thought of tripping once more, but decided against it. Womble might well have me anyway.

'Fuck, you've got big ones, Tasha,' he growled, dispensing with any polite preliminaries. 'Let's have a feel.'

He didn't wait for me to answer, but reached out to take hold of my boobs, fumbling clumsily with the fat sausages of his fingers. I let him grope, wondering how to get him off as quickly as possible. Unfortunately, it almost certainly meant taking him in my mouth, but a glance at his cock was enough to make me think twice. Not only was he huge and very ugly in the way only a man's cock can be, but his skin was covered in fish scales and oil from his outboard where he'd been wanking himself.

'Would you like to fuck them?' I offered, holding my boobs out and trying to sound seductive.

His answer was a growl and to push me down to my knees. I went, as I had no choice, his massive strength far beyond my ability to resist. The boulders were smooth, but hard, making me more determined

178

than ever to make him come quickly as I folded my boobs around his cock, my senses filling with the smells of man and fish and oil all at once. He began to rub in my cleavage, grunting with pleasure and calling me his little pole-dancer as his cock grew swiftly to erection.

He really was huge, his shaft a great tower of flesh, thick at the base and rising to a small bright-red knob, which was soon bobbing up and down between the pale pillows of my breasts. I was already smeared with scales and oil, and tried to put a brave face on it, telling myself that, compared with what I'd just done, deliberately, this was nothing. It didn't work. This was Womble, and he was fucking my boobs and calling me dirty names, and worse.

'That's good, Tasha. Oh you've got lovely big ones, so fucking big, you little pole-dancer you, you little gorgeous fucking little pole-dancer . . . oh yeah, I've got to have you . . . you're going to be mine, ain't you, Tasha, my girl . . . my little dancer . . . my . . .'

I squeezed my boobs tight around his cock and turned my face away, thinking he was going to come, but he stopped, panting, and sat down on a boulder. As his cock slipped from between my breasts, I felt a most unwelcome touch of disappointment. I also got my first proper look at his erection, huge and ugly, like a piece of tree root or something. It was now in his hand, and he was panting as he nursed himself, but still staring at my chest.

'Are you OK?' I asked.

He took a couple of deep breaths before he answered. 'Yeah, yeah, great. I want to spunk up for you, Tasha, only I've got to rest.'

I nodded my understanding, knowing how hard fat men find it to come standing up, and it seemed the perfect opportunity to make my task a lot easier.

'Shall I show off for you?' I offered. 'You can do it in your hand.'

My hands were still on my boobs, and I gave them an encouraging wiggle as I spoke.

Womble licked his lips. 'Would you?' he asked. 'Would you tart for me, for real?'

I hadn't heard the expression before, and I had to admit it had a certain dirty appeal. 'Yes, I'll tart for you,' I promised. 'Do you like my titties then? Did you like me putting them around your big cock?'

He began to wank properly, his tongue flicking out once more to wet his gristly little lips. I leant forwards, letting my boobs hang down into my hands to bounce and jiggle them, at which he gave a long pleased sigh and began to tug harder still at his cock.

'You liked them when I did my pole-dance, didn't you?' I said, catching on to what seemed to be his obsession. 'I bet you wanted to fuck them then, yes?'

He nodded earnestly, his face now starting to go red as he jerked furiously at his erection.

'Yes,' I purred, 'wouldn't that have been fun, to give me a titty fuck down in front of all those other people? I'd have liked that . . .'

'No,' he gasped, 'not other people, just us. I want you dancing just for me . . . just for me . . .'

'OK, alone then, maybe down at your house. I'd do a special strip, just for you, and I wouldn't keep my panties on. I'd go nude for you, Womble –'

'Don't call me that fucking name!'

'Oops, sorry, Paul, I forgot.'

'Shit!'

He'd stopped wanking suddenly. I bit my lip, afraid for the sudden aggression in his voice and feeling stupid too.

'I'm sorry,' I said quickly. 'I'm really sorry, Paul. Why don't you carry on?'

All I got was a grunt, and he turned his face away, but his hand was still on his cock. I stepped forwards a little, to jiggle my boobs in his face, something I was sure he couldn't resist, and a gesture of submission too.

'Come on, please,' I urged. 'I want to see you come.'

I wasn't lying, not entirely, because playing with my breasts and talking dirty had been getting to me. Also, I was stark naked outdoors, showing off my body so that a man could masturbate over me, something too shameful not to affect me. He began to tug again as I rubbed my boobs in his face, and I stood back. It wasn't easy to dance on the uneven rocks, but I tried, wriggling my bottom and posing to show off the curves of my waist and hips, my boobs and bum too. Soon he was tugging frantically, but something was still wrong, because he was only half-hard. With a touch of chagrin but also a touch of desire, I came back to him, holding out my hand.

'Shall I do it, maybe?'

He nodded and I took him in hand, feeling his thick greasy shaft and once more catching the smell of fish and oil. It did feel good and dirty, wanking off some overweight fisherman among the rocks, first giving him a titty fuck, then tarting for him, a lovely phrase, then wanking him off, maybe wanking him off over my tits.

'Where's your bikini? I love that little yellow bikini you wear, 'cause it's like your bum and tits are trying to get out of it all the time. Do me with that, yeah, the bottom bit?'

'Um ... I, er, they're all wet, and, er, I lost it, anyway, I think ... I –'

'Lost them? What, around here? I'll find 'em.'

'No, no, no ... um ... look, come indoors and I'll use a pair of my panties. Wouldn't that be dirty?'

'Yeah, a panty wank, let's do it.'

He immediately began to scramble up the rock ledge, indifferent to being stark naked, half-erect and visible from the shore. I hesitated, but only for a moment, because a picture of a stark-naked Womble trying to get in at the gate of my house was surely going to be worth publishing, if only in the *National Geographic*. Jamming my sun hat down over my face, I followed, vaulting up on to the rock and streaking for the front of the fort. There was an awful moment while I tried to find which rock I'd hidden my keys under, and another as I fought to open the door with a man walking his dog in direct view across the water, but then I was through, holding the door for Womble before slamming it behind him.

'Yeah, panty wank, panty wank!' he chanted, obviously not giving a damn that we'd just been seen running stark naked around the edge of *Les Hommeaux Florains*.

I was shaking my head in despair as I led him indoors, now worried about Pensler to add to my woes, but really with little choice other than to find a pair of panties and toss him off with them.

'Dirty ones,' he said with relish as we came into my kitchen, 'white, so I can see where your cunt's leaked.'

I grimaced as I went to the laundry, wondering if maybe I should have tossed him off in my dirty bikini bottoms after all. He had pushed back one of the kitchen chairs by the time I came back with a pair of spanking panties from my laundry basket, which he immediately took hold of, sniffing the crotch. I retrieved them before he could decide to eat them and settled myself on his lap, folding his cock in my panties and tugging at the now limp shaft. His hand found my bottom, kneading my cheeks, with his eyes flickering between his growing cock and my chest as he worked.

'You're nice, you are,' he grunted after a while, 'you give good stuff, and you've got a nice bod too, nice bum . . . nice fat tits . . . I like fat tits.'

'Why don't you touch them?' I offered, eager to get him going and already beginning to admit to myself that once he'd gone I would be playing with myself again, over what he'd made me do for him.

He continued to fondle my bottom, and my boobs too, holding them up as if he couldn't quite believe they were real. Soon his cock was hard, once more a great rigid pole of man flesh, hot and thick in my hand. I changed my grip, encasing his erection in panty material so that with every tug his helmet made a rounded bulge in the white cotton. He'd began to grunt again, and his groping was getting harder, and more intimate. One fat finger slipped between my bum cheeks, touching my hole. Scared he might get ideas about buggering me, I pushed out my bum.

'Put it up my pussy, Paul, finger me.'

In it went, deep up me, a finger as fat as a little cock, wriggling about in my pussy hole as I tossed him in my panties, now as fast as I could, because if he didn't come soon I'd be in danger of losing control. Already I wanted to suck him, and why not? His cock was huge, and very hard, so virile, while surely the least I owed him for his help with Pensler was a blow-job?

I got down, barely knowing what I was doing as I popped his cock out through one of the leg holes of my panties. He gave a sigh of pleasure as I took him in my mouth, sucking on his hot shiny little helmet, nuzzling him against my face, licking at his balls. It felt good, dirty, kneeling nude at a fat man's feet, paying court to his cock and balls. He'd been between my tits, put a finger up my pussy, he'd made me tart for him and wank him with my panties.

He was going to come, soon, grunting and pushing himself up at my face. So was I, because my fingers had gone to my pussy and I was rubbing myself, revelling in my dirty behaviour as I worshipped his cock and balls, licking and sucking and kissing, all the while with my soiled panties wrapped tight around his monster shaft. He slid forwards a little, exposing himself yet more blatantly, and before I could stop myself I'd kissed his bottom hole, just once, a gesture of utter wanton submission, and I was back on his cock, now sucking furiously as I snatched at my sex.

Womble gave a final grunt and he'd come, all over me, in my mouth and in my face, over my chest too as I leant back a little and jerked him off all over my tits. Before he'd finished, both of them were covered in it, great fat creamy blobs of spunk to mix in with the fish scales and oil, and more of it in my face and hair, soiling me utterly. I was smiling happily as he grabbed his cock to milk what he had left into my slimy cleavage, my fingers still busy between my pussy lips.

I rocked back on my heels to show off for him, and for myself, revelling in my own disgusting behaviour as I smeared his spunk over my boobs and face, rubbed it into my nipples and sucked my slimy fingers, splashed it over my eager cunt before I began to rub once more. He took it all in, staring in delight despite having just come. I spread my thighs wide, showing him my open pussy as I masturbated, and my bumhole, still dirty. As he saw, he grinned, sending a shock of erotic humiliation through me, and I was coming.

Maybe it would have been better it he had caught me dirty. Maybe he wouldn't have minded. Maybe he'd have thought it was funny and laughed at me, then made me suck his cock in a squat, with my load swinging in my bikini pants as I got him hard. Maybe he'd even have fucked me in it or, worse, buggered me. Yes, that would have been best, to make me kneel and pull down my soiled bikini pants to show what I'd done in the pouch, then rammed the full fat length of his grotesque cock right up my bum, buggering me in my own filth.

I was screaming, clutching at my cunt and clutching at my boobs, spread naked in front of him, utterly shameless, and rolling back, to spread my bottom for him and, as my body jerked in climax, I inserted a finger slow and deep up my still-slippery bottom hole, as I imagined the unbearable humiliation of sucking his cock with my bulging shit-filled bikini bottoms swinging under my bottom, then being bent over and buggered in it, with Womble laughing at me as his huge cock squelched in my filthy bumhole.

Even as my pleasure began to fade, I was still in myself, easing the top joint of my finger in and out of my nicely slimy ring, and the full horror of how far I'd let myself go only struck as Womble spoke.

'Yeah, that's my tart, that's my girl . . . my girl.'

Eight

I had a bit of a problem. Old-fashioned male possessiveness seemed to be endemic on the island, which was bad enough with Liam, who very definitely regarded me as his girl, however much he liked to watch me being fucked by other men. Saul and John Martell were the same, although allowing Liam precedence, and even Don White, for all my clear agreement that he should spank my bottom in return for having his cock sucked, and notwithstanding the fact that he was married. Now there was Womble, who clearly thought that what I'd done with him marked the end of my relationship with Liam and the beginning of one with him.

After the way I'd behaved in front of him, perhaps it wasn't entirely surprising, but it had been no time for anything he might have interpreted as a put-down. What I wanted was a chance to think as I cleaned up, but he came shambling after me to the shower, babbling about how wonderful I'd been as I struggled for a polite way of pointing out that just because I'd let myself go with him didn't make me his girlfriend. Fortunately, he was feeling guilty about Liam too, which gave me a chance to postpone the inevitable confrontation by telling him it was only fair for the three of us to talk things over in Andy's.

That seemed to satisfy him, but I still had to keep up my pretence, and he didn't seem to be in a hurry to go, pointing out reasonably enough that his clothes were soaked through. I was also nude, my bikini bottoms irretrievably soiled while my top had probably drifted off on the tide. Once I'd showered I made him have one too, but even the huge fluffy bath towels I'd ordered specially from England weren't quite big enough to encompass his girth, leaving him with a great deal of pasty white flesh sticking out as he sat down to drink coffee. I'd put my top back on, along with a pair of panties, which seemed enough when he'd just had me nude and masturbating with a finger up my bum, and I didn't want to give him the impression I was covering up from him.

It was hard to know what to say, but as he explained to me how he chose where to set his lobster pots I kept finding my eyes drawn to his half-covered body and thinking over and over of what we'd done, and after telling myself I wouldn't give in. Not that I'd had much choice, as even Womble was far better than having the fact that I liked to do it in my panties become public knowledge, but by the end I'd really shown him what I was like deep down, far more than I'd shown Liam.

What finally saved me was the tide, not because I could leave the island, but because he had to go before his boat got stuck on the rocks, which was likely to damage it. As it was, he only just made it, with me up to my knees in water to push at the wretched thing as he ran the engine in reverse. Once the boat was free I stood and watched him go, full of chagrin for my predicament but not as unhappy with my experience as I perhaps should have been. After all, it had been wonderfully dirty, from the moment I'd woken up knowing that my morning toilet was going to be in my bikini pants to when I came in front of Womble with my bumhole penetrated and my body filthy with his spunk.

It wouldn't go away either, images of what I'd done flicking through my head despite my best efforts to distract myself, until finally I was forced to go up to my bedroom and lie down with my eyes closed to take a third orgasm as I ran through events in my head. Even that didn't clear my mind entirely, and I was very glad indeed when the tide was finally low enough to allow me to escape.

Womble had spunked all over my new sun hat, so it had gone in the wash, leaving me bare-headed as I started to walk towards town. He was going back for the harbour, and would be in Andy's later in the afternoon, by which time Liam would be behind the bar. With luck, I could use the time to work out some suitably tactful explanation.

I followed the shore, then climbed up on to the great concrete wall from which Pensler had watched me, walking along the top. That made me think of him again, and I made a quick phone call to John Martell. He'd seen Pensler just half-an-hour before, alone, in the dunes behind Bray Beach. That meant the little rat was presumably spending his afternoon peeping at girls, but as I was on the other side of the island I was hopefully safe. The journalist was another matter, and I hurried on to where the cliff walk began from the car park at the far end of the wall.

That meant climbing down through a large bunker at the back of the wall, in at a hatch and down through two rooms before I could get out. In the lower room a gun emplacement covered the bay, affording a broad angle of view, and allowing anyone in there to observe the entire beach without a chance of being seen. Like the slits in the observation tower, it could have been purpose-built for Peeping Toms, and even as I glanced out there was a girl not twenty yards away, changing her bikini after swimming, tits on show and completely unaware that she was being watched. The island really was a pervert's paradise.

As I started up the hill I was wondering just how much advantage Pensler might have taken of the German fortifications, how often he might have been watching me, maybe even photographing me. Possibly he had left Bray and was peering out at me even now, his slimy little cock in his hand as his imagination ran wild. It was certainly possible, with just about every possible field of view covered by one or more pillboxes or bunkers, to say nothing of the wild vegetation.

By the time I reached the top I was beginning to wish I'd kept the yellow sun hat, although the cliff path had to be about the safest place for me, open and lonely, with very little a Peeping Tom might find to interest himself in. I made another phone call, but got laughed at by John, who told me he was sure Pensler was still at Bray, and I at last managed to turn my mind to the problem at hand.

Liam was going to be angry, but I could at least point out that he'd wanted me to go with Womble. Perhaps I could claim that I'd seen the boat before and put on my yellow bikini to make it clear I was available. Yes, that was good. I could even pretend I'd thought they were both on the boat, but hadn't wanted to hurt Womble's feelings by turning him down. Again, that was good. That way, if Liam threw any accusations at me I could throw them right back, pointing out that I'd only done what he wanted me to.

That dealt with Liam, but left Womble feeling rejected. Really that wasn't my problem, now that I was no longer alone with him, but, perhaps if I allowed him to join in with Saul and John next time they had me, hopefully he would be satisfied. It was still an alarming thought, especially after I'd now handled his monstrous cock, but it was a lot easier to accept than it would have been just hours before. It's odd that, the way things seem unimaginable until you've done them, and then you find out it wasn't really so awful after all, like having an injection, or going to the dentist, or getting titty-fucked by a 25-stone Neanderthal.

My idea seemed to work, but I was in no great hurry to get to Andy's. I was tired for one thing, after such an exhausting morning, and the warmth of the day was making me drowsy. Womble presumably had some more lobster pots to check, and might take ages. I really didn't fancy having to explain myself to Liam in advance, or waiting until Womble arrived before making my confession. It was best to take my time.

I'd come out above a little cove, with cliffs all around and huge boulders at the bottom, visible through the pale-green water, with no beach at all. There was nobody about, and by walking just a little way off the path I could lie down among soft grass and relax, my mouth set in a happy smile as I thought of how naughty I'd been, and I drifted slowly off to sleep.

When I woke up, it was gone four o'clock. I felt thirsty and uncomfortably hot, making me wish I'd had the sense to bring a bottle of water with me. Yet it wasn't too far to The Barn, just over the ridge and back down the far side of the hill. I went, and had soon refreshed myself with water and a cup of tea with biscuits, making up for my missed lunch.

Once I'd finished I set off for town, avoiding the road just in case the journalist was about, and instead climbing up on to the central spine of the island, which I'd yet to explore. It was easy at first, walking along the edge of the golf course, but beyond that it got tougher, with a lot of dense bracken and strands of scrubby hawthorn and gorse, also the inevitable bunkers, which could be a serious hazard if you didn't look where you were going.

Eventually, I found a path and followed it along a low ridge that gave a magnificent view over the harbour, and Bray Beach. My thoughts turned to Pensler, just as he stepped out from behind a huge gorse bush, with a camera pointing right at me. I heard the click, and he was grinning with glee.

'Gotcha!' he crowed. 'I've got it, I've got it. I've got me a picture of Aisha Tyler!'

I was frozen, the shock of his sudden appearance and the realisation that he'd taken a photo of me, face on in good light, just too much to let me react physically as well. Then I was running forwards, snatching for his camera, a little silver digital, which I fully intended to smash to pieces. 'Give me that, you little bastard, now!'

He jumped back, surprised, and I stumbled, clutching at him for support. My reaction can't have been what he expected, because he stumbled too, falling back and dropping the camera. It fell on the grass and I was reaching for it immediately, but he was closer and got it, jumped to his feet and danced clumsily backwards to leave me sprawled on the grass with my dress halfway up my back and my knickers on show. I heard the camera click again and knew he had an even worse photo, a candid shot.

My face was hot with anger and embarrassment as I struggled to my feet, and I went straight for him, holding out my hand for the camera. 'Give me that camera, Pensler, now!'

He hesitated, an expression of worry crossing his face before it changed to a look of obstinate pique and he spoke. 'Hey, come on, don't get mad, it's only a picture!'

'Yes, a picture of me, which you have no right to take. Now give me that camera!'

He moved back as I approached him, and suddenly we were running, Pensler racing away down the track between high banks of foliage, and me behind, stumbling in my sandals with my dress catching on every available snag: bracken, gorse and a rusting iron spike left by the bloody Germans, which tore it wide open, right up to the waist. I stopped, fighting to untangle myself, close to tears in my fury and frustration as Pensler disappeared into the distance. He had me, well and truly, and I was forced to swallow my pride and call out. 'Stop! Stop, will you! Let's talk about this, please. Please Pens – please, Aaron?'

He'd stopped, maybe fifty yards down the path, only his head visible above the bracken, his voice defensive as he answered me. 'I only want a picture, that's all, Aisha. I don't mean nothing nasty.'

I shook my head, trying to collect my wits. He still thought I was Aisha Tyler, and that meant the journalist hadn't discovered the truth. If he saw the picture he would. I had to get it back, and if I could only lure him close enough, just for a moment, long enough to grab the camera . . .

. . . which he had thrust into a deep pocket as he came closer. I cursed under my breath as I finally managed to get my dress loose. It was ruined, torn from the hem right up to my tummy, so that I had to hold the front together to stop my knickers showing. It was a nice one too, a Max Hannan I'd picked up in New York. I still managed to smile as I looked up. 'I'm sorry, Pensler – I mean Aaron. You just gave me a bit of a surprise, that's all, but the thing is . . .'

I had no idea what the thing was, and could only extemporise in desperation.

'. . . the thing is, my contract, which . . . which says all pictures of me are supposed to be . . . to be syndicated, centrally syndicated through my agent, so you shouldn't really have taken one, do you see?'

I hadn't thought it through at all, and it didn't work.

'Yeah,' he answered, 'but don't you get photos taken all the time, on the beach and that?'

'Well, yes,' I admitted feebly, wondering frantically what I could say, 'yes, but not like that, not candid ones . . . not showing my knickers. It's not a very dignified look, really, is it, and I'm sure you wouldn't really want to see me like that, would you?'

I was very sure he would, but he at least had the decency to look doubtful before replying. 'I'll delete that one, OK? Maybe . . . you were a bit of a bitch to me, down at the harbour.'

'I'm sorry, I – I suppose I just thought I was being clever. Please could you delete them?'

'Yeah, OK, the one where you're showing your panties, but the first one's all right, yeah?'

'No . . . yes . . . I suppose so, but . . .'

I had no idea what to say. Maybe I could grab him and steal his camera, but maybe not. He was weedy, for a man, but I wasn't at all sure if I was stronger than him, while I'd rather have wrestled with a large earthworm. Whatever happened, I had to stay close, and somehow get at the camera before he met up with the journalist. I forced another smile.

'Look, Aaron, I've torn my dress really badly. I don't suppose you have a needle and thread?'

194

'I've got a stapler.'

'A stapler?'

'Yeah, that would do OK.'

'Um . . . I suppose it would. Are you staying near by?'

'Yeah, just down in Water Lane.'

I had no idea where Water Lane was, but it didn't seem to be far and, ignoring the thought of going about in a designer dress held together with staples, it was a step in the right direction. Surely I could manage to get at his camera, if only long enough to pinch the memory card. Unfortunately, I hadn't reckoned on one thing, a problem I realised as soon as he began to talk, keeping up the pretence of being Aisha Tyler.

'Wow, who'd have thought I'd be walking along with Aisha Tyler. I love your stuff, it is so cool, and your videos, they are way cool! You know, I say you're the best dancer out, and way the best star. So what you doing here, a new vid, yeah?'

'Um . . . no, I just wanted a few weeks' peace and quiet really.'

'Oh yeah, you said. So what's new with Sammie and Latisha?'

'Er . . . I'd really rather not talk shop, if you don't mind. Where is it you're staying, exactly?'

'Down here.'

We'd come to the end of the ridge of land, below which it fell away to a wooded valley maybe a quarter of a mile across at most, with The Royal Hotel visible on the far side. A few new red roofs showed among the trees, evidently holiday cottages. We moved on, the path narrower than ever, so that we had to go in single file. Fortunately, that made it hard for him to ask awkward questions, but my dress was forever catching and I knew that even if I did snatch his camera there was no way I could outrun him in his jeans and trainers.

His house was one of the nearest, and at first I was surprised by how big it was, only to realise it was actually flats. It didn't look like holiday accommodation either, the balcony a complete shambles, with his stuff all over the place. Inside was the same, with posters on the walls, a computer, videos lying on the floor, and just the sort of mess I'd have expected him to live in.

He was openly embarrassed, frantically picking things up and talking at the same time, first to offer me coffee, then beer, then saying he'd find his stapler, then suddenly jumping up and pointing to something in his living room, his face splitting into a satisfied grin. 'I got your poster from *Brit Girls Gone Bad II*.'

'That's nice,' I replied, and came forwards to see what he was pointing to.

There, on the wall, four feet high and in glorious Technicolor, was Aisha Tyler. She looked a lot more like me than she had in the internet image, but that wasn't what had me gaping like a goldfish. It was what she was doing.

For a start she was stark naked, except for a silly plastic bowler hat, the sort you see in Carnaby Street, patterned with a Union Jack. She did have shoes on too, lipstick-red ankle boots with at least six inches of heel. She also had company, two girls, presumably the ones Pensler had mentioned, one to either side, with her hands on their bottoms and their lips pressed to her face. Aisha Tyler was not a pop star at all. She was a porn star.

When I'd finally finished doing my goldfish imitations, I turned to Pensler, imagining the images he'd have had going through his head – me with the other two girl, sucking titties, licking pussies, kissing bum-holes; me with men, sucking cock, having my tits used, getting fucked; and more, so much more, everything from the mildest striptease to goodness knows what, bondage, buggerings, even bestiality for all I knew. I soon found out, some of it, as he began to talk.

'Fucking great video, Aisha, my favourite. That scene with the three of you in the tub, fucking ace! Say, you don't mind me talking dirty and shit, yeah?'

I managed a faint gurgling noise, no longer at all sure what I minded and what I didn't, or whether it made the slightest difference. He seemed to take my silence as a cue for full-flow pornographic verbal diarrhoea as he made for the kitchen.

'I'll get those beers, yeah? I like that black girl you were with, nice ass. I hope she's in your next vid, yeah? I'd like to see you and her do a double on one of the really big guys, Ramon maybe, or Mr Steele . . . not that I'm a faggot or anything, but I love to see a girl take a really big dick, and boy can you take them! I love that scene where Ramon and Peter Pecker double you in the garden, fucking wild! And . . . and when Mr Foot Long catches you in the shower and butt-fucks you with the soap then puts his dong up and all the bubbles are coming out and that. But you know the best bit? When Mr Steele fucks Latisha up the ass when you're giving her head, and pulls it out and sticks it straight in your mouth. I love that stuff! You are just the queen of ass to mouth!'

He finally shut up, his last words running over through my numbed mind – the queen of ass to mouth – and wondering how the real Aisha felt about being famed for sucking cocks that had just been up her bottom, or one of her friends' bottoms. Possibly it turned her on for real, because by the sound of it she was dirtier than me, or as bad anyway, but I would have been willing to bet that she wouldn't have fancied Aaron Pensler.

I glanced at his computer, wondering if I could mess it up so badly he wouldn't be able to download his pictures, maybe format the hard drive or something, but he was already coming back. He had a cold beer in each hand, already open. I took one, seriously wondering if I should hit him over the head with it and steal his camera. Maybe I'd get done for assault and theft, but . . .

The phone rang, not his mobile, but an ordinary land line. He made a face at me and went to it. 'Hi. Yeah, hi, Mr Rattigan . . . er, I've got somebody over right now, a friend, the girl I told you about . . . half-an-hour? Yeah, that's no problem . . .'

He was trying to sound calm, but failing. I could hear the glee in his voice, and I knew there was only one person Mr Rattigan could be, the journalist, and he was going to come round. When he did, I was lost. He'd recognise me, but if I left without the picture he'd recognise me anyway. I tightened my grip on the neck of my bottle, willing myself to smash it over Pensler's head, but I couldn't do it. I had to do something though, now close to panic and filled with self-disgust as I got up, feeling physically sick as I put my arms around Pensler's scrawny body and slid my hands down to his fly. He gave a start, but kept talking even as my fingers found his zip and I whispered into his spare ear. 'Make it an hour. Better still, two hours.'

Pensler swallowed, his oversized Adam's apple bobbing in his throat as I nuzzled his neck. His skin smelt sour, like off-milk, and, as I pulled his cock free, of man, so strong it made me wince. He was already hard. I'd imagined him having a weedy little specimen, but it wasn't. It was worse, thin but very long, and badly bent, a really horrible cock, which I was now wanking as he began to stammer down the phone. 'I . . . er . . . sorry, Mr Rattigan. I . . . could we make that a couple of hours? Yeah, see you.'

I had pushed down his trousers, feeling the hard lump of the camera in his pocket, to add to my burning consternation. Aaron Pensler's cock was erect in my hand, and I was going to have to take it further if I was going to get the camera, to get his trousers right off and take him into the bedroom. Maybe I could just wank him, maybe, if I was lucky, but I had to find an excuse to be alone with his trousers.

'What – what are you doing?' he demanded as he put the phone down.

'Playing with your lovely cock,' I purred, wondering if I could bear what I needed to do, and what was worse, to take him in my mouth or my pussy? As with Womble, maybe it wouldn't be as bad as I feared.

It would, it would be worse. Womble made me feel scared. Aaron Pensler made me feel sick. He made me feel sick, but his long bendy cock was in my hand, already making me want to retch as I tossed at him. I couldn't suck it, I just couldn't. I had to just wank him off, maybe over my tits so I'd have to clean up. Yes, that was it, and I had fantasised about it, after all, but the reality was very, very different.

'Let's have you out of your trousers,' I told him, squatting down to remove them.

He let me, staring down open-mouthed as I tugged his trainers off and pulled his trousers over his feet, all the while with his cock waving in my face. I was sure he would try to put it in my mouth, or just lose control completely and spunk over my head, but he only stared, and was still staring as I stood up and once more took him in hand.

'Come into the bedroom,' I sighed, pulling on his cock to guide him. 'I've got a surprise for you.'

He came after me, first silent, then babbling obscenities. 'It's true, it's fucking true! You are a fucking nympho, you can't get enough cock, can you? What're you going to do, Aisha? What're you going to do, blow me? Oh, tell me you'll blow me, or give me your special, your special where –'

'I'll give you something very special,' I promised.

'The Brit girl special?' he groaned. 'Oh yeah!'

We'd come into his bedroom, a mess of magazines and books, of empty coffee cups and old take-away containers, of discarded clothing and crumpled-up tissues, and all of it smelling thickly of Aaron Pensler. I determined to be quick, and pulled my dress up as I sat down on the bed. He was staring goggle-eyed as I flopped my boobs out of my cups and pulled off my bra, and as I took hold of his cock he gave a long low moan.

'This is what I'm going to do,' I said, my voice sugar-sweet but false even in my own ears. 'I'm going to pull your cock all over my big titties. How would that be?'

'Nice, real nice,' he groaned, 'and then the triple, yeah, do the triple, mouth . . . and cunt . . . and ass, oh yeah, I want to finish up your ass, Aisha, the way you did with Ramon in *Brit Bitch IV* . . .'

'No,' I answered him, 'just a nice wank over my titties. Don't be greedy, Aaron.'

'Yeah but . . . but you always want the triple, and you said you'd do your special, you said!'

He was whining horribly, and suddenly his cock had begun to go limp in my hand. I tugged harder, but it made no difference, the whole shaft dropping forwards as he lost his erection.

'What's the matter?' I demanded. 'Don't you like my breasts?'

'Yeah, but . . . but, please, Aisha, let me do a triple on you, please? You like the triple, you always say you do, and . . . please?'

I had never heard such a wheedling, self-pitying tone, and his cock had gone completely limp in my hand. Bitter frustration was welling up inside me as I tossed furiously at him, but it was like masturbating a cheap pork sausage, limp and greasy.

'Please?' he begged. 'You did it for the three guys in *Nerds get Lucky*, and –'

'OK!' I spat. 'Look, Aaron, I . . . you can have me from behind, if you like, but I'm not going to suck you, because . . . because I had a guy this morning, and he took ages, and my jaw still hurts. So just from behind, yes?'

'Yeah, great!' he answered, his tone changing on the instant. 'Doggy style! Let's fuck doggy style! Who'd you suck this morning, that barman you see, or the big fat guy?'

So he had been watching me, diligently, but that was now the least of my problems as I turned over on the bed. It was just as well he couldn't see my face, because I was finding it impossible not to screw up my features with emotion, a blend of consternation and humiliation so strong I was fighting back sobs. Still I did it, climbing into a kneeling position with my bottom in the air and trying to tell myself that at least I didn't have to look at him.

Maybe, but he could look at me, now with my fresh white spanking panties stretched taut across my bottom cheeks, a privilege I would never have dreamt of giving him, and shortly to be worse, naked, with my pussy and bumhole on plain show. I just hoped Aisha Tyler had a pouty cunt and a brown anus with a pink centre, because he no doubt knew every wrinkle and crease.

He climbed on to the bed behind me, now wanking his cock back to erection as he feasted his gaze on my bottom. I shut my eyes, praying he'd be quick, but knowing full well he wouldn't. His hand found my bum and he was groping me as he wanked, stroking my panty seat and squeezing my flesh.

'Nice panties!' he crowed. 'I love 'em big and white, like what high-school girls wear. I bet you were something at school, Aisha. I bet you were the prom queen and everything. Fuck me, what a butt! I love your butt, Aisha, you're the best, just the best, like in *Bubble Butts in the Desert*, where you're in that pink thong bikini, and you wiggle it right in the camera guy's face, then take them down real slow, then hold your cheeks open to show your butt-hole, then stick the beads up while you suck Ramon hard. I want to rub up them, yeah? Then I'm going to pull them down.'

He didn't wait for a reply, let alone permission, but pushed his erection to the seat of my panties, rubbing on the cotton to press it into my crease, tickling. His balls were slapping on my pussy pouch too, a sensation I couldn't ignore for all my disgust, and a horrible realisation came to me, that if he carried on I might get genuinely responsive. No, I wasn't going to let it happen. It was too shameful. Womble maybe. Womble was a man, at least, but not Pensler . . . not Pensler . . .

My agony broke as he spoke again, his awful voice breaking the spell of my purely physical arousal. 'Now the panties come down! Oh yeah, oh yeah, oh yeah, I'm pulling down Aisha Tyler's panties, I'm pulling down Aisha Tyler's panties!'

I'd thought my sense of consternation was bad as I got into position, but it grew far, far worse as Pensler took hold of my panties, held them out so that he could see down the back and peeled them down off my bum with deliberate taunting slowness. God knows I've had my panties pulled down by a lot of men, and often to show the full moon of my bottom as I was stripped, but there was something incomparably humiliating about having him do it, and knowing what he could now see.

'Fuck me, what a butt!' Pensler repeated. 'I'm going to love this!'

It was all I could do to fight down my sobs as my panties were settled around my thighs, well down, so that he could see everything. I thought of how my cheeks would look, round and pink and flaunted, a disgraceful display for a woman to be making at any time, never mind in front of Aaron Pensler. I thought of how my pussy would show, my lips pouted out from between my thighs, pink and wrinkly and wet in the middle, because for all my feelings I was starting to juice. I thought of how my bumhole would look, a neat brown and pink pucker between my cheeks, twitching a little in the agony of my emotions, again something I had no control over whatsoever.

'Nice!' Pensler drooled. 'Cute brown-eye, Aisha, I always said you had a cute brown-eye, and you look so tight. I mean, after all those guys who've fucked you in the ass, how do you manage to keep it so tight? I mean, I've seen this programme, right, where they were talking to Blondie Sirocco, and she said, like, how she couldn't keep her butt-hole closed any more, so she had to wear a fanny rag to stop all the shit and that dribbling out –'

'Aaron, shut up! Fuck me, yes, if you have to, but just shut up!'

'Yeah, right. Sorry, Aisha.'

I'd broken, sobbing in raw humiliation at his words. My whole body was shivering, but he didn't seem to notice, or took it for excitement. Even as he talked he'd been nursing his cock, with his knuckles brushing on the tuck of my bottom cheeks as he wanked. Now he put it to my pussy first in completely the wrong place so that his helmet jabbed against my clitty and made me gasp, then up me, right up me, with one hard shove. I had Aaron Pensler's cock in my body.

It was enough to make any girl weep, and I was sobbing and clutching the bed as he began to fuck me. Yet even before he'd got his rhythm up I could feel my body starting to betray me, the feel of a hard cock in my pussy, really too good to be denied, while my burning shame and consternation was having its inevitable effect. I bit my lip, telling myself I would not get turned on, that I wouldn't let myself enjoy my fucking, that above all I wouldn't lose control the way I'd done for Womble and end up masturbating in front of Pensler.

He began to row me steadily, in and out, in and out, all the while groping my bottom and occasionally mounting up on my back to take hold of my dangling titties, thoroughly enjoying himself with my body and in no hurry whatsoever to come. I began to worry about Rattigan arriving early as well as my helpless pleasure, wishing Pensler would come, only not up my pussy, because, if there was one thing that made every other conceivable humiliation he could inflict on me seem trivial, it was the thought of him making me pregnant. Yet he was just the sort of idiot who'd spunk in a girl's pussy without even thinking about the consequences.

'I – I want you to come, Aaron,' I managed, panting, 'but don't – don't do it in me.'

'Be cool,' he answered. 'Aaron V Pensler knows all the moves. He is the man! Just let me get my monkey spank cream.'

I twisted my head around as his cock pulled from my pussy, to see him lean towards his bedside table. He picked up a fat pink tube, which I realised had to be the cream he used when he masturbated at night, adding one more humiliating touch to my degradation. Yet at least it would soon be over, and as he seemed to want to wank over my bum it would give me the perfect excuse to run for the bathroom as soon as he was done.

That did very little to dull the shame of having to stick my bum up for him to toss over, and my face was set in a self-pitying grimace as I pulled my back in and pushed up my hips, making the rudest possible show of myself in the hope it would make him come quicker. Behind me again, he had stuck his cock back up my pussy, fucking me with short clumsy thrusts as he struggled to get the top off the tube of cream. I waited patiently, only to squeak as what must have been most of the contents of the tube suddenly erupted all over my bottom with a loud farting noise.

'Watch what you're doing!' I demanded.

Most of the cream was in my crease, cold and slimy against my bumhole and squelching in my pussy where some had dribbled down on to his cock. I shook my head in despair, then buried my face in his coverlet as he once more extracted his cock from my hole, this time to settle it between my bum cheeks. A fresh stab of humiliation caught me as he began to rut in my crease instead of using his hand, but I kept my peace, remembering how he'd gone limp when I defied him before.

He took hold of his cock, his knuckles bumping my pussy as he used my crease, his shaft slipping in the thick cream between my cheeks. Again I bit my lip, trying desperately to ignore the little jolts to my clitty and the sensation of having hot slippery cock flesh rubbed on my bumhole. It was not easy, and I could feel my anal ring starting to twitch, reminding me how nice a finger felt inside, and a cock . . .

Which was exactly what Pensler planned to do, suddenly pushing his helmet to my bumhole. I gasped in shock, but I was too slimy to stop him, my ring already open on the tip of his penis, and stretching wider as he pushed again, grunting.

'Hey, no, Aaron, not . . . oh, God . . . oh you have, you fucking little bastard, you –'

I broke off with a cry as he gave another shove, filling my bum ring with hard slippery penis, and he was in me, buggering me, Aaron Pensler's cock up my bottom, lubricated with his wanking cream. At that thought I gave in, sobbing bitterly into his bed covers as he began to jam his horrible bendy cock in up my bumhole. He'd got me, pushed too far, unable to help myself as my bottom was fucked, my pleasure rising despite my burning resentment, my tears hot in my eyes and yet holding myself still to have my rectum filled with cock. As if that wasn't bad enough, he began to talk.

'I love this part, where you see the dick go in up the girl's butt-hole. Oh yeah, you are so hot, and so tight, so fucking tight! Yeah, it's all in now, Aisha, my whole fucking cock, right up your ass. Can I be dirty with you, Aisha? Can I pull it out and stick it back in and that stuff? Can I?'

'If – if you have to!' I managed, gasping as he began to bugger me faster.

'Yeah, cool!' he answered. 'That's the best, like in *Backdoor Brothers* where Mr Steele does you and you're sucking Mr Big, or in *Blazing Buttholes*, or in –'

'Do – do as you like,' I gasped, 'only please shut up, please!'

'You got it, baby doll.'

He took my hips, his thumbs on my bum cheeks to hold them open so he could watch his shaft move in my straining ring. I could feel the bend in his cock as my bumhole pulled in and out, a sensation at once truly disgusting and utterly compelling. My fingers were locked tight in the bedclothes, my mouth wide with ecstasy despite myself, and wider still as he began to pull out, easing himself slowly free, a sensation so strong it set me whimpering, but no longer only in shame.

I wanted to reach back, to rub my aching slippery pussy as he buggered me, but I was still fighting, telling myself I wouldn't do it, that I'd retain that final scrap of pride, however good it would feel to surrender it. As his cock slipped free, I gasped in shock, and again as he filled me once more, pushing in his helmet, only to pull it out immediately. Again he did the same, and again entering my now gaping bumhole with a thick dirty squelch each time.

'Yeah, nice,' he drawled, 'just like –'

'Shut up, Pensler!'

'Right, sorry,' he said and pulled out one more time to leave my anus a burning open ring, ready to be fucked again any time he chose.

I thought of how I'd look, kneeling, my bum stuck in the air, my pussy sopping with juice and my bumhole a gaping black cavity between my cheeks, and with that geek, that nerd, that ugly little monkey of a man, a man who'd spied on me and wanked over me as I sunbathed, Aaron Pensler, about to drive the full length of his erection back up my dirty slippery bottom hole.

In it went, hard this time, to push the breath from my lungs, and right in, all the way to his balls, which began to slap on my empty pussy as my buggering began again, this time in earnest. I knew I was going to come immediately. I just couldn't help myself.

Every push smacked his ball sac on to my open pussy, sending a jolt of pleasure through me, enough to get me there, enough, if only I pushed back a little, maybe wiggled my bottom on his cock to encourage him, maybe . . .

No, I wasn't going to do it, I really wasn't, not unless he rubbed me off, in which case the choice was no longer mine. He'd just take me, make me come despite myself and I'd be left with at least that tiny scrap of pride. No, he was going to bugger me long and hard, to work my bumhole until I could stand it no more, until I was snatching at my sex and begging him to ram his horrid cock deeper up my rectum.

He slowed, and for a moment my dizzy ecstasy had begun to fade, just a little, allowing my chagrin to well up once more, for what was being done to me and my inability to control myself. The shame was unbearable, not because of what I'd done any more, but because I was enjoying it, and because if he pushed me just a little further I'd be rubbing my dirty little cunt again, made a tart for Pensler on the same day I'd been made a tart for Womble.

I cried out loud as he picked up his pace again, the movement of his cock in my bumhole brushing aside all rational thought, to leave me gasping for air and grunting like a pig. It was too much. I couldn't stop myself. My hand was going back, to the soft wet mush of my overexcited cunt, slippery with Pensler's wank cream, and with a final wail of despair I began to masturbate, only for my ecstasy to break at the sound of Pensler's voice.

'Yeah . . . oh yeah . . . I'm going to spunk, Aisha. I'm going to spunk . . .'

'Do it then,' I sobbed, 'do it up my bum . . .'

'No,' he gurgled. 'Ass to mouth, ass to mouth, let me do an ass to mouth!'

'No, Aaron, I – oh God, no, not that . . .'

He was already pulling his cock from my bumhole, and I couldn't fight it, my fingers busy with my cunt again, a thin voice at the back of my mind screaming at me for what I was about to do even as my mouth came wide. As my bumhole closed with a soft fart, I turned around, to find his face twisted in demented glee, his cock standing proud in front of my face, slimy and foul, with bubbles of pre-come at the tip, and before I could stop myself I'd done it, taking Aaron Pensler's dirty ugly penis, straight from my own well-buggered anus into my mouth. My eyes popped as my senses filled with the taste of my own bottom, but I didn't care. It was lovely, so dirty, just what I needed as my orgasm welled up and burst, singing in my head as I mouthed on his filthy cock, sucking with demented urgency as he jerked at his shaft, and pulled out with a crow of perverted delight.

'Yay, ass to mouth, ass to mouth, with the queen, and a facial for the money shot!'

One final grunt and he'd come, right in my face. My mouth was still open, gaping for his cock, and most of his spunk went in. More splashed across my face, over one cheek and into my eye, and more, in my hair, and my mouth again as I grabbed him and stuck him back in, to suck and suck and suck, swallowing down his spunk and my own dirty taste as I rode my orgasm, until finally it began to fade and a wave of shame hit me full on, to leave me wracked with sobs as he pulled out, wiped his cock across my face and collapsed back on to his bed, panting.

I could do nothing, only squat there, dribbling at back and front and fighting for breath. He lay back and put his hands behind his head, looking unbelievably smug, his horrible cock still standing proud over his skinny belly, glistening wet with spit and spunk and slime. I managed to roll on to my side, shaking so badly I knew I'd have to wait a little before I could even stand, my head spinning and spots dancing in front of my eyes as I forced myself to think of what I was supposed to be doing.

'Is that cool, or what?' he sighed. 'I just butt-fucked Aisha Tyler!'

'Good . . . good for you,' I managed. 'Now, I need to clean up, Aaron, so be a good boy and let a girl have her privacy, please?'

'Sure,' he answered. 'Aw, shit, I should have remembered to give you a Dirty Sanchez, like Ramon does in *Blazing Buttholes*, yeah? You looked fucking comic, you did, sucking his cock with a big dirty bean-feaster moustache of your own poop! Grab us a beer on the way back, yeah?'

I didn't answer, but climbed down unsteadily from the bed and waddled from the room. My bottom hole stung and I was dribbling into my panties, which he'd never even bothered to take off, but there was a sense of triumph rising within me as I saw his trousers, lying on the floor where I'd left them. I pushed the bedroom door to behind me and ducked down, burrowing feverishly into his pocket.

Out came the camera. I flicked the right port open first time and extracted the memory card, which I slipped down the front of my panties before staggering into the bathroom.

Nine

Aaron Pensler had made me come. He'd done a lot more as well, but that was the thought I couldn't get out of my head as I walked back up the hill. Anything else, even taking his cock from my bumhole to my mouth, and I could pretend I'd had no choice, but not that. I'd been willing, more than willing, eager, his tart, rubbing at myself as he used my body in the most disgusting way, and my orgasm had been superb, among my best ever. Worse still, I couldn't bring myself to hate what I'd done, but only promise that nobody would ever, ever discover it.

I was still in a mess too, because I'd had to make my excuses and leave before either Rattigan turned up or Pensler realised that his memory card was missing. He'd found his stapler, and my torn dress was held together, but my panties were sticky and uncomfortable, while I was waddling badly from my buggering. I was late too. Liam and Womble would already be in Andy's, but I could hardly turn up in a ripped dress and squelchy panties.

Not that I was in any mood for trying to sort out relationship difficulties. For all I cared, they could beat each other senseless, the winner could call himself my boyfriend, and if that was sure to be Womble it really wasn't going to make much difference after what I'd been through that day. I was going home anyway, for a long hot bath and a bottle of wine, with my phone switched off.

In fact, the sooner I got home the better, because Rattigan was going to want to see Pensler's photos and they would immediately discover the theft. I had an hour at most, and by then I wanted to be safely back in *Les Hommeaux Florains*. By the time I got to the road I was walking as fast as I could, despite knowing that from behind I would look like some sort of demented goose.

I'd reached the junction of the Whitegates road when a familiar battered Cortina drew up beside me and the great bald dome of Don White's head pushed out from the window. 'In a hurry, darling?' he asked. 'Need a lift?'

'Please, yes,' I answered with gratitude, 'out to *Les Hommeaux Florains.*'

'Be right there. You all right? You look like you've been dragged through a hedge backwards.'

'Something like that. I thought I'd explore the middle bit of the island, but it was much rougher than I'd expected.'

'That's right, that is. A lot of bunkers up there, there is, and . . .'

He began to prattle on, but I wasn't listening, instead just staring out at the window and wondering what would happen when Pensler found out he'd been robbed. Only when Don slowed to drop me off at the top of my track did I return my attention to him.

'Thanks, Don. How much is that?'

'Not a penny, love,' he answered, 'only, I don't suppose you fancy . . . you know, a smacked arse and a bit of the other for me?'

'Not now,' I told him, 'maybe tomorrow or the day after, OK?'

He gave me a big beaming smile and a thumbs up, then drove off. I could feel the last of my energy draining away as I walked across the causeway, so tired it was an effort to open the wicket gate. Only my need to see what Pensler – Aaron now, I supposed, as he'd had me – had on his memory card keeping me going. I'd transferred the card from my panties to my bag as soon as it was safe, and spent an anxious moment scrabbling for it among lipsticks and tissues and coins and receipts before I managed to find it.

My laptop was in one of the boxes and I set it up, my fingers shaking so badly I had to have a glass of brandy before I could finish the connections. With the last USB lead in place I slipped the card into my reader and sat back, clicking as ordered until a series of thumbnails appeared on my screen. I scrolled down immediately, to pull up the first picture he'd taken of me, and as it came up in full size I was blowing my breath out in relief. It was perfect, showing me full length, looking right at the camera with an expression of mild surprise on my face, my identity unmistakable to anyone who knew me. Whatever I'd endured on Pensler's cock, it had been worth it.

The candid one would have sold too, because it not only showed me sprawled on the ground with my panties on show but also gave a reasonable view of my face. Side by side, with my flame-coloured summer dress, it was obviously me. Any of the magazines who'd been stalking me would have published them like a shot. There were more too, of me walking along the ridge before Pensler had caught me, distant shots taken as he walked up from the dunes, and I realised my mistake.

From Braye I'd have been visible on the skyline, tiny, but scarlet against green and blue, while no doubt he was well acquainted with my wardrobe. He'd seen me and climbed up the hill to cut me off, sneaking through the tall bracken to make sure he wasn't seen himself. It was hardly a surprise to discover for certain that he'd been spying on me, but it deepened my sense of chagrin. He'd stalked me, peeped on me, wanked over me, and what had I done? I'd let him bugger me.

The other pictures on the card made my chagrin deeper still, but also my sense of relief. It was a 512K card, and he hadn't taken the pictures off for ages. The first dated from shortly before I'd arrived on the island. There were plenty of me, at *Les Hommeaux Florains* and elsewhere, walking, sunbathing or just minding my own business, but not a single one would have been worth having for the journalist, save only the last pair. I was in the clear, at least for the moment.

His other pictures were mainly of girls on the beaches, in bikinis or getting changed, and many of them obviously taken through the observation slits and gun ports of German fortifications. Others were attempts at scenic shots, or typical holiday snaps, except for a very peculiar set I couldn't figure out at all. He'd been taking photographs of the new radio mast at the airport as it was erected, dozens of them, also of two other masts elsewhere on the island, as if he was making a collection.

I shrugged, telling myself that, if people can be sad enough to collect the numbers of trains and even buses, then why not radio masts? Pensler, after all, was a prime case, as sad as they come, his entire life devolved on to people he didn't know, like Aisha Tyler, although obviously he now thought he did, and intimately.

Now that I knew she was a porn star, it all made sense, the facts clicking slowly into place in my head as I went to slump on the sofa with a glass of wine; that I'd never heard of her, Pensler's lack of surprise at seeing me in a strip show, the way he acted towards me as if my naked body was public property, her revealing picture on the net, that my accent was like hers, the fact that Cheryl had never heard of her. Evidently, she was an English girl who'd gone to the States and made a career in porn, using her British origin as a trademark.

It did seem odd that a reporter would come all the way out to the island in pursuit of a girl who was presumably more than happy to be photographed, but I was too tired to try to puzzle that out. In fact, if I didn't haul myself off to bed immediately I was going to fall asleep on the sofa.

I did fall asleep on the sofa, and woke to near darkness from a dream in which Aaron Pensler and four men with improbably large cocks were gluing my panties to my pussy and telling me it was the latest thing in dirty videos. After a moment of disorientation, I discovered that the gluing part at least was true, and staggered off to shower before making for my bed. It took ages for me to get to sleep again, what with Liam and Womble, and Pensler and Rattigan, and what Percy was going to make of it all. It was dawn before I managed it, and when I woke again the tide was already over the causeway, as high and strong as the day before.

There was nothing to do but wait, sitting on the battlements sipping coffee and staring out across the island and the sea. Even with all my worries it was impossible not to appreciate the lonely beauty of the place, and not for the first time I promised myself that I would stick it out and make *Les Hommeaux Florains* my home, whatever the world had to throw at me.

It wasn't until well after lunch that I remembered my phone was off, by which time the causeway was nearly uncovered. I decided not to turn it on, but to make my way up to Andy's and sort things out with Liam face to face. As I drove up to town, my apprehension was rising fast as I wondered what might have happened the day before. Being Monday, Frank was supposed to have come down to me, and it was all too easy to find the excuse of visiting him first. It turned out that the carpets they were supposed to be fitting in my second turret simply hadn't arrived, but I left the car outside his yard and walked down to Andy's.

Liam was there, looking bored behind the bar with just three tourists drinking at the outside tables. I approached him, feeling extremely nervous, and was pleased to be greeted by a big smile and a kiss. He gave me a beer and I sat down on one of the bar stools, wondering just how much he knew and deciding to make a cautious enquiry. 'Is Womble about? I mean Paul.'

'He's out in the boat, I think. We've got to talk, Tasha.'

I nodded, cautious, but relieved by the lack of aggression in his voice. If anything, he sounded as nervous as I felt.

'It's like this,' he began, and he was fidgeting with the label of a beer bottle as he spoke. 'What you did for Paul was really great ... I mean, you know, he doesn't get a lot, 'cause ... 'cause he's Paul, and I know you didn't want to, so, you know, it was really great of you and that.'

He stopped, and again I nodded, wondering where he was leading.

'Paul's a great guy,' he went on suddenly, 'a really great guy. We've been mates all our lives. He'd never fuck me around, never, like he said yesterday, he wouldn't nick you off me ... I mean, I know that's stupid anyway, but –'

'Of course,' I put in, catching the doubt in his voice, which vanished as he went on.

'If you want to, you know, go with him, or Saul, or John, that's all right with me, only do you mind if I, you know ... 'cause you're not really into being faithful and that, are you?'

What he meant was that I was a little slut, but at least he was trying to phrase it nicely. I could tell what was coming too.

'Do you mind if I, maybe, see other girls now and then, just tourists and that, you know, and it doesn't mean ... Do you remember Tanya, who did a strip the same night you did? I –'

I put my hands up to stop him and he immediately looked worried. It was tempting to torment him, and I couldn't help but feel a pang of annoyance, however irrational it was after what I'd been up to. 'That's fine, Liam. You go to bed with Tanya if you want to. In fact, let's both do just as we like, that way it won't be awkward when my boyfriend from England visits.'

He looked crestfallen, as if I'd hurt his pride by not getting jealous over him, but he knew when he was on to a good thing and forced a smile. I clinked my bottle against his, determined to cling on to a situation that was in fact ideal. Now I could play with him whenever I wanted, and also Saul and John, even Womble, which had to be enough male virility to keep me satisfied, and yet not one of them would be able to claim the right to invade my space. Just for once, things had worked out properly, and as I took a swallow of my beer I was telling myself it was just as well I was such a bad girl.

Liam grinned and nodded towards the loos. 'So how about a blow-job?'

There was a touch of chagrin as he led me to the loo. I knew I'd soon have a bad reputation, but then I'd been going in that direction anyway. Maybe it had been inevitable. On the island, as elsewhere, it seemed I had to make the choice between being a good little mouse and the real me. It's not really a choice at all because, while having people calling me a slut may hurt my pride, if I was to play the mouse I'd soon have no pride left to hurt.

Liam was headed for the Gents, but I steered him next door and into a cubicle. He was eager, immediately sitting down and pulling out his cock, the pale shaft already half-stiff, also with a telltale trace of cherry-red lipstick around the base. I took him in my mouth, rubbing my tongue under his foreskin and sucking gently as I let my feelings build.

It was deliciously humiliating, to be on my knees to him in a lavatory, sucking his penis after he'd been with another girl, presumably Tanya, and just the night before. I focused on that as he grew in my mouth, enjoying the shame of it and wondering if he was thinking about her as I sucked his cock. Maybe he was, maybe he wasn't, but it made a great fantasy, to imagine him having a night of wild sex with her, in bed together, and me, having to relieve him of the excess sexual energy she'd inspired, down on my knees in a lavatory to take his lipstick-stained penis in my mouth and swallow his spunk.

As soon as he was hard, I took him out, to kiss and lick at his balls as I masturbated him, all the while with my own excitement rising, until at last I'd tugged up my dress and slipped a hand down the front of my panties. His response was to pull my dress higher still and flop my tits out of my bra, feeling them as I sucked and calling me a slut. He was right, and it was what I wanted to be, a dirty little slut, his to be ordered down to my knees whenever he wanted, or by Saul, or John, Frank, Womble, Don, Mick, all of them, making me tart for them, as they said, making me dance striptease in private and in seedy pubs, but, best of all, making me suck their cocks, whenever they wanted.

I gave a little wriggle against my hand, now thoroughly enjoying myself. Liam was getting urgent, and I wanted to come before he did, with his lovely cock still in my mouth. I now had some of Tanya's lipstick on my own face, adding an exquisite touch to my humiliation, and I focused on it as I rubbed harder. They'd been to bed, no doubt for some nice clean sex, the sort our moral guardians in the magazines say we can have. Not me. I ended up down on my knees on the hard tiled floor of a public lavatory, sucking his cock as he thought of how wonderful it had been with her ... sucking his cock still smeared with her lipstick ... her lipstick which was now on my face ...

My muscles went tight and I was coming, a lingering orgasm as I sucked as much of his cock into my mouth as I could get. I was still high when he came, grunting out loud as his spunk erupted into my mouth. Even as I swallowed my slimy mouthful, I was thinking how good it felt, being made to eat the spunk he'd done in my mouth over thoughts of his night with her.

He needed to get back to the bar, and I had a little cleaning up to do, so it was a good five minutes before I followed, walking casually out of the Ladies to find Liam serving drinks ... to Aaron Pensler and the journalist, Mr Rattigan. They saw me immediately and I stopped, hesitant, not knowing whether to run for it or try to brazen it out.

'Hi, Aisha,' Pensler greeted me, all smiles, 'I'd like you to meet Mr Rattigan.'

'Hi,' the journalist added, extending a hand. 'So you're Aisha Tyler? Well I never. Call me Myles, please.'

I extended my hand with my face frozen in a rictus grin and my mind working overtime. Rattigan thought I was Aisha Tyler, or was pretending he did, but Liam was about to say something, no doubt something that would give the game away.

'That's me!' I said brightly. 'Pleased to meet you, Myles.'

'Yeah, but . . .' Liam began, looking puzzled.

'It – it is actually a stage name I use,' I said frantically, telling myself I could sort it out later. 'I know I should have told you, but you know . . . I just wanted a bit of peace and quiet.'

'Told me what?' he asked, and I was wondering if Womble really was the stupidest man on the island.

'Told you what?' Pensler chimed in. 'Don't you know? She's one of the biggest porno stars in the States, man!'

I could hardly deny it, not in front of Rattigan, and gave what I hoped was a modest shrug, while praying that Liam would catch on to what was happening.

'You are?' he asked, looking more dumbstruck than ever.

'Hardly one of the biggest stars,' I began, only to be cut off by Pensler.

'Oh you are! You're the best anyway, just the best!'

'And it's a real pleasure –' Rattigan began, obviously keen to chat me up, with his hand still extended.

'What, you're in porn films and that?' Liam queried, interrupting the journalist.

'A few,' I admitted, taking Rattigan's hand, which felt like a piece of boiled fish.

'A few?' Pensler laughed. 'Sixty-four, yeah? From *Brit Babes in the Woods* to *Mega Meat Suck Show*, yeah? I've got fifty-seven and I've got the three *Leg Show* ones you did on order with legslegslegs.com, and . . .'

'Shit!' Liam responded, now staring at me as Pensler rattled on.

I gave another shrug, completely lost for what to say. Rattigan was ogling me, and I was just waiting for him to say I reminded him of somebody else, or for Liam to call me Natasha, or for the ghost of Philippe Fauçon to come in, rattling his chains and calling me a thief. It didn't, but something nearly as bad did – Womble, rolling through the door with a large bucket half-full of what for one horrible moment I thought was spunk, until I saw the tentacles and realised he'd been catching small squid.

Liam called out as he saw his friend. 'Hi, Paul. Tasha's a porn star, and she never said, you know that?'

I froze. He'd said my real name, in front of Pensler and, worse, Rattigan, but they took no notice.

'She sure sucks like one,' Womble answered Liam, laughing. 'Don't you, darling? Look, I got a load of squid. Don't get them normally.'

I'd gone pink from what he'd said, but all four men were laughing, until Womble recognised Pensler.

'What you doing in here, you little shit?' he demanded, reaching out to close one massive fish-smeared hand on the nape of Pensler's neck. 'You want I should smash his face in, Tasha?'

'No, no, no,' I said hurriedly. 'I've sorted all that out. It was all a mistake.'

'Yeah?' Womble queried, not letting go of the wriggling Pensler. 'You touch my friend Natasha, and I'll fucking have you, got that?'

Womble released his grip, reluctantly. If I'd been Pensler, I'd have run for it, but he was made of sterner stuff, that or plain stupid.

'I have touched her, actually,' he said, his high squeaky tone for all the world like a schoolboy claiming he'd fingered the prettiest girl in the class. 'She did the triple with me, and ass to mouth, so go fuck yourself, Womble.'

I felt the blood rush to my face, but it was nothing to the transformation that came over Womble's. His skin had gone puce, his little round mouth had gone wide and his eyes were staring from his head, yet he seemed to be rooted to the spot, perhaps unable to fully take in what had been said to him. Now Pensler ran.

'I'll fucking kill him!' Womble roared, and he was in pursuit.

So was I, not with any intention of catching them, but to get away from Rattigan and because I had no desire whatsoever to explain what the triple was to Liam, never mind ass to mouth, open relationship or no open relationship.

Outside, both Pensler and Womble were well up the street, and it was obvious who to bet on. Pensler was light, in jeans and trainers, and probably used to running away from bullies, at least if he made a habit of telling them to fuck themselves. Womble must have weighed more than twice as much, was in overalls and sea boots, and still carrying his bucket of squid. By the time I'd reached the Italian restaurant, Pensler had vanished around the corner, but Womble wasn't giving up, lumbering after his prey and shouting threats as he went.

I followed, not wanting Pensler to end up in hospital for all my ill feelings about him. Soon I'd caught up with Womble, but he took no notice of my entreaties, still muttering threats even when Pensler had disappeared from view along the track to the cliffs. We followed, out on to the Blay, with the corn fields all around us, empty.

'Where's the little bastard gone?' Womble queried.

He looked around, scanning the corn and the distant line of gorse and scrubby hawthorn that marked the cliffs. I had a fair idea where Pensler would be, but I wasn't saying anything. Unfortunately, Womble wasn't as dim as he looked.

'He's gone down a bunker. Hold this, Tasha.'

I took the bucket of squid he'd thrust out towards me, holding it tentatively as he scrambled over a barbed-wire fence and started down the side of a field towards the nearest emplacements. When I called out he ignored me, and I wasn't climbing over the old German barbed wire for anything, especially not in a dress. I stayed put, waiting nervously and hoping Womble wouldn't catch Pensler, or that I'd be able to talk him out of going too far.

Womble disappeared from view, presumably into a bunker, but, just as I was wondering if I should risk the wire after all, Rattigan appeared, puffing along the track and looking around him as he approached. I cursed silently, but there was nothing for it but to behave normally, or at least what passed for normal in the circumstances.

'What happened?' he demanded.

'Aaron ran off,' I told him. 'Womble's looking for him, in a bunker, over there.'

I pointed, hoping Rattigan would go, but he turned to me instead.

'I'm glad we got a chance to talk alone, because I've got a little proposition I'd like to put to you ... Natasha.'

I froze. He knew, and he was about to blackmail me. I wondered what I'd have to pay to buy his silence. Obviously more than the papers would for my photos, maybe a thousand, maybe more. He would keep coming back too, I knew, but there was nothing I could do but attempt to placate him. 'How much?' I asked weakly.

'I like that,' he answered, 'straight up, no bullshit. How does a hundred pounds sound?'

'A hundred?' I queried, astonished he should ask for so little.

'A hundred's good, yeah?' he demanded. 'But you have to do what I say, exactly what I say.'

I swallowed hard, the tears already starting in my eyes. Just as I'd feared, he wanted sex too.

'Deal?' he demanded.

'OK,' I answered, and hung my head in defeat.

'Fucking ace!' he went on, not making the slightest effort to hide his triumph. 'I want a strip first, down to your panties, then a nice slow blow-job, you little fuck toy, you.'

I didn't answer immediately, not wanting to admit to myself that I was really going to have to do it, but there was no choice. 'All right,' I sighed. 'Come on, I'll do it in one of the bunkers.'

I glanced around. The last thing I wanted was Womble catching me sucking Myles Rattigan's cock, and Pensler would just have to look after himself. We hadn't heard any screams, so presumably he'd got away, and he was the least of my worries as I hurried out to where the track met the cliff path. I felt numb, and full of self-pity, wishing Rattigan to hell, Pensler too, wishing the media had never latched on to me, wishing I'd never stolen Fauçon's paintings in the first place. Now I was going to spend my life sucking cock on demand, maybe worse, because if he dug deep he'd soon realise he could do as he liked with me. Reality was very different from the fantasy.

He could bleed me dry and make me do what he'd said – his fuck toy, a crude expression I was sure described only too well how he'd treat me, used on demand, in any position he wanted, in my mouth and in my pussy, no doubt up my bum too. Maybe there was a limit, a point at which I could take it no more and would tell him to do his worst, risking prison. Maybe, but I hadn't reached it, not for now. For now I was going to suck his cock.

I was determined nobody should know, and led him out to the cliffs. There was a bunker I'd spotted before, sited on a rocky promontory overlooking a stony bay and broken cliffs. It was ideal for what I had to do, with a wide gun slit looking out over the bay and also back the way we'd come. Inside, it was also bigger than I'd expected, with the black concrete mouth of a doorway and a single small gun slit leading into the hillside. I put down Womble's bucket of squid, which I hadn't dared discard, and turned to Rattigan, who was standing in the doorway.

'Well, come on then,' he demanded, 'behave like you're enjoying it.'

All I could manage was a weak grimace. He leant against the wall, leering at me and squeezing his crotch. My sense of being numb had spread, leaving me feeling oddly detached, perhaps a defence against being made to perform for him, and a sensation completely and utterly different to all my fantasies. I realised I had to be strong, or he would ruin that for me as well, but it was not so easy to do, and I felt weak and hesitant as I stepped to the middle of the bunker.

'You – you want me to do a strip?' I managed. 'Naked?'

'No, down to your panties. I like a girl in just her panties.'

He was almost drooling, his voice thick with lust, and we hadn't even started. There was a round concrete gun-mounting in the middle of the floor. I climbed up on it and began to dance, feeling utterly foolish, and yet it was easy to fall into the familiar rhythm of a strip, something I'd done so often for Percy, and for other men, but never like this. Yet I did it, barely aware of my body, the sense of numb detachment my sole emotion. He just watched, occasionally squeezing his crotch, but his eyes never leaving my body as I made a slow display of my legs and hips, lifting my dress only gradually, before slipping my bra off down my sleeve to tease him. Still he failed to react, merely staring, with a little bit of spit running out of one side of his mouth.

He was worse than Pensler, infinitely worse, creepier by far. Pensler might look awful, but at least his desire was honest, and ultimately he had turned me on. Rattigan wouldn't, not ever, and there was no question of me having to fight my own feelings. I had none.

Nor did he seem to. Even when I finally pulled off my dress to go topless he stayed as he was, just rubbing himself through his trousers and goggling at my near-naked body. I kept on dancing, not knowing what else to do, not wanting to give him more, wishing he'd respond so that I could get it over with. When I could stand it no more, I pushed out my bum and began to ease my panties down over my cheeks, just like a good little stripper should, and finally he reacted. 'Don't do that. The panties stay on.'

'OK,' I answered, in relief, tugging them up again. 'What now? I can't suck you if you don't take out your cock.'

He should have heard the bitterness and the hurt in my voice, maybe felt guilty, but he gave no reaction, simply unzipping himself, to pull out one of the most pathetic cocks I'd ever seen, short and wrinkly, still only half-stiff despite my striptease. Remembering what had happened with Pensler, I said nothing, but squatted down in front of him as he made himself comfortable against the wall. As I took him in my mouth I tried to blank my mind, to see it as a nasty job, like unblocking a drain, to be done as quickly and efficiently as possible.

Despite my best efforts he took forever to get hard. I was sucking on his helmet and teasing the underside of his foreskin with the tip of my tongue, tickling his balls and holding up my boobs for him, normally enough to get any man rock solid in seconds. Not Rattigan, but I worked on it, making fake noises of pleasure in my throat and even pretending to play with myself through my panties as I struggled to turn him on.

Finally, he was hard, all of four inches of stiff little cock in my mouth. My knees hurt, and I had to change position, kneeling instead, the concrete cold and hard against my skin. For the first time he showed some emotion, a little gasp, and I stuck my bottom out a bit more, showing off my panties. At that he gave a low moan and his hand came down, to take his cock between two fingers. I was sucking on the tip of it as he began to wank into my mouth, my lips working on the little fleshy cherry of his helmet. My hands went back to stroke my panty seat and again he groaned, now staring down at my bum, his face bright red, and giving a final gasp as he came in my mouth.

I rocked back on my heels, my mouth clogged with spunk and more running down my chin, making it impossible to speak. Normally I'd have swallowed, enjoying the intimacy of eating a man's spunk, or the humiliation of being made to if that was the game. Not now, not with Rattigan. I spat, coughing up the filthy mess he'd done in my mouth and flicking what was on my face off with my fingers.

He paid no attention at all, but put his cock away as quickly as he could, tossed something on the floor and left. I was still on my knees, retching spunk on to the concrete, my vision hazy with tears as my emotions finally began to come to the boil. Only when I'd wiped my eyes on the hem of my dress and stood up in a futile effort to be strong about it did I see what he'd left, a slim sheaf of twenty-pound notes, five in all. I picked them up, utterly confused. Why would he want to give me money? Surely he should have been demanding it from me? It made no sense, unless . . .

No, that was just wishful thinking. He'd called me Natasha, after all. Natasha, yes, but not Natasha Linnet. No, it was too much to hope for, that he still hadn't made the connection. He was a journalist, after all, and my picture had been in a dozen magazines and most of the papers. Yet he was American, perhaps even some sort of specialist in the porn industry. At the least I had to find out.

I pulled on my dress and ran from the bunker, sure I was about to make a bigger fool of myself than I already felt as I called out after him. He was halfway up the slope, where he hesitated, looked around, and would have gone on had I not called out again. I followed, picking my way carefully among the thorny bushes as I tried to decide what to say and prayed I was right about what he'd done.

'I – I think we may have got off on the wrong foot, rather, Mr Rattigan . . . Myles, that is,' I said as I approached him.

'Dead right,' he answered, his tone none too friendly. 'I thought you were supposed to be well up

228

for it? That's what Aaron said, but I've never had such a cold whore.'

'That ... it's ... I'm just a bit moody today,' I tried. 'PMT. I'm sorry. Look, you can have your money back.'

I held it out to him, but he shook his head. 'No, you keep it, but, next time, how about a bit more enthusiasm? Like in your videos.'

I managed a weak smile and a nod, then turned away, not wanting him to see my emotion.

'I – I left something, I think,' I told him, and started back towards the bunker.

He didn't follow, and the moment he'd gone from sight I sat down on a bulge of grass, not knowing whether to laugh or cry. My body wanted to do both, and I couldn't stop myself, the tears bursting out and streaming down my face, my body shaking with sobs and with laughter too, laughter with a hysterical edge. I tried to stop myself, but I couldn't, and gave in, pouring out my battered emotions to the empty cliffs until at last my tears had run dry and my sobbing had died to wet gulps.

I no longer cared about Pensler, or Womble, or anything much else except for myself. Maybe I wasn't in trouble, yet the fact was taking its time to sink in, and there was something else too. In my desperate efforts to escape what I knew most would have considered my just deserts, I had managed to prostitute myself. I needed to think about what I'd done, and alone.

When I finally felt ready I got to my feet. Womble, Pensler and possibly others were still somewhere up on the Blay, and if they saw me they were sure to come down. I didn't want to see any of them, but only to come to terms with myself in my own time. My first thought was to go back to the bunker, but the thought of the puddle of Rattigan's spunk on the floor put me off. Unlike with Pensler, there was no compulsion, only distaste.

I did retrieve Womble's bucket of squid, because I couldn't face the inevitable explanations if I abandoned it. Walking on along an even fainter path, I quickly found another bunker, the twin to the first, but in mirror image on the far side of the little promontory. It was heavily overgrown, more so than the other, and the inside was cool and dim, with most of the gun-slit overhung with trailing brambles. I sat down on the mounting with my chin in my hands, thinking.

What was most important, I told myself, was that Rattigan had no idea who I really was. Maybe there was still a danger he would find out, but it was faint. That was an immense relief, yet it carried two implications, two deeply humiliating implications. First, I'd prostituted myself to Rattigan for no good reason and, second, I needn't have had sex with Pensler at all, never mind been so utterly filthy.

I tried to tell myself that I had actually followed the sensible course of action, behaving, hopefully, as the real Aisha Tyler would have done. Unfortunately, I was fairly sure she'd have done nothing of the kind. Why should she? As a porn star, she was presumably reasonably well paid, and would have treated Rattigan's offer with the contempt it deserved. Also presumably, she'd have had so much sex she'd either be permanently satisfied or jaded and, compared with the sort of men she was used to, Pensler would have seemed a pretty miserable specimen.

She wouldn't have looked at him twice. I had. I'd come over the thought of him spunking over my tits. I'd let him rub his ugly cock between them. I'd let him fuck me from behind. I'd let him grease my

230

bottom hole with the cream he used to wank with. I'd let him bugger me and stick his cock straight from up my bottom into my mouth. I'd come while I sucked it.

For Rattigan? For Rattigan, setting my misunderstanding aside, I'd stripped to my panties and sucked his penis for a hundred pounds, a miserable one hundred pounds, less than I'd spend on a half-decent bottle of wine. It was only a shame he hadn't made me do it for a tenner.

With that thought I finally managed a smile. That was more like me, thoroughly naughty, not content to get off on merely degrading myself, but wanting to do it in style. A hundred pounds was far too much to pay me for a strip and blow-job. If I was going to be made a whore, it should be done in style, maybe ten pounds for a striptease and full sex, maybe a pound to do what Pensler had done, bugger me and make me suck his dirty cock.

A flush of genuine shame hit me at the thought of what I was doing, but I forced it down. If I allowed what had happened with Rattigan to make me less of a bad girl then it meant he had damaged me, spoilt a part of my freedom to think and behave as I pleased. That was not going to happen. I would enjoy it, make it a fantasy, not over him, and not for him, but for myself.

I made myself a little more comfortable on the gun-mounting and closed my eyes, determined to do it. A really dirty way for me to be used had occurred to me, being put in a public lavatory, the paying kind, and made available to anyone with the money to come in, maybe twenty pence. Maybe there was one on the island. All the locals would come, men and women too, to make me suck cock and lick pussy at twenty pence a time.

They'd film me doing it, and have posters stuck up showing me seated naked on the loo with a cock in either hand and my face plastered with spunk, with something like 'Cheap Tart – She Sucks for 20p!' underneath so that the tourists would know where to go for their blow-jobs. There would be a queue in no time, and by the time I'd finished my entire body would be dripping in spunk, my face plastered, my hair clogged with it, my boobs slimy and foul.

Then again, why should they bother to pay me at all? Maybe I should be made to do it just to eat. It might have been during the war, with me left alone on the island as a sop to the German troops. I'd simply have been requisitioned, like a car or a house, and put to whatever use they felt me best suited to, in this case their amusement. They'd have made me do little rude burlesques, dolled up in bright-red lipstick and high heels, maybe a short black jacket over big white panties, and jackboots, definitely jackboots.

That was better still, ideal in fact, because it went so well with the setting. I stood up and glanced out of the gun slit to make sure I was completely alone, then peeled my dress up over my head. My excitement had began to rise, making me feel triumphant, which encouraged me in turn. I felt really good, and I began to strut up and down across the bunker, imagining how the soldiers would make me march and drill in just panties and sandals, just as I was doing.

It felt rude, deliciously rude, but it could get ruder. They'd have no respect for me whatsoever, seeing me purely as a set of pleasing curves, put there to amuse them. Even after I'd sucked them all off, they'd find it amusing to torment me. One would have been fishing and caught some squid, which would just happen to be in the bunker where I'd been made to parade for them and suck their cocks. I wouldn't have been allowed to put my dress on, and after a while they'd start making fun of me, laughing about the shape of the squid and how well they'd fit up me.

I'd try to run, the worst possible thing to do. They'd catch me easily, two of them holding me without any real effort at all despite my frantic struggles, a third pulling down my panties to bare my pussy and bum, a fourth forcing my kicking legs wide, a fifth easing in a fat cold squid up my pussy, a sixth forcing another squid up my bumhole. How they'd laugh, as I was bent over, to show off my rear view, my bare pink bum out of my panties and two sets of squid tentacles hanging down obscenely from my cunt and anus.

That was dirty, gloriously dirty. I could do it too. I was going to do it. Why stop? Why hold myself back at all? Rattigan hadn't spoilt me, I was as bad as ever, grimacing in mingled delight and disgust as I plunged my hands into the bucket of squid, feeling their cold slimy bodies against my skin. I took two of the fattest, the accusing stare from their dead eyes making me hesitate, but only for a moment. Their shape was just too tempting, their bodies tapering to rounded ends, perfect for insertion in a bad girl's fuck holes.

I was shaking badly as I stuck out my bottom and pushed my already slimy fingers into the waistband of my panties. As I tugged them down, I was thinking of how the soldier would do it, with one sharp tug to get me bare, laughing at the sight of my round meaty bottom, jiggling right in his face to the motion of my struggles. Maybe he'd slap me a few times, to try to shut me up and stop me fighting, but it would make no difference, because I'd be in a state of blind, stupid panic.

My mouth came open in bliss as I touched the squid between my cheeks. It felt cold and slippery, like a little icy cock with the head wet with spit or pussy juice, delightful against my pouted sex lips, and between, on my clitty and in up my wet eager hole. It went in easily, the full plump body lodging deep in my vagina to leave just the head and tentacles lolling out behind, a sight I knew would be both truly obscene and truly absurd.

Reaching back, I took a moment to fuck myself with the squid, thinking of how the troopers would laugh to see me as I was. Not that I'd be being rude with myself, but struggling frantically, with not just my bottom jiggling stupidly about, but the tentacles of the squid too, hanging from my penetrated cunt like some absurd beard, all ten jumping to every kick and wriggle I made. They'd hold me like that, bent well over so they could all see, laughing uproariously. One would start to spank me, tell me I had to be punished for being such a slut, as if it was my fault. Another would take a handful of squid slime and slap it between my bottom cheeks to grease up their next target, my anus.

I took the second squid, my legs now braced well apart and my bum stuck right out as I put it between my cheeks. My bumhole was already a bit open, slippery with my own juice and squid slime, but I wiped a little more of both on and slipped the tip of one finger up before trying the squid. At first my ring spread easily, accommodating a good deal of the squid before it stuck. Determined to get it in, I began to bugger myself, my mouth wide in ecstasy as the body of the squid moved in my bumhole. Slowly my muscle gave, with just a twinge of pain as the fattest bit went up, and the squid was in, lodged in me, so that I now had two sets of tentacles hanging out behind.

To be like that felt utterly, perfectly filthy, and I was ready to come, but I could go a little further first. For one thing, my mouth tasted of Rattigan's spunk, and raw squid had to be better. I stuck one in, sucking on the fat turgid body. It felt horribly rubbery and didn't taste so very different from the spunk, but I kept it in, imagining how I'd look, plugged with squid for the crude amusement of German troopers.

One more thing remained. Spreading my legs to stretch my lowered panties out between my thighs, I scooped up as many squid as I could and dropped them into the pouch of cotton hanging down beneath me. Most of them stayed in, creating that same lovely dirty sense of weight as when I'd soiled myself. With that thought, I pulled them up, sighing in pleasure as the fat squashy mass pressed against my bottom, to make a huge heavy panty bulge, which I reached down to touch, amazed at just how dirty I could be, but thoroughly enjoying myself.

The troopers would definitely have done that to me, pouring the entire bucket of squid down the back of my panties and forcing me to parade like that, all six of them laughing so hard they'd be clutching their sides and cracking jokes about how it looked as if I'd shit in my panties. They'd slap my bulge too, and use more squid to whip my breasts and belly and thighs, smacking the tentacles down on my flesh.

I began to parade for real, marching back and forth across the bunker with the squid squashing in my panties. Every step made the ones in my pussy and bum move, in my holes and out, the tentacles squirming against my flesh as if they were alive. I stopped and reached down to my panties, to adjust the one up my cunt, so that the tentacles were between my sex lips. As I took a couple of experimental steps, the tiny suckers were rubbing on my clit. I could come, just by marching, not easily, but I could, and when I did it would be wonderfully intense.

That orgasm was just what I needed to take my stress away and make me believe in myself once again. I began to masturbate, stroking my breasts and the front of my panties, then to march up and down once more. I thought of the troopers watching me, men who hadn't had a woman in years, their cocks already hard in their trousers again as I paraded and posed for them, my pussy and bumhole and mouth stuffed with squid, my panties bulging obscenely beneath me. My holes would already be well greased with the squid slime, in anticipation of the good hard fucking they'd give me when they grew tired of laughing at me, cocks in my mouth and in my pussy and up my bum, all six of them to satisfy, big virile sex-hungry men ...

I stopped at a noise, no more than the tiniest of scraping sounds, but it had come from within the deeper part of the bunker. My visions of virile young soldiers shattered to become skeletons dressed in the rags of once smart uniforms, as I'd imagined before. The noise came again, this time unmistakable and my heart came up into my mouth as something moved in the darkness ...

... Aaron Pensler, who stepped out of the door, his long, bendy cock erect in his hand. 'Fuck me, you really are something else, ain't you, Aisha?'

I had gone scarlet, crimson, beetroot, the blood flaming in my cheeks as my mouth fell slowly open to release the squid I'd put in it, which landed on the floor with a wet plop.

'That's nasty, that is,' he said, his eyes flicking down to the huge bulge of the squid bodies in my panties. 'You want I should put my cock in, yeah?'

236

I could only stare, speechless with embarrassment, but I'd been right on the edge of orgasm, so close the muscles of my thighs and my bum cheeks were still twitching, and he was offering to put his cock in me, the cock with which he'd already brought me to one of the best orgasms of my life. I nodded weakly.

'Yay, well cool! Kneel down on that bit of concrete then. I'll fuck you from behind.'

I knelt, barely aware of what I was doing as I stuck out my squashy squid-filled panty seat towards Aaron and his erection. He got down behind me, jerking at himself one-handed as he took hold of my panties with the other.

'There – there's a squid in my pussy,' I managed, my last word breaking to a sob.

'I know,' he said, chuckling. 'I saw you put it up, and up your Hershey highway. Oh yeah, nasty or what!'

He'd pulled down my knickers, spilling out the squid all over the floor, also over his cock. I watched as he caught some up around his shaft, masturbating in them with his little monkey face set in a demented grin. He was worse than me, comprehensively perverted, but at least that made it easier to take what he was about to give me.

'Do as you like,' I sighed. 'Come on.'

'You got it, girl!' he crowed, and took hold of the squid in my pussy, easing it free before immediately replacing it with his cock.

I was gasping at once, brought back on heat in just seconds as he fucked me, first fondling my slimy bottom cheeks as he did it, then climbing on top of my back to grope at my dangling boobs and smear them with slime. That way I could feel the body of the squid in my anus, pushing up me with every shove and driving my ecstasy higher still, until I couldn't help myself at all, grunting and panting and begging him to fuck me harder. He obliged, ramming himself into me and clutching at my slimy tits until I was screaming with passion. I was too far gone to care even if he came up me, but he remembered, suddenly whipping his cock out to leave me begging.

'No, don't stop! Put it back . . . oh, God!'

I could feel the squid being pulled from my bumhole, and that could only mean one thing. His cock was going up instead. I didn't protest, I couldn't, but just hung my head in shame as the squid was eased out to leave my anus gaping and ready. I felt his cock head touch, just as I'd started to close, and push in, invading my bottom, deep and deeper still, until his balls were pressed to my empty slimy cunt.

'Oh yeah!' he called out. 'One up the ass for Aisha, up your ass then in your mouth, yeah? That's how you like it, yeah?'

'Yes, do it,' I managed, a whimper of noise that broke to grunting as he began to pump himself into my bottom.

He was going to do it, and I was going to like it. This time I had no compulsion, no excuse. I was going to do it because I wanted to, because I'm a dirty little bitch, his dirty little bitch. I knew I'd be full too, to make it worse, but I wanted it that way, just as humiliating as it could possibly be. What did it matter, after the way he'd seen me? Parading up and down in my panties with my pouch and both holes full of squid, one in my mouth even. It didn't matter. He liked it. He liked everything, everything rude, everything dirty. Not like prissy, stupid Liam, who wouldn't even smack my bottom. Aaron would. I was sure he would. The slightest excuse and over I'd go, panties down for a thoroughly humiliating spanking and a cock up my bum afterwards for good measure.

'Spank me!' I demanded. 'Spank me while you fuck my bum!'

There were no stupid questions, no hesitation. He just did it, spanking both my cheeks and laughing gleefully as he watched my bottom wobble, all the while still easing his cock in and out of my straining anus. I screamed out, overcome with sheer joy for what was being done to me, spanked and buggered at the same time. His balls were pushing to my cunt lips too, driving me ever closer towards orgasm, and as the smacks grew firmer and the pace of his cock in my rectum faster I could wait no more.

My hand went back, briefly touching my panty pouch where it hung between my legs, still heavy with squid, before I found my pussy and began to masturbate. Aaron saw and gave a gleeful cackle as he took hold of my bottom to ease his cock free, and I was babbling and pleading. 'No . . . no, Aaron, do it up my bum . . . spunk up my bum while you spank me, please? I beg you . . . please!'

'Yeah, but –'

'Just do it, I'll do anything!'

He didn't answer, but he'd began to bugger me again, ramming his cock deep in, and to spank me, slapping hard at my cheeks. I was nearly there anyway, my fingers busy between my lips, rubbing hard on my clitty, brought closer to orgasm with every touch, with every smack, with every thrust of his cock up my bottom hole. My mouth came wide in a piercing scream and I was there, wriggling myself desperately on his cock for extra friction as he went into a wild thrusting frenzy, his hands smacking down on my bum with all his force.

Again and again I screamed, riding my orgasm on and on, a fresh peak every time he jammed his cock deep, until my vision had gone and I could no longer hold my body off the concrete. All the time I thought of what a bad, dirty little bitch I was, letting the local nerd bugger me and spank me, begging for it too, in return for complete use of my body, and as my orgasm finally began to fade I realised that was precisely what he was going to take. He hadn't come, his cock still rock hard up my bottom and moving with a slow deliberate motion inside me.

'Nice,' he said, panting just a little, 'now your ass to mouth, and I'm going to give you a Dirty Sanchez.'

I knew what he meant, he'd told me, in detail, a disgusting thing to do to a girl, but all I could manage was a weak sob as he began to ease his cock out of my bottom hole. I'd collapsed, my knees wide apart, my tits squashed out on the concrete, my face in a pool of squid slime, but too far gone to move. My knees ached, my cheeks stung, my anus was a ring of pain, but I was going to do it, in meek doglike gratitude for what he'd done. His cock pulled free of my bumhole and my mouth had come wide, eager to be made to suck dirty cock and have my mouth spunked in for all my exhaustion.

His hand closed in my hair, he pushed his cock in my face and wiped the knob across my upper lip, twice, painting on a Mexican-style moustache with what he'd just drawn out from my bottom. As he looked down, he laughed, and gave me a thumbs-up sign before pushing his cock into my mouth, as much of the slimy reeking pole as would fit. I was sucking immediately, my head spinning with the taste of man and squid and my own bumhole. Not that I could do it properly, because his helmet was jammed down the back of my throat. I could barely even breathe, my snot bubbling from my nose as I fought for air and running down on to his shaft. He didn't care, staring down at my cock-filled mouth and my dirty stupid shit moustache in demented glee as he fucked my head, one hand holding me by the hair, the other wanking at the base of his erection, and talking.

'Yay, Dirty Sanchez, Dirty Sanchez! I've done a Dirty Sanchez on you, you dirty bitch, Aisha, you lovely dirty bitch! Now suck my dick, suck it good, Aisha, straight from your ass . . . taste it straight from your ass, Aisha, you dirty bitch . . . suck it and taste your own poop, Aisha . . . suck!'

I struggled to obey, doing my best to be a good little bitch for him, but he didn't really need me, having fun with my mouth regardless, his hand smacking on my chin as he wanked, my lips smeared with goo as he pumped himself into me, my mouth full of it, and spunk too as he came, first down my throat, then in my face, great dollops of it, until I was plastered and filthy, with bits in my hair and hanging from my nose, caked in my eyes and smeared over my cheeks.

As he pulled back I collapsed completely, unable to move, indifferent to the filthy state I was in. My hand was still between my legs, kneading my pussy in sleepy, exhausted contentment. Only when he gave my bottom a resounding slap did I move, sitting painfully up on the gun-mounting and looking up at him with a weak grin through hazy eyes.

'Thank you, Aaron. I needed that. Now, would you give me a hand down to the sea?'

'Yeah, sure,' he answered. 'You look like you need a wash.'

He laughed his squeaky, irritating little laugh. I found myself smiling as I climbed unsteadily to my feet and peered from the gun slit. The path and the cliffs beyond were as empty as before.

'Do you know the way down?' I asked.

'Sure,' he answered, joining me at the slit. 'I often come here, 'cause sometimes girls go in nude. What happened to that fat bastard Womble?'

'I don't know. He's probably still looking for you.'

He bit his lip, a trifle pensive, and not surprising.

'It's all right,' I promised. 'I'll make sure he doesn't hurt you, but you really must learn not to tell human gorillas to go and fuck themselves. He doesn't like to be reminded that he looks like a giant womble either.'

We shared a grin.

He helped get my things together and we made our way down to the sea, Aaron scouting ahead and me feeling deliciously naughty because I was in nothing but badly soiled panties and sandals. I went in nude, enjoying the cool water as I washed, rubbing myself down and winkling bits of squid tentacle out of crevices. Aaron watched, taking in every moment as if he still couldn't get enough of my body despite what we'd just done.

I didn't mind any more, because to me he was now a human being, and one with whom I shared a very dirty secret. Not only that, but with the intimacy between us there was every chance I could make him get rid of Rattigan once and for all, a subject I broached as soon as I was dry. 'About Mr Rattigan, can I ask you a favour?'

'Sure, Aisha, anything. Can I keep your panties as a souvenir?'

'Um . . . yes, I suppose so, if you like. About Mr Rattigan –'

'I love the white panties you wear, so much sexier than the thongs you have in most of your vids.'

'Never mind my panties. Mr Rattigan –'

'Miserable fucker, ain't he? He's not bad as a boss though, just boring.'

'I suppose he is rather, but . . . hold on, what did you say?'

'Which bit?'

'About Rattigan. You said he was your boss.'

'Yeah, sure. We've got the contracts for all the new masts, right round the Channel Isles, we have.'

'Who have?'

'My firm, S-Sat Communications. I'm IT and Mr Rattigan's my site boss. Didn't you know that?'

'No. I didn't. I thought . . . no, never mind. Here, have my panties.'

'Yay, cool!'

I put my dress on, not sure what to say, not sure what to think. Aaron was telling the truth, his honesty plain, and more interested in securing my panties than what I was saying. Besides, his story explained why he'd been taking photos of radio masts. He wasn't a tourist at all, he was on a work contract, and Mr Rattigan was not a journalist. It was hard to take in, but the whole thing had been a product of my paranoia, which meant . . .

Which meant that I'd had two of the dirtiest, most satisfying sexual experiences of my life and collected enough fantasy material to keep my pussy sore for life. It also meant I was in the clear, as free as a bird. I gave Aaron a big kiss and stuck my panties over his head, so much relief and so much joy welling up inside me that I didn't even care that I was stark naked and that two men were approaching down the path from the cliffs. It was only when I recognised them that I stopped jumping up and down in delight – it was Don White, and Percy, who hailed me as he reached the final slope of rock leading down to the stones. 'Good afternoon, my dear, and may I say that you seem remarkably exuberant.'

I ran over to kiss him, leaving his shirt front damp from my wet skin. Aaron had managed to remove my panties but was looking rather doubtfully at the two men, so I quickly made the introductions.

'Aaron, you probably know Don White, and this is my boyfriend, Percy Ottershaw. Percy, this is Aaron Pensler, an IT engineer who's been keeping me company.'

'Yeah, right,' Aaron answered, looking more doubtful than ever as his eyes flicked from my naked body to Percy.

'Please don't concern yourself, young fellow,' Percy told him. 'Natasha and I have a most informal relationship.'

'Yeah, that figures,' Aaron answered. 'You'd have to, wouldn't you?'

Percy looked mildly puzzled but continued happily enough. 'I thought I'd give you a little surprise, my dear, by coming over a little early.'

'You did surprise me. But how did you know I was down here?'

'Mr White stopped to intervene in an altercation between two young men by the road,' Percy explained, 'a cousin of his and one other. They said you were somewhere around here, and we saw you from the cliff top.'

'Was one of them a big fat guy?' Aaron asked.

'Looks like a womble,' I added.

'Paul, yes,' Don answered, addressing Aaron, 'he was trying to get that mate of yours to tell him where you were.'

'Did he find out?' Aaron asked.

'I told him to go home,' Don answered, 'but you want to watch out –'

'I don't care,' Aaron cut in, 'I'm off tomorrow, just as long as he's not waiting around for me.'

'You're going?' I asked.

'Yeah,' Aaron answered me, 'we finished this

lunchtime. That's why we came in to Andy's, to have a beer to celebrate.'

I nodded, both disappointed and relieved at one and the same time. The buggerings were good, but so much else about him was unbearable, while sooner or later he was sure to realise I wasn't really Aisha Tyler. I'd have had to tell him, which would have been awkward, but now I could leave him in blissful ignorance.

'I'd better get on, as it goes,' he said. 'Got to pack.'

'Be careful,' I advised and went to kiss him again, this time goodbye.

As he hugged me his hands slid down to take a cheeky squeeze of my bare bottom. I kissed him again and pulled away, leaving him to start back up the path as I pulled my dress on over my head and slipped into a fresh pair of spanking panties from my bag. Don White had followed him up the slant of rock, presumably to offer some much needed advice, giving me a chance to talk to Percy.

'So you got over OK? No problems?'

'None at all,' he assured me. 'I came in on the Guernsey plane. I reached Guernsey from Nantes, which in turn I reached from Tours, after driving down through the vineyards, a route I flatter myself only the most determined of reporters could have followed. Besides, since your departure they have been thin on the ground. There is no mileage in fat old wine writers, you know, unless they happen to be spanking pretty girls.'

'Good,' I told him, 'Penny and Cheryl said much the same, so it looks like I'm clear.'

'So it would seem,' he said, 'at least, in so far as reporters are concerned.'

'How do you mean?'

'How do I mean? Is that not clear? Cavorting naked on the beach in full view and with a boy? I think that deserves a spanking, don't you? Also, I learn from young Penny Birch that you have reached a certain accommodation?'

He lifted an eyebrow as he spoke. I knew what he meant, my tummy already fluttering at the prospect as Don White returned to us.

'As I was saying in the car, Mr White,' Percy went on, 'it would give me great pleasure if you were to join me in taking my brat here across our knees and spanking her bottom.'

I could see from the look on Don White's face what his answer was going to be.

My knickers were coming down, which is what happens to bad girls.

The leading publisher of fetish and adult fiction

TELL US WHAT YOU THINK!

Readers' ideas and opinions matter to us. Take a few minutes to fill in the questionnaire below and you'll be entered into a prize draw to win a year's worth of Nexus books (36 titles)

Terms and conditions apply – see end of questionnaire.

1. Sex: Are you male ☐ female ☐ a couple ☐?

2. Age: Under 21 ☐ 21–30 ☐ 31–40 ☐ 41–50 ☐ 51–60 ☐ over 60 ☐

3. Where do you buy your Nexus books from?

☐ A chain book shop. If so, which one(s)?

_____

☐ An independent book shop. If so, which one(s)?

_____

☐ A used book shop/charity shop
☐ Online book store. If so, which one(s)?

_____

4. How did you find out about Nexus books?

☐ Browsing in a book shop
☐ A review in a magazine
☐ Online
☐ Recommendation
☐ Other _____

5. In terms of settings, which do you prefer? (Tick as many as you like)

☐ Down to earth and as realistic as possible
☐ Historical settings. If so, which period do you prefer?

_____

☐ Fantasy settings – barbarian worlds

- ☐ Completely escapist/surreal fantasy
- ☐ Institutional or secret academy
- ☐ Futuristic/sci fi
- ☐ Escapist but still believable
- ☐ Any settings you dislike?

_____

- ☐ Where would you like to see an adult novel set?

_____

6. In terms of storylines, would you prefer:

- ☐ Simple stories that concentrate on adult interests?
- ☐ More plot and character-driven stories with less explicit adult activity?
- ☐ We value your ideas, so give us your opinion of this book:

_____

_____

_____

7. In terms of your adult interests, what do you like to read about? (Tick as many as you like)

- ☐ Traditional corporal punishment (CP)
- ☐ Modern corporal punishment
- ☐ Spanking
- ☐ Restraint/bondage
- ☐ Rope bondage
- ☐ Latex/rubber
- ☐ Leather
- ☐ Female domination and male submission
- ☐ Female domination and female submission
- ☐ Male domination and female submission
- ☐ Willing captivity
- ☐ Uniforms
- ☐ Lingerie/underwear/hosiery/footwear (boots and high heels)
- ☐ Sex rituals
- ☐ Vanilla sex
- ☐ Swinging
- ☐ Cross-dressing/TV

☐ Enforced feminisation
☐ Others – tell us what you don't see enough of in adult fiction:

_____

_____

_____

8. Would you prefer books with a more specialised approach to your interests, i.e. a novel specifically about uniforms? If so, which subject(s) would you like to read a Nexus novel about?

_____

_____

_____

9. Would you like to read true stories in Nexus books? For instance, the true story of a submissive woman, or a male slave? Tell us which true revelations you would most like to read about:

_____

_____

_____

10. What do you like best about Nexus books?

_____

_____

11. What do you like least about Nexus books?

_____

_____

12. Which are your favourite titles?

_____

_____

13. Who are your favourite authors?

_____

_____

14. **Which covers do you prefer? Those featuring:**
    (tick as many as you like)

☐ Fetish outfits
☐ More nudity
☐ Two models
☐ Unusual models or settings
☐ Classic erotic photography
☐ More contemporary images and poses
☐ A blank/non-erotic cover
☐ What would your ideal cover look like?

_____

15. **Describe your ideal Nexus novel in the space provided:**

_____
_____
_____
_____

16. **Which celebrity would feature in one of your Nexus-style fantasies?**
    We'll post the best suggestions on our website – anonymously!

_____

THANKS FOR YOUR TIME

Now simply write the title of this book in the space below and cut out the
questionnaire pages. Post to: Nexus, Marketing Dept., Thames Wharf Studios,
Rainville Rd, London W6 9HA

Book title: _____

TERMS AND CONDITIONS

1. The competition is open to UK residents only, excluding employees of Nexus and Virgin, their
families, agents and anyone connected with the promotion of the competition. 2. Entrants
must be aged 18 years or over. 3. Closing date for receipt of entries is 31 December 2006.
4. The first entry drawn on 7 January 2007 will be declared the winner and notified by Nexus.
5. The decision of the judges is final. No correspondence will be entered into. 6. No purchase
necessary. Entries restricted to one per household. 7. The prize is non-transferable and non-
refundable and no alternatives can be substituted. 8. Nexus reserves the right to amend or
terminate any part of the promotion without prior notice. 9. No responsibility is accepted for
fraudulent, damaged, illegible or incomplete entries. Proof of sending is not proof of receipt.
10. The winner's name will be available from the above address from 9 January 2007.

Promoter: Nexus, Thames Wharf Studios, Rainville Road, London, W6 9HA

NEXUS NEW BOOKS

To be published in June 2006

UNEARTHLY DESIRES
Ray Gordon

When Alison comes into money, she uses the small fortune to buy a country home. A house unlike any other she has ever experienced. From the discovery of a sinister playroom in the basement, to the strange men who call upon the house and request unusual and bizarre services, Alison begins to wonder about the previous owner. And herself, when she is compelled to oblige the visitors' demands.

Both the mystery, and Alison's alarm, ratchets-up another notch when she realises her country retreat was once a house of ill-repute, run by an elderly madam. And as she and her friend, Sally, sink further and further into committing depraved sexual acts with their guests, she becomes certain that the previous owner is still in control . . .

£6.99   ISBN 0 352 34036 3

EXPOSE
Laura Bowen

Lisa is a successful book illustrator with a secret that could ruin her reputation. The two sides of her life – the professional and the erotic – have always been strictly separated. Divided until mysterious events begin to act powerfully on her imagination. And when her secret is discovered, she is drawn inexorably into circumstances ruled by her own unrestrained desire in which her fantasies, however extreme, become real.

£6.99   ISBN 0 352 34035 5

THE DOMINO TATTOO
Cyrian Amberlake

Into this world comes Josephine Morrow, a young woman beset with a strange restlessness. At Estwych she finds a cruelty and a gentleness she has never known.

A cruelty that will test her body to its limits and a gentleness that will set her heart free. An experience that will change her utterly. An experience granted only to those with the domino tattoo ...

£6.99   ISBN 0 352 34037 1

If you would like more information about Nexus titles, please visit our website at www.nexus-books.co.uk, or send a large stamped addressed envelope to:
  Nexus, Thames Wharf Studios,
  Rainville Road, London W6 9HA

NEXUS BACKLIST

This information is correct at time of printing. For up-to-date information, please visit our website at www.nexus-books.co.uk

All books are priced at £6.99 unless another price is given.

ABANDONED ALICE	Adriana Arden 0 352 33969 1	☐
ALICE IN CHAINS	Adriana Arden 0 352 33908 X	☐
AMAZON SLAVE	Lisette Ashton 0 352 33916 0	☐
ANGEL	Lindsay Gordon 0 352 34009 6	☐
AQUA DOMINATION	William Doughty 0 352 34020 7	☐
THE ART OF CORRECTION	Tara Black 0 352 33895 4	☐
THE ART OF SURRENDER	Madeline Bastinado 0 352 34013 4	☐
AT THE END OF HER TETHER	G.C. Scott 0 352 33857 1	☐
BELINDA BARES UP	Yolanda Celbridge 0 352 33926 8	☐
BENCH MARKS	Tara Black 0 352 33797 4	☐
BINDING PROMISES	G.C. Scott 0 352 34014 2	☐
THE BLACK GARTER	Lisette Ashton 0 352 33919 5	☐
THE BLACK MASQUE	Lisette Ashton 0 352 33977 2	☐
THE BLACK ROOM	Lisette Ashton 0 352 33914 4	☐
THE BLACK WIDOW	Lisette Ashton 0 352 33973 X	☐
THE BOND	Lindsay Gordon 0 352 33996 9	☐